NO ESCAPE

NO ESCAPE

No Justice Series: Book 2

NOLON KING
DAVID WRIGHT

STERLING & STONE

To YOU, the reader.
Thank you for your support.
Thank you for the wonderful emails.
Thank you for the thoughtful reviews.
Thank you for reading and loving our stories.

Prologue

MORNING DEW STILL HUGGED the grass as the man approached the baseball diamond, cell phone streaming his ill intent on the LiveLyfe app.

He arrived just after the Spring Baseball Opening Day ceremonies. But he wasn't here for that bullshit, with the league owners trotting out their bratty kids, praise the flag and fucking sponsors, while parents pretended to care. And the ones who did cared *waaaay* too much.

No, he was here for the game about to take place on Field Four between a pair of nine and ten-year-old teams, the Hawks and the Rays. Approaching the stands, he scanned the home team crowd, laughing at the disparity between the over-invested parents and those glued to their smart phones, checking statuses from people they probably usually ignored. A hit of stimuli because the game, which meant so much to their kids, wasn't enough to shake them from their lazy, privileged malaise.

He broadcast the pathetic display to his viewers, now numbering 413, and sighed. Then he turned the phone back to himself, careful to keep his face hidden. He typed: *Who first?*

He turned the camera back to the stands, slowly panning the clueless parents, and wondered about the odds of someone in that crowd watching his stream. Perhaps, but he'd said nothing to surrender his plans.

Of course, commenters on the LiveLyfe video weren't exactly subtle.

Kill the foreign fucks first! one commenter said.

Responses were coming from people who'd followed the link he'd posted to /KillEveryone, a members-only sub board on NonAMus, a message board harboring some of the internet's most infamous trolls, miscreants, addicts, and perverts. If NonAMus and its popular content of hate speech, doxing, negative public opinion, and the most heinous, degrading, or illegal porn traffic, was in the gutter, then /KillEveryone was the rot festering in the sewer beneath it.

It was a snuff buff's wet dream, with photos and videos of murder and mayhem, the shit you couldn't find in the internet's more respectable corners. The kind of place you'd find pictures of mutilated children. And, as if that wasn't enough, commenters always posted despicable shit like, *Mmm … tasty* or *looks like Timmy lost his head* or *got nudes?*

He went by the handle, Orestes666 — a name he chose at random four months ago after stumbling into the community and his unexpected plan. He ingratiated himself to the group and its moderators by finding the most disgusting photos and videos online, then regularly posting with a clever comment or two. Members of /KillEveryone liked the gore but seemed to appreciate a biting punchline even more.

Orestes666 found the community tasteless. Pics of dead people, especially kids, weren't his thing. After all, these weren't the people who pissed him off. He wondered how many of /KillEveryone's members were only there for the LULZ, and how many were psychopaths who truly got off on this shit.

A week ago, he posted: *Who wants to see me go on a killing spree?*

Which was met with *extreme* enthusiasm. Of course.

One of the moderators pointed out that the board doesn't endorse illegal activity, but he didn't close the thread. A slap on the wrist for the sake of appearances. After all, most people talked a lot of shit on the board; but, so far as Orestes666 figured, nobody was *doing* any of the horrible things they talked about.

Shaming someone for their particular fantasy would only get that person labeled a fag or newfag, and likely booted from the community.

Orestes666 was surprised by the group's almost fierce community spirit. Who would have thought that such fucked up people could form a close-knit group?

He figured it was a board where its members were frustrated in their daily lives and held no true power, forced to do the bidding of their parents, spouses, and employers. /KillEveryone was a place to fantasize about what you would do if you genuinely stopped giving fucks.

Orestes666 had stopped giving fucks a year ago when his life spiraled right into hell.

Now he was ready to *do* something about it.

To make others feel his pain.

He looked at the thread and laughed at more of the comments.

Someone going by the handle of RightHandofOdd, wrote, *Don't kill 'dat blonde in the red shirt. Save her for me. Wanna suck on 'dem titties!*

He turned the camera back to the stands and started

walking, keeping an eye out for anyone who might be watching his livestream. Anyone who seemed like they were would need to go first. And unfortunately, that would ruin his show.

He passed the concession stand, eyeing the fat woman and her fat, half-retarded looking kid with disgust, walking away with giant sodas and hot dogs lathered in enough cheese sauce to bury the buns. The retard had cheese running down his bright green shirt.

Either one would be a mercy kill.

Orestes666 turned his camera on them to get commenter reaction.

Someone posted: *LOL! WHALE ALERT!*

Then someone else: *Hope you brought enuff ammo to bring down those elephants!*

Orestess666 smiled and kept walking, finding a spot along the right field fence, next to the home team dugout.

He watched the kids finish practicing, then head into the dugout for their pep talk from an obese, balding, over producing testosterone coach.

"Alright, this is what we've been working toward. This is why our practice matters! On three, I wanna hear you say. *Let's go, Hawks!*"

The kids shouted, "Let's go Hawks!" then scrambled onto the field.

Orestes666 focused on the kids, then turned the camera back to himself, still obscuring his face. "What should I do first?"

Someone commented: *Go grab the ball from the pitcher!*

Someone else commented: *Then shoot him!*

Orestes666 put the phone camera-side down on the ground, then he reached into his jacket and pulled out a rubber monkey mask. He picked up the phone and waited as the pitcher threw a few practice throws to the catcher.

He scanned the other dugout, saw a redhead waiting on-deck for a turn at bat that would never come.

Sorry, kids. Show's over.

The umpire told the batter to step into the batting box. Orestes666 hopped the fence and strode towards the pitcher's mound, aiming his phone at the crowds, capturing the players' confused expressions, the nervous laughter, then the angry faces of coaches, one in the home dugout, another in front of the away team dugout.

Orestes666 approached the pitcher and held out his hand, asking for the ball.

The pitcher, a young blond about nine-years-old, looked confused, first at Orestes666, then his coach.

"Get off the field!" yelled a steroid-case in a red team tee from the stands.

Orestes666 stared back at the crowd, still aiming his camera.

Then he looked at the screen and typed: *Which one?*

Dozens of commenters competed to either leave a witty comment or a first kill suggestion. Nobody suggested that he not do it.

The first commenter wrote: *Fugly bitch with blue shirt and red hat in the front row.*

Orestes666 reached into his pocket. He looked at the pitcher, still holding the ball, staring at him nervously. "If I were you, I'd run."

The kid's eyes widened as he saw the gun.

He dropped the ball and sprinted.

Orestes666 aimed at the "fugly old bitch" and fired.

Direct hit in the chest.

She pounded the ground. Her drink bled into the dirt.

The bleachers cleared in chaos.

Kids ran from the field screaming.

Orestes666 spotted an attractive woman he'd seen

glued to her cell phone earlier, now running toward the parking lot, and doing a shit job in her high heels.

He laughed as he fired off two shots.

The first missed.

The second hit her in the neck.

She fell to the ground screaming.

A rush of adrenaline coursed through him, freebasing God into his body.

The rush!

He'd imagined how it would feel to do something like this so many times in the last year. But never did he conceive that killing could feel *this* powerful. *This* liberating.

His heart raced, scanning the chaos, searching for someone else with a gun — it was Florida, after all — or his actual target. The person he came here to kill.

Sure enough, an older man with salt in his hair but only pepper in his beard aimed a pistol back at Orestes666 and fired.

And missed.

Orestes666 did not.

He fired back, catching the fucker right between the eyes.

Orestes666 scanned the dispersing crowd.

Anybody else wanna take a shot?

Anyone?

Then he finally spied his target, thirty-nine-year-old Chip Halverson, running into the home dugout, trying to get his daughter, Carrie, to safety.

Orestes666 ran to the dugout as a fat kid scrambled past him, clutching a Gatorade as if it were Kevlar.

Orestes666 tripped the kid, just to scare him.

The kid cried out as he hit the ground.

Orestes666 ignored him, cornering Chip and his

daughter, cowering at the other end of the dugout. There was an opening to their right, but only chain link between them and Orestes666.

Chip raised his hand. "Please, please don't. I'll give you whatever you want."

Orestes666 smiled, though its effect was lost behind the monkey mask. "Good, because I *want* you to die. But I'm going to give you a choice: Who should live, you or your daughter?"

Chip's eyes widened with panic. "Please, you don't have—"

Orestes666 fired a shot at the girl's leg.

She cried out and hit the ground.

"You fuck!" Chip screamed and started to charge.

Orestes666 aimed at his face and stopped him cold. "Last chance to choose. Three seconds. Three …"

Tears streamed down Chip's face as he blubbered and begged.

"Two…"

"Kill me! If you have to shoot any of us, shoot—"

Orestes666 fired two shots, one in the face, another in the chest, then watched the bastard slump to the ground.

"Daddy!"

Orestes666 looked down to see the comments streaming.

KILL HER TOO
BRUTAL!
Now kill yourself, FAG!
This can't be real!
Where is this?
Pete, why are you doing this?

Orestes666 looked to the crowd, searching for heroes. But everyone was either running or hiding. The fat kid was frozen on the ground, piss soaking the front of his pants.

He saw a few people who thought they were hidden —
a fat man behind a tree, a few kids quivering behind a row
of giant boulders at the entrance of the field.

Cars were fleeing the lot.

It wouldn't be long before the adults attending games
at the other two fields made their way over. Maybe another
hero looking for glory.

Sirens screamed in the distance.

He didn't have long.

Orestes666 looked at the screen.

A commenter said: *Run, Forest, run!*

He did, toward the woods and his stolen escape truck.

Chapter 1 - Mallory Black

"WHAT DO WE HAVE?" Mal asked Jamie Murphy, as she and Mike arrived at the killing fields. The crime scene tech met them in the parking lot and escorted them to Field Four.

Passing the bleachers, Mal spotted the outlines of bodies lying in front of the first base line, all of them under a tarp. Then her eyes traveled over the spilled drinks, food, clothing, and purses abandoned by the scattered crowd.

She imagined the terror. Parents searching for their children, struggling to get them to safety. The gunman stepping toward the bleachers, gun aimed, firing.

What kind of monster opens fire on a crowd of people, especially a crowd with so many children?

Mal wondered if this was terrorism.

Creek County had never had an incident of terror, but with the internet, any angry loner could be recruited, no matter the locale. Then any fool could make a name for themselves or advance a twisted ideology. All they needed was enough hate and a loaded weapon.

"Four dead, all adults," Jamie said.

"No kids? I guess there's a silver lining." Mal looked from the bodies, hidden to preserve a bit of dignity from the bystanders' cameras and news crews massed along the crime scene's edges, hoping to glimpse whatever they could, as if sight could ever provide understanding.

Another cop, Angus Pearson, came over and gave them the details gathered so far.

"Witnesses?" Mike asked.

"Over there." Jamie pointed to a second field full of parents and kids. There were easily fifty or more.

"Do we have victim names yet?"

"Yes," Angus said, reading off a list of names.

"Any relations stand out?"

"Other than all of them being moms and dads of kids here, no. But this has to run deeper than an angry parent on a rival team."

Mal sighed, eying the tarp and its terrible treasure, picturing the scene in her head. "And you said he had a monkey mask?"

Angus nodded. "Yes."

"Anyone get pictures or video?"

"Yeah, we're processing everything now. I'll let you know the minute we have anything useful."

"Okay, I want all footage sent to me, no matter how mundane."

"Got it," Angus said.

"Take me through it."

Angus pointed toward the right field fence. "The gunman came from there. He stepped through this gate over here and onto the field."

Mal nodded, looking at the gate. "We got photos and evidence tagged?"

"Yes."

"Okay, let's see what you've got."

She and Mike followed Angus through the gate and onto the field, passing fallen hats left behind by fleeing children.

"Seems he was recording the whole thing on his phone."

"Did we find his phone?" Mal asked.

"Not sure. We're still processing everything. But he went up to the pitcher's mound and asked the pitcher for the ball."

"What were his exact words?"

"Uh ..." Angus took out his notebook and looked down at his notes. "Nothing at first. He just held out his hand."

"What next?"

"He took out the gun and told the kid, 'If I were you, I'd run.' Then he began shooting.

"He gave the kid a chance to get away? Did he aim at the kid?"

"I don't know."

"Who was the first vic?"

"Belinda Thompson, 51, grandmother of one of the players, Zachary Thompson," Angus said as they walked back to the home team bleachers.

Angus lifted the tarp. The woman was lying face up, a bullet wound to her chest, dead eyes wide open, a crushed cup on the ground beside her, soda and blood staining the pavement.

"Who's next?"

Angus looked down at his notes, then pointed at another body between the bleachers and the concession stand.

"Claire Lambert, 29, a friend of one of the other kid's mothers. She got clipped making a run for the parking lot."

"What about the friend?"

"Becky Thompson, mother of the pitcher, Sam Thompson. Said she and Claire got split up when she went running toward the field to get her son." He turned to the dugout. "Then we've got Chip Halverson, 39, back in the dugout. His daughter, Carrie, nine, was shot in the leg. She's in stable condition and on her way to the hospital."

"Did we get a statement?" Mal asked.

"Not much. She was hysterical. Watched the man shoot her father."

"What happened?"

"We have a few different accounts from people who saw it. The killer apparently said something to Chip, though nobody heard what. He shot the girl; then there were more words exchanged between the two men before he killed Chip."

"Hmm," Mal said, exchanging a glance with Mike.

Mike asked, "Is Chip the only one that the killer spoke to?"

"Other than the pitcher, yes."

"I want to talk to the daughter the minute she's able."

"Okay," Angus said, scribbling in his notebook.

Mike's phone rang. He looked at the screen, then answered the call. "Cortez." His brow furrowed. "Okay, send it over." Again, he looked at the screen, waiting.

"What is it?" Mal asked.

"Batra is sending us a link to a LiveLyfe video. The killer wasn't recording. He was broadcasting *live*."

The video played.

Mal watched the scene unfold, her stomach knotting as kids screamed and scrambled on camera.

Then the first *POP!*

She watched all the way through.

The phone muted before the killer's words with Chip,

making their exchange all the more mysterious, and suspicious.

Mike brought the phone back to his ear, talking to their tech guru, Aanya Batra. "Peter Kincaid? What do you have?"

A moment of silence as Mike listened, then, "You are awesome!" He hung up, his eyes bright. "We've got a name and an address. Peter Kincaid, a girls' soccer coach. He's got a wife and two kids, lives over on 1215 Randolph. We're staging at the middle school."

Mal turned to Angus. "Looks like our suspect has a name. Going to bring him in. Can you get statements from the witnesses?"

Angus nodded.

Mal turned to Jamie. "How long until you can work these?"

"There a rush? Bodies aren't going anywhere over the weekend."

Mal rolled her eyes. "So, Monday morning?"

"Monday afternoon, like six-ish."

"Six is *afternoon* now? Shit, I need your hours."

Jamie laughed.

Mal and Mike headed back to the parking lot, got in the unmarked car, and headed to the staging area. Mike drove. Mal kept looking at the video, listening as loud as the phone would let her, hoping that she'd pick up on something useful. After the video played a few times, she scrolled through the comments.

"Jesus, you see this? These people were egging him on. Telling the guy who to kill. What the hell is wrong with people?"

"How long you got?"

"Hey, usually I'm the pessimist."

"What can I say, you're rubbing off on me," Mike joked.

The more Mal looked at the video, then at the profile page of the coach turned suspected killer, the more confused she became. But she couldn't quite put her finger on *what* wasn't adding up.

And then it hit her. "How many LiveLyfe friends do you have?"

"Hell, I dunno," Mike shrugged." I only use it to keep up with a few family members. Nobody can just call anyone anymore. It's gotta be LiveLyfe chat or video calls. What about you?"

"I don't have an account. Deleted it after Ashley died. Too many trolls."

"Why do you ask?"

"Well, the coach has five hundred friends, which seems normal, I guess, for someone involved in the community. But there are a ton of commenters on this video, and they don't appear to be his friends."

"*None* of them?"

"Well, none that I've seen so far. Most of the people commenting aren't using their real names. They're using either handles or obvious fake names like Ronald Reagan or Sir Charles BigCock."

"Ah, Chuck BigCock, he won the Nobel prize in '09, right?"

Mal laughed.

Then she called Batra and told her the same thing she'd just told Mike. "Any idea why he'd have so many live viewers and commenters? And why none of them were his actual friends?"

"It might have made the front page of Reddit or some site like that."

"Can you look into it?"

"I'm on it. I'm also going through his whole page, copying and saving it all in case it gets taken down. I have calls into LiveLyfe to get everything we can — IP addresses, private messages, anything we might need. I'll also look into the commenters, see if there's anything worthwhile."

"Thanks, Aanya."

They pulled into the school parking lot. The undercover SWAT truck was idling. A current of dread rippled through Mal, forcing her thoughts to the raid gone wrong on Paul Dodd. How the bastard had rigged explosives and murdered three sheriff's deputies, and seriously injured two others.

This would be Mal's first raid since returning to duty four months ago. The SWAT team was most frequently used for narcotics, not homicides. Then again, the county didn't usually have many of the latter, and not mass murderers.

She hoped they weren't walking into another trap.

Chapter 2 - Mallory Black

THE HOUSE WAS a single-story home in Pine Ridge, an older community built out in the eighties and nineties in an unincorporated part of the county surrounded by Pine Harbour on three sides. A burg caught in a perpetual tug-of-war between the county and the city seeking to annex it for the valuable property running along State Road 110 — widely regarded as the municipality's next big commercial expansion.

In many ways, Pine Ridge was frozen in time, a neighborhood holding out against the modern homes, shops, and strip malls that had exploded around it during the last building boom. Residents clung to their sovereign rights, wanting to park cars on their lawns, paint their homes in garish colors, and buck against every other code or policy that Pine Harbour enforced upon its residents.

Under such chaos, it was common to find a million dollar palace sharing the street with a hovel that ought to be condemned.

The coach's home was one of the nicer, more modern builds on a street with several eyesores, a single-story house with a well-manicured lawn full of flowering bushes, a neat brick walkway, a wrought iron fence, and a wooden bench in the front yard.

Of all the houses, it was the one she'd least expect a monster to live in.

Most of the Sheriff's office vehicles parked at the end of the street.

The SWAT truck rolled up to the house, the unit splitting. Some deputies took the rear while others stormed the front.

A deputy knocked twice, loud.

No answer.

No waiting.

They battered the front door with a battering ram and surged into the home, guns drawn.

Mal watched from two houses over, on edge in an unmarked car, waiting with Mike for their turn.

She flashed back, watching her fellow officers storm Paul Dodd's house only to be murdered by his fiery trap.

A part of her waited for another explosion, even though bombs and traps weren't something they usually had to worry about. But once it happened to your siblings in blue, it was hard to approach another raid the same way.

But there were no explosions. She listened to the deputies' voices crackling over the radio, saying "clear" after checking each room. One said, "The house is clear. We've got a white male, possible suspect, dead, gunshot wound to the head."

Mal and Mike headed into the house, slipping on gloves and booties. She immediately saw why the officer had said "possible" suspect.

Slumped, dead in the living room recliner, was a white man in a tee and boxers, his jaw blown away at the bottom. An exit painted the wall behind his skull in chunks of bone, blood, and brain.

In his right hand, slumped over his lap, he held a Smith & Wesson Shield 45ACP.

She pulled out a recorder and spoke into it, "No obvious signs of rigor or lividity, blood is slightly congealed ..."

Mal took some preliminary photos of the corpse and crime scene, using her phone before the crime tech arrived with an actual camera.

On the coffee table, next to two open bottles of beer, was a note.

She snapped a photo, then read:

I MAY BE A SICK MAN, but NOBODY has the right to judge me.
Nobody but my maker.
Sorry to anyone I may have hurt.
Peter Kincaid

MIKE STARED AT THE LETTER. "Well, that looks like a confession if ever I saw one." He looked back up at Mal.

"Yeah, but *what's* he confessing to? Does that sound like it came from a guy who just shot up a baseball game?"

There was also a phone, face down on the table. She wanted to pick it up, pour through every megabyte, searching for evidence to close the case. But it would be best if she left that for Aanya.

Evidence collection rules were specific when it came to computers, phones, and other devices where data could be erased with a keystroke. Fail to enter the right password, and you might find the phone's data wiped. And while there were methods of retrieval, they were never surefire and could cause issues when entering the device as evidence in a trial.

Sometimes Mal wished she were born fifty years earlier when tech didn't offer lazy criminals easy tools to commit crimes in relative anonymity. Once upon a time, a perp had to leave his house to rob, extort, or abuse someone.

Mike went outside to update Gloria Bell — the sheriff — while Mal walked the house, snapping additional pictures and searching for evidence without disturbing the scene. As tempting as it might be to call this a suicide and then wrap the case (and the shooting at the baseball field), every death had to be investigated as a possible homicide.

The coach's home was spotless. A nice three-bedroom, built within the last six years or so, with too many sconces and a master bedroom with a studio apartment's worth of wasted space. The bed was unmade, clothes on the floor. The room's only personality lived on the two shelves holding trophies for a girls' soccer team. There were also a couple of team photos from the coach's two previous seasons. The other two bedrooms were spare, and reeked of recent divorce, providing a cold room with little comfort for refugees of a domestic civil war.

There was another small room that could have been an office. It looked like a small hotel room waiting for its guest. The bed was neatly made, and there was a night stand with only a vase and a single flower, a small desk topped with issues of Elle and Real Simple, a dresser without any knick-knacks.

Was this room for a relative? A girlfriend?

There was nothing in the room to indicate a regular guest. The magazines were current, with the labels addressed to Peter Kincaid.

Mal returned to the bedroom, saw four pillows on the bed. It was hard to tell if two people had been sleeping there or not. There were no indentations in either the pillows or the bed.

She stepped around toward the left side of the bed, looked in the trash can and saw a used condom.

She remembered the bottles of beer on the coffee table.

Mal stepped back out into the living room, past the body, and reached down to carefully touch the bottles without moving them.

They weren't cold..

But someone had likely been with him last night. Could it be the killer? Or had he slept with someone, then the two went their separate ways in the morning, with the suspect going off to kill a bunch of people?

Who was his guest?

And what did they know about him?

She needed to find out.

She stepped outside the house, told Gloria and Mike what she'd found, then said, "We need to find out who he had over last night or this morning. See what they know."

"So, do we like him as our shooter?" Gloria asked.

"I won't know anything until tech gets a look at stuff."

"But what does your gut say?" They rarely saw Gloria at a crime scene, especially on the weekend. She wanted this case off of everyone's desk yesterday. The last thing she needed with the election in seven months was a community thinking it wasn't safe to bring your kids to a baseball game. Her challengers would exploit fear to get themselves elected.

No single person could keep an entire community safe. A sheriff's job amounted to policies. What kind of work did the sheriff believe was best? Before Gloria, the sheriff's department wasn't exactly known for its neighborhood involvement. Deputies only went to Butler for arrests. But after Gloria stepped in, deputies became more community-oriented, getting to know the residents, business, and civic leaders within each city.

It had helped to reduce the crime numbers, but there were always those who thought the old traditions and the disgraced sheriff's ways were The Right Way to Do Things. They didn't think that Gloria was tough enough on crime, and jumped at every opportunity to make her appear weak or ineffective.

Nobody wanted a feeble sheriff.

"My gut?" Mal said. "My gut says let's wait to see what we've got here."

Gloria sighed. "Okay, we've had two shootings in one day, and I need to get the hell out of here before the media shows up asking *me* what the hell is going on. Which means I need answers from you two, ASAP. I can't stomach another, 'It's an ongoing investigation.'"

The bodies aren't even cold, and you want the case closed?

Mal wanted to tell Gloria to give them some breathing room — fuck the media. But Mike's look said, *Don't engage. Just let her vent and move along.*

Mal bit her tongue, holding back any of the smart-ass comments she might make if an election weren't already kissing the horizon.

"We'll keep you in the loop," Mike assured her.

"Thank you," Gloria said, then got into her SUV and tore away from the scene before the news could arrive.

Most of the neighbors were already out, peeking over, trying to get a look. Mal turned to Mike. "We may as well interview them until Jamie gets here. Maybe someone will know something so we can give the boss lady some answers."

Mike smiled.

Chapter 3 - Mallory Black

MIKE AND MAL split their interviews, Mal talking to the women on the street while Mike took the men. No reason to double their efforts. While there were times you might want to have somebody else interview a witness, it was usually best not to add additional work. Witness accounts were hit and miss enough already.

Mal was on the sidewalk across the street from the Kincaid's, talking to Sue Peterson. Sue was a heavyset woman in a grease-stained red tank top, clutching a sloppy-faced one-year-old on her hip. When she spotted a man making a beeline toward them, she dropped her cigarette and squished the butt into the sidewalk with her ratty blue flip-flop.

He was in his late thirties or early forties, tall, stocky, skin like leather, with a dirty blond buzz cut, sideburns, bushy albino caterpillar eyebrows, and intense chestnut colored eyes. He was wearing blue coveralls with a circular patch: *Sal's Towing*.

Sue shifted her baby to the other arm and looked at him. "Hey, Daryl. How's it going?"

"Okay," he said in the Southern drawl that was a lot more common before all the city folk from New York and South Florida ruined things for the locals. "What's going on?"

"Coach Kincaid is dead."

"What?" Daryl's eyebrows furrowed above his crooked nose. "What happened?"

Mal already had everything she was likely to get from Sue. She thanked her, then turned her attention to Daryl. "How do you know Mr. Kincaid?"

"He coached my daughter's soccer team. What happened? How'd he die?"

"A gunshot wound."

"Shit. A break-in? I bet it was those fucking Mexicans on the next street! You look into them yet? There's like fifty in one house."

"No, Coach K done shot up a buncha people at the baseball field earlier," Sue said, still hovering with her kid. She lit another cigarette, not realizing, or caring, that she was blowing smoke in her baby's face.

Mal had to look away from the woman or else she was likely to give her a lecture about the dangers of second-hand smoke. On the list of casual abuses she saw from parents, smoking was low on the list. Mal would occasionally speak her mind as a patrol cop, but it never went well, and always made things more difficult. It also probably earned the kids a wallop out of spite.

"It's still early in the investigation. That's why we're talking to neighbors. What's your name, sir?" Mal readied her notebook and pen, already scribbling *Daryl*.

"Daryl." He looked confused. "Daryl Turner. What's all this about shooting up a baseball field?"

"We believe that Mr. Kincaid shot four people earlier this morning. We're still investigating the matter."

Sue piped up again. "He livestreamed it on LiveLyfe! Dude fucking snapped!"

"Shit, I always knew something was wrong with that guy. Seemed a little too nice. My wife and daughter said I was too paranoid. *Hah!* Figured he was either queer or a pervert. What man has two boys and volunteers to coach a bunch of high school girls?"

"You said your daughter is on his team?"

"Yeah."

"What's her name?"

"Katie, with an 'ie.'" Color fled his face. His eyes went wide. He looked toward his house, then back at Mal. "Was anyone with him? When you found him? I know his wife and kids are outta town, but ...."

"No. Why?"

Daryl sighed, long and heavy. "Katie sometimes goes over to practice in his back yard."

The baby started crying. Mal wondered if he realized his mother was a horrible person. "Okay, okay," Sue said to the kid, then, "I gotta go feed Brandon. If you need anything else, you got my number."

"Yes, ma'am. Thank you," Mal said, glad to have her gone.

Sue waddled away in her cloud of smoke.

Mal turned back to Daryl. "You said that you thought something was wrong with the coach. Did he do or say anything to make you suspicious?"

"Nah, if he did, I wouldn't have let Katie on the team. Sometimes people just give you a vibe, ya' know?"

She did. Mal was getting one now. Daryl was a racist homophobe.

"The man was always acting like he was better than me, and stuff."

"How so?" Mal asked, taking notes.

24

"I dunno, just the way he'd look at me. He had money, not sure where he got it, but I doubt he ever worked a *real* job. And he loved to flaunt it — he'd take the kids out to eat at expensive restaurants after games. He even bought Katie an iPhone for her fourteenth birthday. Who buys a phone like that for someone else's kid?"

"An *iPhone?* Kind of an expensive gift."

"That's what *I* said. I told her to give it back."

"Did she?"

"Of course," he said with the authority of a man who had complete dominion over his teenage daughter. Mal wondered if he truly exerted that much control or if it was only delusion.

"Did you ever see him act inappropriately with any of the girls?"

"No. He was a bit of a fruit; you know what I'm saying?"

Mal nodded, hiding her disdain.

"Why you askin'? Did you guys find anything?"

"It's still early in the investigation," Mal said for what felt like the hundredth time that hour. "We're looking at all possibilities. Would it be possible to talk to Katie? Is she home?"

Daryl looked from the house to Mal.

"I dunno. My wife's car is gone, but we can check." Daryl turned and headed back toward his house.

Mal followed.

EVERY MEMBER of law enforcement has seen places where it didn't seem possible for humans to live. Houses that looked nice on the outside but were nightmares inside. Filthy, full of vermin, a reek that lingered for days.

But occasionally, Mal was pleasantly surprised.

Some homes looked old and decrepit on the outside but were nice on the inside. That was the situation with Daryl's single-story ranch-style house. The lawn was over-grown. A pair of broken cars marred the driveway, and a third was killing the grass. The garage door was crumbling and slightly ajar. The home's chipped paint was best described as a hopeless beige.

Mal and Mike followed Daryl through the front door. She was expecting dark and dusty, knee-deep in a hoarder's sea of miseries. But the interior of the small house was immaculate. Relatively bright. Furniture and appliances were all at least a decade old but in excellent condition. The carpet was clean, free of debris, animal hair, or the stains Mal would have expected to see in a run-down home. The living room opened to a kitchen on the right and another pair of bedrooms on the left.

Two things jumped out immediately to Mal: the giant wooden cross in the living room, and its location — directly on the wall facing the couch, the spot where most family homes had a TV.

Unless they had televisions in their bedrooms, they appeared to be one of few homes Mal had been in without one.

Nor did she see a computer, tablet, or cell phone.

Sitting on the coffee table was a selection of knitting, sewing, and magazines — all arts and crafts titles. Beside them, a large Bible.

There were two chairs in addition to the couch. One was a small armchair, and the other was a plush brown leather recliner. Beside that was a wooden stand stuffed with newspapers and hunting magazines.

"Katie!" her father bellowed, much louder than he needed to.

One of the bedroom doors opened to Katie, a scrawny blonde wearing a long dress like something out of Little House on the Prairie. Her hair was pulled back in a loose pony tail. Fifteen or sixteen years old.

Katie's eyes weren't red. But they were puffy. Mal suspected she had been crying or had allergies.

"Yes, father?" Her voice timid, eyes worried like she was in trouble.

"The police here would like to talk to you about Coach Kincaid."

The girl looked spooked. She knew something for sure.

"Hello, Katie. I'm Detective Mallory Black, and this is my partner, Mike Cortez. We'd just like to talk to you about your coach. Is there a place we could sit down?"

Daryl walked to the kitchen and pointed to a small table. "You all can chat here."

Mal and Mike sat on one side of the rectangular table, Katie sat on the other.

"You all want a drink?" Daryl asked.

"No thanks," said Mike and Mal together.

Daryl grabbed a Coke from the fridge, popped the tab, then sat beside his daughter. He scraped the chair against the floor, sat with his elbows claiming most of the table, and looked at them as he guzzled his drink.

At first, Daryl had seemed rightly concerned about his daughter being around the coach suspected of shooting up a ball field before ending his own life. But his body language now said something else: Daryl was threatened by their presence.

And Mal wanted to know why.

Did he have something to do with the coach's death? Did he find out the coach was abusing his daughter, so he handled the matter himself?

Mal would have to find out where he'd been this morning, but—

Daryl reached over to put an arm around Katie. She flinched ever-so-slightly.

Mal *knew* that flinch. She'd seen it countless times. In wives and girlfriends living with a domineering or abusive man.

Mal's heart sank further. "How well did you know Coach Kincaid?"

Katie looked at her dad as if seeking permission to open her mouth. He nodded, took another drink, and started eyeballing Mike.

"He's been my coach for two years."

"I told her mother she didn't need to be on some damned soccer team. But *noooo*, she thought it was good to interact with kids her age."

Mal and Mike traded glances.

"What do you mean 'interact with kids her age?'" Mike asked.

"We homeschool Katie. And Lynn, bless her naive heart, thought Katie needed to be around more kids her age. I told her the church has plenty of kids."

"They're not my age," Katie said. "They're all either way younger or way older."

"What about that Kenny kid? He's in the same grade as you."

"Kenny is a dork," Katie whined.

"Well, at least he's not in a gang or one of those skanks on your soccer team."

Katie said nothing. This was clearly an ancient argument.

Mal steered the conversation back to the coach. "So, your father said you'd go to his house, and he'd coach you."

"Yes. He was very nice."

Mal noted her use of past-tense. Maybe a neighbor had called the house and told her what had happened, or Katie had seen the sheriff's deputies or news crews surrounding the crime scene. But Mal suspected something else.

Getting to that something else in front of her father was delicate. She didn't want to get the girl in trouble. But a case needed to be worked, and Mal couldn't concern herself too much with the kid's possible fallout.

"So, how did you meet?" Mal asked.

"The soccer league had put some flyers up at our church."

"Does he go there?"

"Sometimes. It's one of those teams that'll take anyone, no matter how good you are. But I spent my first year on the bench. And I was awful the few times I did get to play. I was about to quit, but he talked me into staying, and offered to help me practice a few times a week."

"Did you ever see him act inappropriately with any of the girls? Or maybe heard rumors?"

"Oh, no, ma'am. Everybody loved him."

Daryl snickered, stood, then went to the fridge for another Coke. She spotted several cases of Budweiser in the fridge and bet he couldn't wait for her to leave so he could get good and drunk.

"Did he ever act inappropriately toward you?"

The slightest hesitation in the girl's response.

"No, ma'am."

"Did he have any enemies?"

"I don't think so. Like I said, everybody liked him. He was nice."

Again, past tense. And not once did the girl ask why they were asking about her coach.

Mal asked a few more questions, scribbling in her note-book while Daryl paced the kitchen.

He cut in, "So, how exactly did he die? You're asking us all these questions, but we'd like some answers. I wanna know if I need to be worried about leaving my family home while I'm at work."

Mal gave him a pleasant smile. "Could you excuse us for a moment?"

"Yes," the girl said.

Mal got Mike's attention, leading him toward the living room. She could feel Daryl's eyes as she whispered, "Could you get me some alone time with her? Maybe keep the dad busy for a few minutes?"

Mike nodded.

They returned to the kitchen and sat. Daryl eyed them.

"Sorry, I just had to ask him how much we could say in front of your daughter," Mal said. "Mike will give you more details if the two of you would like to go outside."

"Alright," Daryl said, obviously annoyed, but curious.

Once alone, Mal met Katie's eyes.

"Why didn't you ask what happened to the coach?"

"What do you mean?" Katie crossed her arms, avoiding eye contact. A shit liar.

"We never said what happened to your coach, but you were talking about him in the past tense like you already knew that he's dead."

"I saw the cop cars and the news vans. I guess I assumed."

Mal shook her head. "Whatever you're not saying, you can tell me. You won't get in trouble."

Katie shook her head, lips trembling. "I don't know anything."

Mal leaned forward, trying to decide between the

threat of punishment or understanding. Compassion was probably the key.

"Did he touch you?"

Katie's eyes began to well up. "I told you, I don't know anything."

"Bullshit."

The girl's eyes widened.

"I wasn't lying when I said that you wouldn't be in trouble. But if we find out that you are withholding information, we *can* charge you with obstruction of justice. Maybe more. I don't want to do that, Katie."

She squeezed her eyes shut, trying to stem the flow of welling tears. But it only made things worse.

Katie finally opened her terrified eyes. "You don't know my father. How mad he will be."

"We can help you," Mal said.

"No," she shook her head. "Nobody can."

Mal heard the front door open.

Shit!

She reached into her pocket, palmed a card and handed it to Katie. "If you change your mind, call or text me," she whispered. "Anytime, day or night."

Behind her, Daryl asked, "What the hell's going on here? What did you say to my daughter?"

"Nothing. She was just upset about the coach."

Katie nodded, "All of a sudden, it just hit me. He's gone."

Daryl stared at Katie, then at Mal. "Are you all done here? Did you get everything you needed?"

"Yes, thank you for your help," Mal said, offering her hand to Katie.

The girl's handshake was tentative and weak, her flesh cold.

Mal offered her hand to Daryl. He firmly shook it, his eyes boring into hers: *I'm on to you, bitch.*

Mal and Mike left.

And as they did, Mal was certain that their best lead might never pick up the phone.

Chapter 4 - Jasper Parish

JASPER PARISH SAT in the shadows of a battered van, nearly invisible in the rear of the parking lot that served as overflow for the beachside bars and clubs oozing between Sixth and Eighth along A1A in Coral Cove. His van faced an old wooden fence, its paint chipped and weathered from years of salty air.

He watched the parking lot entrance in his side view mirror, awaiting his victim's arrival.

Unlike St. Augustine and Jacksonville, parking was still free in the Cove, without the ten to twenty dollar hustle for the privilege of getting a temporary space within a block of wherever you wanted to eat or drink at. Parking lots were unattended, no security hanging around. Jasper could wait for Calum Kozack as long as he wanted. Eventually, he'd stumble out to his red Lamborghini, parked to the left of Jasper's van.

Calum was the son of Oliver Kozack, one of Creek County's most powerful businessmen. Calum had a bulletproof vest when it came to the law. Not only had he been responsible for Jasper's daughter, Jordyn's death, but he'd recently skated on a rape charge because there hadn't been enough evidence to charge him — code for the DA's office didn't have the guts to bring charges against Oliver Kozack's son.

Jasper had let the boy go once.

He would never make that mistake again.

He glanced at his watch: *9:40 PM*.

Calum usually started his Saturday nights at Vibes — a club owned by his friend, Mickey Cerano — before heading into Jacksonville for action.

Jasper had considered abducting Calum in Jacksonville but didn't know the area nearly as well. The clubs there were far busier, making an ambush more difficult. And Calum probably wouldn't return to his beach house alone.

This was the best place to grab him.

Jasper just hoped that Calum would leave before the Coral Cops started their rounds. He probably had another hour or so before the first patrol car cruised by, assuming none were called out to an accident nearby.

On the side of Jasper's van was a magnet, one of several for various non-existent out-of-town businesses. This one read: *Johnny B's Handyman Services*, with a Daytona phone number below. The van was untraceable, designed to blend in. The last thing Jasper needed was to get pulled over for another crime, especially if the police did a thorough search and found the hidden recess under the shelving unit, where Calum would live out his last moments on the way to Jasper's kill site.

Lights swept the parking lot.

Jasper prepared to get out of the car in case he drew suspicion, and head to the bar on the south side of Sixth. A working stiff eager for a drink.

The car, a black Mercedes, pulled in and parked four spots from Jasper.

A balding muscular man in a tight black tee emerged with a bleach bottle blonde in a tight dress and tacky heels. They glanced over at him.

Jasper pretended to be talking on his phone, waving his hand and not looking their way.

He waited a bit, then glanced over.

They were already gone.

Calum entered the lot, talking loudly on his cell, calling the person on the other end, "bro" and "dude" a dozen times in half the seconds, it seemed.

Jasper climbed into the back of the van and slid open the right side panel door, exposing the driver's side of Calum's red Lambo.

He hopped out of the van, pretending to root around for something as he listened, trying to determine Calum's proximity. About twenty feet away, judging from his voice.

Jasper steeled himself. He would have to be quick if he hoped to render Calum unconscious before the punk could fight back.

Calum was six-foot-five, wide, and muscular. He could've easily had a football scholarship to Florida State if he'd had even the tiniest ounce of self-discipline to do anything more than work out and party. As it was, he was about three inches taller and much younger than Jasper — he'd probably be a problem if Jasper tried to take him down without any aid.

Jasper reached into the bucket on the floor, unscrewed the bottle of chloroform, doused a rag, and waited, his back to Calum's car. Listened as the footsteps drew closer.

Listened as Calum said, "I know, bro. She's such a bitch. But that's okay. I told Stacy everything. Pre-empted that shit hard."

With his left hand clutching the rag, Jasper reached

into his pants pocket with the right and clicked on the signal jammer.

Calum spilled another few sentences before his voice grew agitated. "Hey, dickbag, did you hear me?"

Silence.

Calum stood just in front of Jasper's van, looking at his phone, confused. He brought it back to his ear, "Hello? You there? Fucking signal!"

Calum approached his car door.

Jasper didn't turn back to acknowledge the man, but he imagined Calum rolling his eyes at the black man with his dirty van having the audacity to park so close to his shiny red sports car.

Calum's car alarm beeped as he unlocked it.

Jasper heard Calum squeeze past him and open his door.

Jasper sprang into action, coming at Calum from behind, shoving the chloroform rag tightly against his mouth and nose.

Calum struggled, banging Jasper hard into the rear of his van.

He elbowed him hard in the ribs and stomped on Jasper's foot.

Despite the steel toe boots, Jasper held him tight.

He couldn't let go.

Calum tried to scream.

That's it, open up and breathe in, boy.

Calum went limp and slumped backward.

Jasper held the rag, long enough to make sure the man wasn't faking it.

Once certain, he pulled Calum into the van.

~

JASPER WAS fifteen minutes away from the beachside parking lot when Jordyn appeared in the passenger seat.

"You can't do this," she pleaded.

Jasper slammed on the brakes, nearly losing control of the van and running off the road.

He stared at his dead daughter sitting in the seat beside him.

"No, no, you're dead. You're not here."

"And yet, here I am. Maybe someone forgot to take their meds. Maybe you wanted to see me."

"No," he said, shaking his head, trying to remember the last time he'd taken his pills.

This morning?

"You're not real."

"Come on, Dad, admit it — you missed me."

Jasper hadn't seen Jordyn in six months, the longest she'd been gone since her death. He hadn't seen her since Detective Mallory Black had asked him who he was talking to.

His delusion cracked.

And the aftermath had been hell, forcing Jasper to remember his daughter's death. *How* she had died. He was forced to remember his illness. And visit his shrink. Get medicated again before he went off the deep end.

A car raced past them, its horn blaring.

Jasper had to get moving again before he drew attention from the authorities. If they pulled him over now, there was no way he could hide his racing heart, crazed thoughts, or the ghost in his passenger seat.

He reached into his pockets, even though he knew he hadn't brought any pills.

"Come on, Dad, you don't want me to go, do you?"

He looked at her, sitting there just as real as the road

beneath him. He returned his eyes to the windshield, trying to straighten his thoughts enough so that he didn't get lost.

What road am I looking to get off at?

He glanced back at Jordyn. Despite being a figment of his imagination, there was an odd comfort in seeing her again. It was bizarre to find comfort in a lie, but Jasper couldn't help how he felt. Seeing her there, sitting in her jeans, black shirt and jacket, her hair colored purple under a black knit cap, smiling at him, she seemed so damned real. Hell, he could smell her shampoo.

Jordyn continued, "You can't kill him."

"Yes, I can."

"If you kill him, you *will* get caught."

"Nope. They'll never find his body. They'll think he took off."

"Dad, you don't really believe that they'll stop looking for Calum Fucking Kozack, do you? Every department in the city, hell, in the state, will be looking for him."

"They won't find him. No body, no murder."

"Maybe not, but they'll be onto you. *She'll* be onto you. How long do you think you can sneak around killing people with her watching?"

"Who?" he asked.

"That detective you saved. Mallory Black. She's going to put two and two together, and when she does, she's going to come for you."

"Don't you get it? I'm doing this for you?"

"For me?" Jordyn laughed. "For me?"

"Yes, for you. It's his fault you're dead. And he needs to pay. Don't you *want* him to pay?"

"Not if it lands you in jail."

"It won't."

"You're not thinking clearly. You can only kill bad guys because you're not connected to them. You do your homework. You don't go after targets that'll lead back to you. Like Calum will."

"Someone has to stop him. He just got off *again*. How long do I just sit back and watch him ruin young women?"

"Not now, Dad. You need to wait for a better time."

"There won't *be* a better time. The hard part is done. He's in the back of the van. I already committed a crime, Jordyn. Hell, I'd argue that me letting him go now is *more* likely to get my ass caught. The damage is done. The only way through it is to get through it."

"No. You let him go now. Drive him back to his car, take his wallet or something and make it look like a robbery."

"No."

"Do this, and I'm leaving for good."

He looked over at her expecting to see her pouty face, but she was staring at him, her eyes deadly serious.

"If you do this, I won't come back. I know you think it's the pills that kept me away, but it wasn't. I left because I thought you needed time alone. But then I saw what you're doing with that alone time, and I had to intervene before you screwed up your life for this piece of trash."

"No. You're not here. The pills have kept you away."

"I know what your shrink *thinks* is wrong with you, but it isn't that, Dad. I *am* here. But if you do this, I won't be. And you'll never see me again."

Chapter 5 - Mallory Black

MAL SLIPPED into one of the last pews in the Beacon Community Church just as the Narcotics Anonymous meeting was starting.

She felt like an imposter unworthy of sitting with the dozen or so others up front. It had been more than a month since her last meeting. She'd blown off her sponsor Mary's calls. She hadn't spoken to her ex-husband Ray since he'd gone with her to a meeting six months ago. His calls had been going straight to voicemail, too.

But, despite the missed meetings, Mal had been sober for six months, at least when it came to the pills.

And that was no small accomplishment.

As she sat in the back listening to the meeting, Mal didn't feel like she belonged. She didn't know any of the people up front, and most of them seemed to know each other well.

There were two NA meetings on any given day, with rotating locations. From what her sponsor had said, regulars broke down into two groups: location specific and those that went to many meetings, location agnostic. Both groups had people falling in and out over time as new users joined the fray. Some would relapse, some would return, but if you went enough, you eventually found your family.

A family where most of the others attended meetings and followed the Twelve Steps. But those steps were a large part of what kept Mal from becoming more involved.

Mal didn't want to list all the people she'd wronged. That list was too long, and she had no idea where to start. And hell, most of the people were shit heels who didn't even deserve her apology or the making of amends.

Another problematic part of the Twelve Steps was the whole belief in a higher power thing. Though some of the NA folks said that higher power didn't have to be God, or even spiritual. But you were expected to believe in *something* greater than yourself. Expected to surrender your life to a higher power, and let that power help you.

But there was no higher power.

There certainly wasn't some omniscient God offering to help her, or any of the other poor wretches in the church. Hell, nothing she saw on the job — from drug addicts squandering their lives, to the murderers and abusers of women and children, to the absolute monsters like the man who opened fire at a baseball game that morning — offered any evidence of God, unless He was the cruelest of tricksters.

If Mal wanted something done she only had herself to count on. God wouldn't punch the clock or catch the killers for her. He wouldn't dull Mal's craving for the pills, or bring her daughter, Ashley, back to life.

And where was God when her daughter's murderer, Paul Dodd, came back and kidnapped another little girl, Jessi Price? Where the hell was He when Paul was going to rape Jessi right in front of Mal?

Nowhere.

And it wasn't God who kept her from pulling the trigger despite wanting vengeance for her daughter, and for Jessi.

It was her strength — a strength she had to dive deep to find. The kind of strength that more often than not felt like a flickering candle in the coldest rainstorm. The kind of strength she didn't even know she had, and could only discover once she was already empty.

It had nothing to do with *God*.

No, it was Mal.

It was also human intervention, in the shape of a man whose name Mal didn't know. But he wasn't some fucking angel or messenger of God. He was a man. A hunter. Some crazy vigilante who tried to get Mal to murder Paul.

A woman in the front of the church started recounting her week, thanking God for His help getting through it without using. Anger coursed through Mal. She wasn't even sure *why* she was so angry, but that didn't dim her rage.

Was it anger at people believing in something that she no longer believed in?

Was it that they could so easily have faith while her capacity for hope had withered to memory?

Did Mal even *want* to believe?

Or was it that these people giving credit to a higher power simply didn't deserve what they had? In many ways that abdication of personal responsibility felt to Mal like a future excuse in the making.

Well, obviously I gave in, I'm only human. I need that Higher Power to help me!

Needing a Higher Power was admitting that you couldn't do it on your own. Embracing a weakness that you didn't need to accept. It was buying into someone else's bullshit. Maybe *they* need someone or something greater than them, but Mal certainly didn't.

Fuck that. Don't try to tell me what I need!

Mal didn't need some invisible man in the sky to help her do anything. She'd gotten this far on her own, and every day and every battle came down to her being strong enough to fight. And at least if she failed, she'd place the blame on the person who deserved it: *herself*.

She stood from the pew and made her way out of the church, not even looking to see if anyone had noticed.

She pushed through the front door and bumped into the last person she wanted to run into.

Ray smiled. "Hey, didn't expect to see you here."

"Yeah, I'm, uh, just leaving."

They stood in awkward silence outside the church, both dancing around an awkward moment from six months ago. He'd come to her hotel room after she'd been abducted by Paul Dodd. Mal had needed a friend because she was feeling so damned lost after the ordeal.

One thing led to another, and they kissed.

It might have led to more, but Ray stopped it.

And then he left.

Mal was more than alone. She felt stupid and embarrassed. She'd almost slept with him. Yes, he was her ex-husband, but still, it was wrong. He was with Julie. It would be one thing if they both suddenly realized how much they loved one another. If they were somehow able to surmount the pain of losing a child and all that had followed. If they were in that place, maybe she wouldn't have felt shitty about it. But this wasn't that. Mal wasn't sure what it was, except *not right*.

Mal decided to call her sponsor and attend a meeting that night. It was the last time she'd used. She turned her weakest moment into one of her strongest. But now, seeing

Ray after all this time, Mal was that desperate idiot in the hotel room, making a move and getting rebuffed.

"What are *you* doing here? Are you——?"

"No, I'm not drinking again. Just ... every now and then I need to remember the reasons why."

Alcohol was Ray's drug of choice after Ashley's death, but he preferred NA because he felt the AA meetings were a bit too boisterous for his introverted personality. Mal had a feeling that one of his co-workers at the Chronicle was probably in AA, and that was the real reason he avoided the place, but she never questioned him.

They stood in the awkward moment. Mal's eyes flicked to her car.

But Ray wasn't moving from the doorway. He seemed to be working up the courage to speak. She hoped he wouldn't mention their last encounter.

God, no. Anything but that.

She saw something else in his eyes and caught a whiff of his breath.

"Are you okay?"

He looked at her, then away. He sighed. "I'm *not* drinking again, but I did have a few drinks tonight. Julie and I got into it. And I just had to ... well, get a drink. I was heading home and saw——"

Saw my car?

"The church, and decided maybe it'd be better to come here than go home."

Mal felt even more uncomfortable, unsure of what to say. She didn't want to be involved in whatever was happening between Ray and Julie. But at the same time, he was probably shy of friends he could talk to. He had a few at the paper, and that was more than her, but still, Ray looked like he needed a friend. She wondered if she should go inside the church with him, or if it'd be better to go somewhere else?

She hated the idea of going back inside, especially after having just left. Mal moved out of his way. "Well, don't let me stop you." Immediately regretting how that came out, she added, "Did you want someone to talk to? I mean, I'm not sure if your ex-wife is the ideal person to help you handle problems with your girlfriend, but … I'm here."

"No, I couldn't do that," he said, breaking away from her eyes. "You have enough on your plate."

Another moment of awkward silence.

Mal could tell that he didn't want to go in the church any more than she wanted to stay in there. "Do you wanna grab a coffee? We can both bitch about our days."

Ray laughed.

His eyes were slightly wet, but there was also a spark — the one she sometimes used to see when he stared into her eyes on a lazy Sunday morning. A spark she hadn't seen in a long time.

"Okay," he said.

"I'm driving."

THEY SAT in a booth in the back of Morningstar Diner, Ray slowly eating eggs and home fries while Mal nursed a cup of coffee.

"You sure you don't want any?" Ray was already looking a hell of a lot better than he had outside the church. Some food in his belly, a little less intoxicated, and not quite as awkward. More like the Old Ray.

"Nah. I had a burger with Mike after work."

"You working that baseball shooter case?"

"Yeah. Were you there?"

"They had me in Jacksonville shooting a surfing charity event."

"Be glad," she said. "It was awful."

While most news photographers would chomp at the bit to cover a shooting spree or other tragedy, Ray never had that particular instinct. He preferred a typical puff piece or local youth sports. He had shot some tragic scenes, including the harrowing aftermath of an accident on I-95, but those moments always left him rattled for days.

He considered it a personal weakness to his career, particularly when newsrooms were shedding skilled photographers and handing reporters iPhones to shoot with. But Mal had always seen it as strength. He saw humanity at its worst and still displayed its best, whether that meant a photo of a heroic firefighter carrying a child out of a house or a father and daughter at a Daddy Daughter dance at school. Ray had an eye for moments that touched her soul in the best possible way. The news needed more of that, less of the grim reality that threatened to drown the planet in sorrow and darkness.

"So, how are you holding up? You think the coach did it?"

"I'm okay. As for the coach, I dunno."

Ray looked at Mal as if trying to determine if she didn't know, or couldn't say. One good thing about not being married anymore was avoiding conversations like this.

"You know I can't talk about details."

"Right," he said, shaking his head. "Sorry."

In the ensuing moment of silence, everything unsaid hung like a brewing storm in the air. Mal wasn't sure how to stay in safe waters, especially if what had almost happened between them was in any way responsible for the rift between him and Julie.

"So, um … tonight. What happened?"

He was about to plop a fork full of eggs into his mouth, but instead he dropped the utensil, took a sip of his coffee and said, "You sure you want to hear this? Isn't it a bit weird?"

"We're friends, Ray. That's never going to change. I'm here to talk, even if it's just to tell you that you're being an idiot."

He smiled, wide enough that he probably wanted to laugh.

She was intentional in her use of "friends" so he wouldn't get the wrong idea. Wouldn't think that she was trying to seize on a moment, or that there was any open door to that part of her life. Yes, she'd been weak at the hotel, and for a minute there she might have taken him back if he'd asked. But that was her being vulnerable, and Mal wasn't ever going to let anyone see her that helpless again.

"Well, things haven't been going well between Julie and me."

"Okay, elaborate."

He sighed. "Ever since this whole Paul Dodd thing, I haven't been able to get him out of my head."

"What do you mean?"

"For a long time, we didn't know who killed Ashley. And the not knowing created this hole inside that almost crushed me. Almost made me start drinking again."

He looked down at the table, dark hair falling over his eyes.

Mal gripped her mug tightly in her hands, even though the coffee was gone.

"But Julie saved me. Pulled me out of the darkness, kept me from going off the deep end. Helped me stay sober. After Ashley died, I almost fell off the wagon. I blamed myself. I thought if we hadn't gotten divorced, if I'd still been a part of the family, maybe it never would've happened. But Julie helped me through. Helped me fill that new hole with something other than guilt and pain."

Mal had to fight the old anger starting to rise. Had to resist the urge to say, *How nice it must've been to have someone help you through it. I tried to help you, tried so many times, but you pushed me away. You wouldn't let me.*

The ancient wounds still felt so fresh.

"I'm sorry." He started to stand. "Maybe I should go."

She reached out, put her hand on his. "No. Stay. Finish."

Ray sat, met her gaze.

The pain inside his eyes was a twin of the agony that Mal had carried for years. And despite all the pain he'd caused her, that they'd inflicted upon one another — *who even knew who was most to blame anymore* — she wanted to ease his burden. Wanted to help him repair things with Julie.

"Somehow I managed to stay sober. To carry on with the business of living. I don't know how, and it wasn't always easy, but I was able to find a reason to wake up. But then ... then Paul took you. And there it was, that hole. Turned out it wasn't filled, just spackled over. When I thought you might die, I could only think about how I failed you. How I failed *us*. And how unfair it was that I didn't do more to try to fill that hole inside you. To help you get over Ashley's death. To be there for *you*. And it killed me, not being able to save you from that bastard."

He stopped talking, took another sip of his coffee.

Mal stared down at her mug again, fighting welling eyes and a trembling lip. Not looking up at him, staying hidden behind her long brown curls, she said, "And what does this have to do with you and Julie?"

Please don't tell me you realized you still love me. Please, what-ever you do, do NOT say that.

She braced for his response.

"Well, after what almost happened at the hotel, I went downstairs, got in my car, and fought like hell not to run back up, knock on your door, and be with you that night. I don't know, a part of me always thought we'd end up together again someday in the future. Maybe after we were older and wiser, we'd find our way back. I know it's shitty to think like that, to you and to Julie. But hell, Mal, you were my first love. You were my best friend. And to suddenly almost lose you, it ..."

She swallowed.

"I sat in the car forever. And then I went home. Nothing's been the same between us since. I find myself getting mad at Julie for the silliest reasons. I can't stop thinking about you, and wondering what might have happened if I'd stayed that night."

Ray swallowed, looked down.

Mal could tell he was trying not to cry.

Her gut was on a roller coaster with a drunk carney at the controls. She tried to process — hell, to figure out — what Ray was saying while sorrow and rage fought for the stage in her mind.

"Why are you telling me this?" she asked.

"You asked me to tell you what's wrong."

"Yeah, but I don't know what to do with what you've told me. You're saying that you wish we were still together?"

"I don't know what I'm saying. All I know is that I don't want to lose you."

Mal wanted to yell at him. Wanted to tell him he was too late, that he'd lost her the moment he chose the bottle over his family.

But the addict in her understood something now that she hadn't back then. And another part of her also saw her culpability. She wasn't easy to get along with. She brought her job home and probably could've done more to be there for him.

A small part of Mal wanted to hug him, kiss him, and take him back to her hotel. To steal him back from Julie. Who the hell was Julie, anyway? She hadn't been dating him forever. She wasn't there all those years as they struggled as young parents. She didn't have to bury Ashley.

Who the hell was Julie to be with her Ray?

But, in the end, *he* chose to leave. Mal gave him an ultimatum, straighten up or hit the bricks. And he chose to go.

Mal understood, but she wasn't sure she could ever really forgive.

A part of her would always love him, but going back would be a mistake.

A twisted part of Mal delighted in knowing that she could steal him from Julie. Hell, a part of her wanted to hurt the woman, even though Julie had never intentionally done a thing to hurt her. She was an ad rep at his paper, a beautiful distraction for a crumbling man. From the couple of times they'd run into each other, Julie had seemed perfectly nice. And Mal wanted Ray to be happy, so it was irrational to hate the woman who took her husband.

"Go home to your girlfriend," Mal said, finally meeting his eyes. She hadn't intended to sound so cold, but she also knew that if she allowed this to go on, she'd either snap at him or cry. Hell, she might even wind up bringing him back to her hotel.

Mal needed to be strong, for both of them.

Something shifted in his eyes, maybe Ray realizing that he'd gone too far. "I'm sorry."

He stood, pulled two twenties from his wallet and dropped them on the table. "I'll get a Lyft home."

"Goodnight, Ray."

He walked away, shoulders hunched.

Mal stared into her empty mug.

Chapter 6 - Mallory Black

MAL DROVE from the coffee shop to the Parke Grande —
one of two luxury hotels in Creek County located on the
beach. She'd been staying there since Paul Dodd had
violated her home and nearly murdered her and Jessi
Price.

Some of her co-workers had teased Mal about staying
somewhere so expensive, the kind of place most deputies
couldn't afford for a weekend, let alone live on a regular
basis.

Mike had asked her why she didn't just sell her house if
she couldn't imagine sleeping there. But she brushed him
off, saying she'd sell the house when she was ready. She
hadn't intended to be so short, but couldn't argue the effec-
tiveness of being an occasional bitch.

Besides, it wasn't as if she couldn't afford to treat
herself. She'd won the lottery years ago and had more
money than she could reasonably spend in her lifetime.
She had no children to benefit from an inheritance. Why
not stay at a nice place where your bed was always made,
where you could order a meal anytime day or night, where

you could swim to the edge of the pool to claim your drink?

She parked in the garage, took an elevator to the tenth floor, and walked to room 1040 — the hotel's farthest corner, away from regular foot traffic.

She used the key card, opened the door, then entered the room and dropped her purse on the small table in the kitchen suite.

She went to the fridge, grabbed a Corona, and headed out onto the balcony overlooking a beautiful view of the night sky and ocean below.

She plopped on one of the two lounge chairs, took a swig of Corona, and closed her eyes, allowing the cool salty breeze and the sound of ocean waves to wash over her, sinking into their violent yet calming collision.

The sound drowned the day's gory events.

Washed away the echoes of her life's bloodiest moments.

A part of her wanted to sit here forever, and she could.

Mal didn't need to work.

She didn't have to put in long hours at a thankless, unending job which only existed because people would always continue to murder their friends, neighbors, strangers, and enemies. Even their children. In a perfect world, Mal's job wouldn't even exist.

At the same time, a part of her *needed* to work. Not just any work, but this exact work. Part of her thrived while processing the brutal aftermath of a crime scene. That part of her enjoyed assembling the puzzle, working to discover the how and why that would drive a person to murder. To deliver justice, yes, but also to prevent the murderer from claiming more lives.

But Mal hated how it went today.

Not only did her lead suspect escape punishment by

taking the coward's exit, he may also have left a host of sexual abuse victims in his wake.

And what could she do about that if the man was already dead?

Find more evidence. More heartbreaking crimes that he'd never have to answer for.

Days like today sucked.

Mal took another drink.

Then another.

And as Mal tried to relax, she kept thinking about how much time she'd probably be spending on this case, following leads, with few of them going anywhere.

She stood, restless, then went inside, closed the balcony door, and returned to the fridge.

She had bottled water, a half-gallon of expired two percent milk, and a couple of Coronas.

She didn't even like Corona. It was left over from a six-pack Mike had brought over when he and Gina had come over to hang.

She closed the fridge, went to the closet door and slid it open to the safe.

Inside was the only thing that would calm her.

The pills she hadn't touched in six months.

A full bottle waiting to be opened.

No.

She shed her work clothes, freshened up, slipped into a little black dress, grabbed her purse and key card, then headed downstairs to the bar.

The hotel's restaurant bar was called Oasis at Parke Grande, and was one of the posher places in Creek County. That meant she wouldn't have to deal with assholes or loud music. A place where getting properly drunk before heading upstairs to bed was a straightforward proposition.

Mal found a cozy spot in the back of the room where she could be left alone and hopefully not run into anyone she knew.

She was two stiff whiskeys in when her waiter, wearing the restaurant's all-black pants, shirt, and tie, approached with a third glass of Glenfiddich on the rocks.

"Compliments of Mr. Ramos."

The waiter nodded toward the bar where a young Latin man with long brown hair hanging slightly over his eyes raised his drink to Mal with a boyish smile. Even from this distance, she could see how well his midnight blue suit hugged his lean but muscular body.

She took the drink, raised it, and returned his smile before taking a swallow.

The waiter left. The man at the bar glanced back at Mal.

She smiled again, feeling pleasantly buzzed. Flirty.

He approached her table, carrying a half-full glass of red wine.

She sat up taller, observing his approach, sizing him up. You could tell a lot about a man from his walk. The way a man moved across a room could tease the way he might move between the sheets.

He looked down at the seat across from Mal and spoke with a delicious Spanish accent. "Is this seat taken?"

"No." Mal pushed the bottom of the chair out with her foot, maintaining eye contact, a slight grin playing at the corners of her mouth.

He offered his hand, "My name is Edgar Ramos. And you are?"

"Mallory," she said, taking his hand. His touch was firm, yet gentle. He seemed confident, but not too cocky. A man used to getting what he wanted, but still polite enough to ask nicely.

"Ah, Mallory, a lovely name," he said, claiming the opposite seat.

"What brings you to Creek County?"

"I'm in town meeting a client. And what brings you here?"

"I live here," she said, immediately wishing she'd thought of a lie.

There was nothing worse than hooking up with a guy who knew you stayed at a hotel. He'd eventually start creeping around the bar, hoping for another tumble, at which time she'd have to tell him what was what, which was always uncomfortable. Another reason Mal typically hooked up with dickheads, guys that wouldn't be needy and wondering when they'd see each other again.

Mal neither needed or wanted a relationship.

"What business are you in?" She took a sip, watching Edgar as he spoke. He was easily one of the most handsome men she'd ever seen. His skin was flawless, and his eyes a deep chocolate that begged for her stare, and his teeth gleamed perfect, straight and white. For a moment she was certain he was going to tell her that he was a movie star or model. Maybe a famous athlete.

"Import, export. But we're only in town for a few days. It's a *quaint* city."

"You mean small and boring."

He laughed. "Not at all."

"It's okay; you're not offending me. We're still in the *up* part of the *up and coming* phase. But it's quiet. Probably not at all what you're used to? Where are you from?"

"Madrid. And yes, it's a bit different. Have you ever been to Spain?"

"No, the farthest I've been out of the US is into Mexico for spring break."

"And how was that?"

She laughed. "Honestly? It was awful. I was sick half the trip."

He sipped his wine. "So, what do you do for a living?"

"I'm a librarian."

"Really?" He looked her up and down, surprised. "You don't seem like a librarian."

Mal had barely fixed her hair, but Edgar was eyeing her like she was the hottest woman in the bar.

"Oh, yeah? What do I seem like, then?"

She smiled, and downed the rest of her whiskey, watching him work for a response.

"I was thinking a hitman. Or woman."

She laughed. "Really? And what makes you say that?"

"You look like you've seen a lot."

She nodded. "And?"

"You don't seem like someone who sits in a library all day."

"Okay, you got me. I'm a hitman. I hang out in bars waiting for my target to buy me a drink."

He laughed again.

"Oh, you think I'm kidding? Your boss hired me. Told me to poison your wine. The waiter you asked to bring me a drink? That's Chris. He's my partner. The poison should reach your bloodstream in, say, another five minutes."

He smiled, but his face paled.

She laughed, hard. "I'm kidding."

He laughed, uncomfortably.

She felt like a giant dork, trying to recover from a crash-landed joke. Detectives usually had gallows humor, and sometimes it was hard to remember that most citizens were on a different page.

"So, no, really, what do you do?"

She wasn't about to tell him the truth, even if he'd be gone in a day or so. Telling strangers you were a detective never made things easier. Either they, or a friend or family member, had suffered a bad experience with a cop that is suddenly your fault, or they were one of those people who couldn't stop asking questions. And the question Mal hated most was whether or not she'd ever shot anyone. Most people meant no harm, but it never came off well. It was a highly personal question, and people always seemed excited about what, for most cops, was one of their worst days ever.

"I'm a waitress. I'm not sure what I was thinking, but it's such a boring job. So of course, I picked an even *more* boring one to impress you."

"Well, I'm flattered." His phone buzzed in his jacket pocket. "Do you mind?"

She shrugged.

Edgar stood, and took his call into the lobby.

She was feeling good, but could use another drink. But she was also aroused and didn't want to get wasted.

When Edgar finally returned, Mal stood to meet him. She didn't wait for him to sit for more small talk, exchange witty banter, and dance around the thing they both wanted.

"Are you staying in the hotel?"

"Yes," he said, his eyebrows arching. "Why do you ask?"

She grabbed his tie, pulled him closer, and whispered into his ear.

He smiled as she pulled away. She wouldn't have to ask twice.

IT WAS four in the morning when Mal woke, head pounding, naked beside the beautiful Spaniard.

She crawled out of bed quietly so as not to wake him. Nothing worse than an awkward goodbye to a one-night-stand.

Slipping out of the room was her best approach. Another good reason to live at a hotel, particularly when the men she slept with had no idea she spent a fair share of her life on the top floor.

But fumbling in a dark room for her clothes and purse were never as easy as she wanted.

She slipped on her clothes, crept past him, sneaking one last look at his bare ass before leaving his room.

Thankfully the hallway was empty as she made her way to the elevator.

She pressed the tenth-floor button, then pulled the phone from her purse and eyed the screen, surprised to see that she'd missed two messages, both from just after one in the morning.

They were from Katie Turner.

It's Katie. I need to talk.

Chapter 7 - Jasper Parish

Four years ago

JASPER SWUNG INTO HIS DRIVEWAY, surprised to see a classic red Corvette Stingray, shining like it just left the showroom, in his SUV's usual spot.

Jordyn didn't have any friends as far as he knew, especially one with a driver's license. They had only moved in a few months ago, during summer. In the two weeks since school had started, Jordyn hadn't connected with anyone. She had once been a vibrant child who made friends easily. But ever since her mother's death she'd crawled into a cocoon that Jasper wasn't sure she'd ever emerge from, despite their fresh start.

Excited by the prospect that Jordyn had made a friend, particularly one with such excellent taste in cars, Jasper was buoyed as he parked, grabbed groceries from the back seat, and headed for the front door.

He entered the house and saw Jordyn's new friend sitting beside her on the couch, reading lines from a play. A young man with short blond hair, a preppy shirt tucked deep into his pants. Neat, well put together, not a single piercing or tattoo in sight.

Jordyn popped up from the couch. "Hi, Daddy."

The young man stood, casually, not at all startled to see Jordyn's father standing there. "Hey, Mr. Parish," he said, extending his hand. "Bobby Hollingsworth."

Jasper went from the kitchen to the living room, sizing the young man up, trying to determine his age. Was he seventeen, like Jordyn? He looked at least a year older. Hell, he could've been in college.

God, I hope he's not a college kid.

And why does she have some guy in the house all alone?

He'd never told Jordyn that she couldn't have a boy over. Aside from a few infatuations in grade school, Jordyn had never seemed interested in dating. She was more into her school work, drama, books, and writing stories. Still, Jasper thought it was one of those unspoken rules that she ought to just know.

Jasper had hoped he'd somehow escape this stage, and yet here was *Bobby Hollingsworth*, in all his six-foot-three, chiseled jaw, good looks, standing right next to Jordyn.

How was he supposed to respond? Was he supposed to be nice? Intimidating? Jasper already hated Bobby's cocky smile.

This was Carissa's territory, not his. She'd know how to handle this. He was in uncharted waters, trying not to be the overprotective father chasing away any boy who might come sniffing around his daughter.

Jasper reached out, giving a good, firm handshake while resisting the urge to crush Bobby's bones.

He had a strong handshake and didn't avoid eye contact like a creepy college dude looking to bang the high school girl.

He still has a cocky smile.

Jasper glanced at Jordyn, trying to gauge the situation. She smiled, clearly nervous that he might say something to embarrass her.

"Bobby's in my drama class. He's helping me study for the role of Abigail in The Crucible."

I'll bet he is. Is there a kissing scene?

"Ah, that's great."

"Can I help you put those away?" Bobby asked, glancing behind Jasper.

Oh, now you're just a kiss-ass.

"Nah, I've got it," Jasper said, stepping back into the kitchen.

Bobby and Jordyn stood at the bar separating the kitchen from living room.

"Nice Stingray," Jasper said, filling the fridge with groceries. "Is it a seventy-six?"

"Seventy-seven. It was my dad's. He left it to me for when I turned sixteen."

"Left it to you?"

"Yeah, he passed three years ago. Cancer."

Jasper caught a look in Jordyn's eye and instantly saw how the loss of a parent had probably drawn them together.

"Sorry to hear," Jasper said, "I hope he didn't suffer long."

"No, it was pretty quick," Bobby said. "Where's your bathroom?"

"I'll show you," Jordyn said, leading him toward the downstairs guest bathroom.

Jasper finished putting the perishables away, then started stowing boxes and cans in the pantry. Moments later, Jordyn came back to the kitchen and grabbed a can of Diet Coke from the fridge.

She stood at the bar, staring out the sliding glass doors leading out to the pool and deck — avoiding eye contact.

"So," Jasper began, "Bobby?"

She turned, face flush. "Please don't embarrass me."

"Embarrass you how?" Jasper asked intentionally loud, smiling.

Jordyn's eyes widened, "Oh. My. God. Please stop!"

"Stop what?" he teased. "Oh, I've got an idea. We should show Bobby some video from when you were little. Maybe some video of you at Seven Mile Beach? When you were afraid of the stingray?"

"I knew I should've met him at the library."

Jasper smiled, then winked. "Don't worry, honey, I won't embarrass you in front of … *Bobby*."

She rolled her eyes and made a face just like her mother used to make when Jasper teased her or did something stupid.

He heard Bobby step out of the bathroom, then shut off the light and exhaust fan before he returned to the kitchen.

Jordyn asked, "Want a drink?"

"No thanks. I told my mom I'd pick up Alfonso's for dinner."

"Oh, they have the best pizza," Jordyn said, more enthusiastically than Jasper had heard her say anything to anyone. Maybe ever.

He had to throttle the smile as it tugged at his lips.

Jordyn glanced over as if to scold him, as if she were reading his mind. Just like her mother. Then she returned her attention to Bobby. "Thanks for helping me."

"You've got this, Jordyn. Ms. Franks would be insane not to give you the role."

"Thanks," she said, blushing, looking down at her feet and putting one purple Converse atop the other.

"It was nice to meet you, Mr. Parish."

"You too, Bobby."

Jasper shook the kid's hand again. Noticed that he maintained eye contact with a seemingly genuine smile. You could tell a lot about a kid by the way they greeted an adult. You could also tell about what kind of family they grew up in. And despite that cocky smile, Bobby seemed like a decent kid.

Of course, Jasper would do some digging online, just to verify. In case things were going the way he thought they probably would be.

Jordyn walked Bobby to the door, then followed him outside.

Jasper resisted the urge to follow, or peek out the living room window. The curtains were open, and there was no way to stay invisible. No way that Jordyn wouldn't be mortified when she returned.

As much as he wasn't ready for his daughter to start dating, it was nice to see Jordyn bring someone home. Nice to see her acting like a normal 17-year-old, rather than one ghost mourning another.

Jasper grabbed a bottle of water from the fridge and took a seat on the recliner, waiting for Jordyn's return.

He was almost done with the water by the time she was back inside.

"So," he said, "Bobby?"

"Don't even start," she said, somewhere between laughing and frustration.

She started past him toward the kitchen.

"Hold up."

She stopped, then turned, "What? Are you mad that I had a boy over?"

"Should I be?"

"What are you asking?"

"Well, you two weren't doing anything, were you?"

"Oh, God, *really*, Dad? I barely even know him! Give me some credit."

"It's not you I'm worried about."

"He's a good kid."

"Yeah? How old is he?"

"Just turned eighteen."

"So, he's a senior?"

"Yeah, and?"

"You're a junior."

"So, what's your point?"

"Just making an observation."

"Thanks, but I don't need you *observing* anything."

"It's my job."

"Hmph," she said, heading into the kitchen.

"What does that mean?" he called out, getting out of the chair.

"Nothing!" she snapped, opening the fridge fast enough to rattle the bottles living inside the door.

She opened another Diet Coke and slammed the fridge.

He was going to point out that she'd already opened one, which was right on the counter to her left, but then she turned and saw it. At least he thought she saw it. Hard to tell when she was already headed toward the stairs.

"I'm going to study for my test on Monday."

"We're not done."

She stopped at the foot of the stairs, frozen, waiting, but refusing to meet Jasper's eyes. He would've wondered where all the hostility was coming from, but in recent months she'd been as unpredictably moody as, well, a temperamental teenage girl.

"So, what's the deal with Bobby?"

"What do you mean, *deal?*" she asked, turning to him with a look of disgust.

"Do you like him?"

"Can we not talk about this now?"

"Why not?"

"Because I don't know how I feel about him. He's the first friend I made at school. He's in drama, and he's nice. He offered to help with my lines."

"Well, he's smitten with you."

"Smitten?" Jordyn said, her eyebrows arched as if he'd just said the dumbest thing a dad had ever said. "Who even says smitten anymore?"

"Lots of people."

"Name one."

"Me."

"Name another."

"I don't know. People."

Jordyn's anger finally cracked into a laugh. "You are ridiculous. You know that, right?"

"So I've been told. By your mother. On a number of occasions."

"I'll bet."

"Hey, I'm just looking out for my baby girl."

"Are you saying I'm not allowed to see him?"

"Are you saying you *want* to?"

"No. I'm just trying to figure out how crazy you're going to be about this."

"Who said I'm going to be crazy?"

"Um, Chris Encarcio."

"Who?"

"The boy I liked in third grade. The boy who kissed me on the playground and you went and made a big scene with his parents."

"I did not make a scene."

"Oh, yes you did!"

"First of all, it was more than a kiss. He shoved you off a swing, too. *That* was why I went to talk to his dad. Not the kiss."

"Mm, hmm," she said, crossing her arms while waiting at the bottom of the stairs for Jasper to finish grilling her.

"So, do you like Bobby? He didn't push you off a swing, did he?"

She laughed again. "You're such an idiot."

"Again, tell me something I haven't heard."

"I don't even know if he thinks anything about me. He's like super popular, and I'm, well, dorky old me."

"You're a smart, funny, beautiful young woman. And he's smitten."

Jordyn laughed again. "Shut up."

"He is."

"Boys and girls *can* be just friends, you know?"

"Yeah, but boys his age only have one thing on their mind."

"Yeah?" she asked with a smirk, now trying to make *him* uncomfortable. "What's that?"

"You know."

"Video games?" She teased. "Sports?"

"No, women."

"Ah, of course. Things aren't like they were back in the olden days when you were a kid. These days lots of boys and girls are just friends."

"So, you're telling me that in the eighteen or so years since I was a teenager, that thousands of years of biology have gone out the window and boys are no longer horn dogs?"

"Horn dogs? Where do you even get these terms?"

"That's not what they say?"

"No."

"What do they say?"

"I dunno. Can I go study now?"

"Yeah, go study," he said, waving a hand at her.

She ran up the stairs, two at a time. He wasn't sure if she was giddy or craving escape.

He took another drink of water.

And then he heard his wife's voice. "You've got to let her grow up."

Carissa sat on the couch, looking at him. She was wearing her favorite blue dress with white flowers — the one he buried her in.

"Easy for you to say. You don't have to deal with the mood swings."

"She's better now, isn't she? Since you moved up here?"

"I guess," he sighed, staring at Carissa. He missed her so much. He wanted to sit beside her — hold her, hug her, kiss her. But attempting touch only made her vanish.

The doctors said she wasn't real. That it was likely a result of some post-traumatic stress or something. They gave Jasper pills that he hated to take. They made him feel fuzzy during the best times and murderous during the worst. Too often, they chased his true love away.

He'd rather be a little crazy and see her, even if she might not really be there, than be sane and alone.

Jasper wasn't convinced that some part of her wasn't there with him. Maybe he was seeing some part of her spirit left behind. He didn't trust the doctors. They doubted psychic phenomena, but Jasper had seen enough visions come true to know better.

"What's wrong?" Carissa pressed.

"I don't know. But the moment she walked Bobby out to his car, I got a bad feeling."

"A vision?"

"No. Just a bad feeling. I don't know. I feel like so much

has changed, too quickly. And I'm afraid that it's all going to fall apart, again."

"It doesn't have to fall apart. You can be happy. But you need to make an effort. You need to believe. Jordyn is looking for you to guide her. And you can't let her see your fear. You can't let your fear stop our daughter from living."

"You're right," he said.

Suddenly, Jasper realized he wasn't alone.

Jordyn was in the kitchen behind him, getting a banana from the counter.

Jasper said nothing as she got it, then walked back upstairs.

Carissa looked at him. "I think she heard you."

Jasper sighed. "How the hell am I supposed to guide her when I can't even get my head straight?"

"You'll find a way."

Jasper squeezed his eyes shut, leaned back in the chair and let out a deep sigh. "I'm glad one of us is confident."

No response from Carissa.

He opened his eyes.

She was gone.

Chapter 8 - Mallory Black

MAL ARRIVED at the park to find Katie doing lazy half-circles on a swing, making patterns by dragging her shoes in the dirt. She was in yesterday's dress, but now her long blonde hair was no longer in a ponytail.

Mal came alone, as requested, and took a seat on the swing beside her.

"How are you doing?" Mal asked in her most gentle voice.

"I couldn't sleep last night," Katie said, staring at the circles in the sand.

"Why not?"

"I kept wondering if I should cancel."

"You're doing the right thing," Mal said, feeling uncomfortable coaxing information from a kid, especially when her father wasn't around.

Katie finally looked up at her, dark circles ringing her eyes. "Coach didn't kill those people in the park. And he didn't kill himself."

"How do you know?"

Katie swallowed. "If I talk, can you promise that my father won't find out?"

"I'll do my very best."

"But you can't promise?"

"I don't want to make any promises that I can't keep. But I will do absolutely everything in my power to keep this between you and me."

"Not good enough," Katie said, getting up and starting to walk away.

"Wait."

Katie turned around.

"Why don't you want your father to know?"

"He will kill me."

Lots of kids say their parents will kill them, but few said it with the gravity in Katie's eyes.

Mal got off the swing and went over to Katie. "Does he hit you?"

"I don't want to get him in trouble."

"We can help you."

Katie shook her head, biting her lip. "No. Nobody can help us. My mom called the police before. But she wouldn't file charges. She *couldn't*. So he got out of jail and was back in no time. He said if she did again, he'd kill us both."

Mal sighed. "I can help if you let me. I can talk to your mother. And if she won't help, at least maybe I can get you out of there."

"No, I can't leave her there with him. He'll take it all out on her."

"Do you want this to stop?"

Katie nodded.

"Then let me help you."

"What would you do?"

"We can get a protective order to keep him away from

you and your mother. We can lock him up for what he's done. There's place you can go for help, too. None of it is an easy road, but it's a hell of a lot easier than doing nothing. This won't end well if you just let things go. It never does.

Katie said nothing.

"You know that what he's doing is wrong, don't you?" Mal pressed.

Finally, Katie nodded.

"Then let me help you."

"I dunno."

Mal could feel the girl slipping away, and taking her secrets with her. She didn't want to force Katie to talk, but she was starting to think she might have to.

Katie returned to the swing and sat, returning her gaze to the ground.

Mal took the swing beside her.

"Coach Kincaid didn't kill them because I was with him yesterday morning."

"Practicing soccer?" Mal asked, even though she suspected the answer.

"No," she said, long hair covering her face. "We were together."

"Oh," Mal said. "And your parents don't know?"

"Like I said, my father would kill me."

"Where were your parents?"

"Working. My dad works for Sal's Towing. My mother works at Walmart. They don't know anything."

"So, you two were … what? Dating?"

"He loved me," Katie said defensively.

Mal swallowed the sickening feeling in her throat. She wanted to explain that *No*, he didn't love her. Peter Kincaid was abusing her. She was still a child, and he was a grown man.

But Katie surely faced a steady stream of criticism

from her father. And maybe her mother. She wore insecurity in her posture, in her penchant for keeping her eyes on the ground. A good kid with a shitty life, the perfect victim for Coach to exploit.

But if Mal tried to explain any of that to her now, Katie would close up. It was best to keep their rapport open. A counselor could help Katie get through this all at a later date. Right now, it was about learning what she knew.

Mal took out her notebook. "So, when were you with him?"

"My dad leaves the house at five on Saturday. My mom left at six. I waited a bit, then went over at seven."

"And what happened next? How long were you there?"

"Well, at first, I was helping him look for his phone. He couldn't find it anywhere. After a while, he gave up, figuring he probably left it at work. We watched some TV. Then we started kissing, and *stuff*."

Mal's stomach churned, thinking of this man exploiting this naive child's need for love. Her reverential tone was no different from any little girl speaking of her crush.

"And how long were you with him?"

"Until after noon."

"You were with him the entire time? And he never left or went to the baseball fields?"

"No. Saturdays were our day, the only time when we had so many hours together, alone."

Katie sobbed.

Mal reached over and put a hand on the girl's shoulder.

She flinched, but then let Mal pat her back.

Mal wondered if she was spinning this tale to protect the coach with an alibi. She didn't think that Katie was lying, but she'd seen the girlfriends and wives of murderers interfere with investigations. Usually, they were trying to keep their lover out of prison.

The coach was dead. He wasn't coming back. There was no decent reason for Katie to risk meeting with Mal, and confessing her affair with the coach.

"What happened next?"

"Then the guy came."

"What guy?"

"The guy who killed him."

Mal's heart raced with the latest twist — a confirmation of her gnawing suspicion that there was much more to this than what they'd seen thus far.

"What happened?"

"We were in bed, just lying there like he liked to do, after. And all of a sudden, someone started banging on his door. At first, I thought it was my dad, and I was freaking out, getting dressed as fast as I could. But then the guy started yelling."

"What was he yelling?"

"He said, 'I know what you did pervert. Open up, or I'm airing this out for all your neighbors.'"

"Do you know what he was talking about? Did Coach Kincaid seem to know who he was?"

"No," Katie said, finally looking up at Mal. "He seemed confused, but I think maybe he thought it was one of our neighbors who'd realized what was going on with us, so he figured he'd better open the door and try to settle the guy down. He told me to hide in his spare room closet. I did, and then he let the guy in. They started arguing, but I could barely hear any of it."

"Did he seem to know the man? Did you recognize the guy's voice?"

"No. But after a few minutes, I realized that I'd left my iPhone in the bedroom."

"Wait? Your iPhone? The one that Coach gave you?"

"Yes, ma'am. How did you know about it?"

"Your father said that he gave you the phone, but that he made you give it back."

She looked down, guilty. "I tried to, but Peter wouldn't take it. He said I needed contact with the outside world, and a tool in case my dad ever got out of hand again. He knew about the problems we were having."

"What do you mean contact with the outside world?"

"My dad is super religious. He won't let us have a TV, a computer, or a smart phone. Not me or my mother. Because they're gateways to hell."

Mal wondered if Katie knew that her father was just using his twisted version of religion to control them. Or did she believe what she'd been taught?

"So I hid it. The phone was usually off, and always on silent. I'd take it out at night, when I went to bed, and go on the internet. Sometimes I'd video chat with Peter."

"Do you have the phone with you now?"

Katie pulled the iPhone out of her pocket and handed it to Mallory, not making eye contact.

Mal wondered if the coach had given her the phone because he wanted the girl to have access to the modern world that most other kids had, in addition to being able to call the sheriff's office on her father, or if he was only using the phone to groom the girl.

Mal was disgusted by both of the men in Katie's life. Was it any wonder that there were so many shitty people in the world? They were raised by shitty parents, and preyed upon by shitty predators? What hope did kids like Katie have without a decent adult in their life?

Mal had seen so many kids like Katie caught in the cycle, living a loop of awful decisions, or worse, becoming just like the monsters who made them —

abusing their kids or doing drugs. It was a shit show, and Mal wished there was more she could do to put an end to it all.

"I was sneaking into his room when I saw them," Katie continued. "The guy had a gun to Peter's head in the living room, and he was forcing him to write something."

"Did you see the man?"

"Not his face. Only his back. He was wearing a mask."

"What kind of mask? What color? Did it have anything on it, like a team name or logo or something?"

"It was black. A ski mask, I think. I don't remember anything about it, though. And I couldn't see the front."

"What was he wearing? What else can you tell me about him?"

"He was heavy. Not fat, but stocky. And I think he was a bit shorter than Coach. He was wearing black dress pants and a black jacket."

"Any rings? Did you see any tattoos?"

"No, not that I can remember."

"Then what?"

"I couldn't hear everything, but then he handed a second gun to Coach and told him that he knew what he had to do."

"What was he trying to get him to do?"

"To kill himself. If Peter didn't do it, then the guy said that he would. And then he'd expose all of the coach's secrets. To everyone. Said he knew about the swinger's club he went to in Jacksonville and the kiddie porn on his computer. He'd destroy Coach K's wife and kids' lives. Peter was crying. Begging him not to hurt them. And the guy said, 'It's your choice.' Then ... Peter put the gun in his mouth and fired."

Katie caught her breath, spent a few seconds trying not to cry, then continued. "I wanted to do something. But I could only stand in the doorway, trying not to scream. And then I hid."

Katie collapsed into tears.

Mal stood and hugged her, wondering who the hell was behind this. She was already processing the new information, working to determine if the man who murdered the coach was also the person at the ball field.

Mal let the girl cry on her shoulder until she was empty.

Then she asked, "What happened next?"

"The front door slammed closed. Then I heard a car starting. I ran to Coach's bedroom window and looked outside. I saw the killer's car."

"You did?" Mal said, thrilled to hear it.

"Yeah. It was blue. I'm not sure what kind, but I might know it if I saw it again. I also got part of the license plate number."

Katie reached into her dress pocket, then handed Mal a folded up piece of scrap paper.

She opened it and saw two letters and a number. "Was this the first part of the plate or last?"

"First."

"Oh, wow, Katie. That's amazing that you could focus in a moment like that. This is such a huge help. What happened after that?"

"I ran out of the house and went home. Am I in trouble?"

"Trouble? For what?"

"Leaving the scene of a crime?"

"No, don't worry," Mal said. "Thank you, for your bravery, and for getting this."

"Can I have my phone back?"

"I'm sorry, Katie, but we'll need to keep it for the investigation."

"Will you be able to catch him?"

"We're going to try."

"Is there any way he knows I was there? Am I in any danger?"

"I'm going to see if we can put you in protective custody."

"What about my mother?"

"We'll figure that out," Mal said, changing the subject. "When you were in the coach's house, you said he was looking for his phone. Did you ever find it?"

"No."

"When we arrived at the scene, it was near him. Did you happen to see it when you left?"

"No. I couldn't even look at Peter. I felt bad, leaving and all, but I could tell he was dead and there was nothing I could do. Right?"

"No," Mal said, "there was nothing you could do."

She hugged Katie again, her mind sifting through the facts, trying to decide the next step, eager to send her new info back to headquarters and find the suspect's car. But first, she needed to deal with the girl's father.

She told Katie to sit tight on the swing as she called Carrie Thompson in Victim Services.

"Hey, Carrie. I need your help with something."

Chapter 9 - Jordyn Parish

JORDYN COULDN'T LOOK at the call sheet pinned to the rear wall of the stage, even though it was finally announcing parts for the upcoming play.

Most of the class had leaped from their seats and raced to the stage before Ms. Franks had finished posting it.

Bobby, standing behind Jordyn, nudged her. "Come on. Go look."

Brianna Gilchrest squealed. A bubbly blonde senior who sincerely believed she was the next Meryl Streep, even though she stood onstage like a wood chipper. "I got Abigail!"

Her little clique congratulated her, while other kids walked away from the sheet either dejected or smiling.

Bobby prodded her again. "Come on."

"What's the point? I probably didn't get anything."

Bobby ran to the stage, looked at the sheet, then waved Jordyn over.

She approached, ignoring Brianna and her group, bragging about their roles and how Brianna was a *perfect* Abigail.

Bobby pointed to the sheet. "You got Tituba."

"The slave? *Really?*" She shook her head, disgusted.

"You totally should've gotten Abigail. Not her."

"Whatever." Jordyn tried to hide her disappointment behind an artificial smile. She didn't want Brianna or her friends seeing her upset. Jordyn hadn't had any run-ins with Brianna, but the girl gave her dirty looks like they were on sale. And when Jordyn read Abigail's part in front of the class, Brianna and her snobby friends were all giggling.

"What did you get?" Jordyn asked.

"John Proctor," he said matter-of-factly, trying to play down that he got the leading male role.

"Wow, that's awesome! Congratulations."

"Thanks."

As most of the rest of the class broke into groups, chatting through the final minutes before the lunch bell, Bobby led Jordyn to stage left, away from everyone.

"Do you have plans for lunch?"

"Maybe," Jordyn said, playing coy, but also not wanting him to ask her to sit with him. He always hung out in the quad with a big group of the school's most popular kids. She wouldn't fit in.

They were the preps, jocks, and the beautiful people. Jordyn was a freaky little emo chick with purple hair. Not a good fit.

"Meeting up with a boyfriend?"

"Maybe," she said being coy.

"That's too bad."

"Why?" she asked, a part of her wanting him to invite her even if she planned to say no.

"Well, I hate to chase a taken girl."

Jordyn laughed, a bit too loud. She could feel eyes on

her but didn't dare to steal a look. She wasn't sure how to respond, couldn't believe this conversation was happening.

Bobby wasn't just popular; he was best friends with Calum Kozack —pretty much *the* most popular kid in school. Bobby was good looking, smart, and nice despite the odds. She figured they might be friends, but that was the most she could hope for.

Jordyn had been what her father called a "social butterfly" as a kid. But that was before her teen years. Before puberty hit her earlier than anyone she knew. Before the unwanted attention, the feeling too tall, and being too awkward. Before she was such a total dork.

Jordyn had never found a group to fit in. She'd made a few friends back home, but then her mother passed away and they moved north, where she felt like a square in a world full of circles.

But now Bobby Freaking Hollingsworth was "chasing" her?

She felt her cheeks flush with embarrassment. Felt like everyone was watching them. Felt the stage lights baking her skin.

She wanted to run away, pretend this wasn't happening.

"What?" Bobby asked, his face concerned.

"Nothing."

"So, you want to go to lunch with me?"

"I dunno. I like to—"

She stopped. It sounded like a stupid reason to reject his offer, and he might be insulted.

"Like to what?"

"I usually pack a lunch and read in the hall outside my next class."

Bobby laughed, then with his movie star smile said,

"So, you'd rather read than hang out with the star of *The Crucible?*"

Another laugh. "I didn't say that. I, just … I dunno."

His smile faded. "What?"

"I don't think your friends would like me."

"That's the dumbest thing I ever heard."

She glanced at Brianna, one of the cool kids that hung out with Bobby and his crew at lunch.

"I think she hates me."

"Well, she's a bitch. She hates everyone, unless Nate or Calum or I like them, in which case, she'll kiss their ass."

"Yeah, right!" Jordyn said.

"You don't believe me?"

"No. She stares daggers at me all the time. Like I pissed in her Corn Flakes or something."

"Come with me." Bobby offered his arm.

Her heart pounded. Jordyn thought she might hyperventilate.

Keep calm and play along.

Jordyn played a mental game when she was anxious. She'd say something like "keep calm and play along" and would pretend that *this* was happening to someone else, another girl that she was guiding along. It was something her father had taught her years ago, after her first panic attack.

She slid into Bobby's arm, walking with him to Brianna and her friends.

This soooo isn't happening.

"Hey, Bri, Jordyn's gonna come to lunch with us today. Cool?"

Jordyn thought she was about to unleash a fiery red laser blast, one that would incinerate her in a second. It was only there for a second, but long enough to give Jordyn an Initial Glimpse into her heart. She was used to shitty Initial Glimpses from closet racists. It didn't happen as much in South Florida, but she'd had a few ugly Initial Glimpses in her new school already.

Not that she thought Brianna was a racist. One of her inner circle was black and another Latina, so Jordyn figured she was just an elitist bitch who didn't like Jordyn because of her style or hair. Maybe she could see straight through to Jordyn's insecurity. Bullies could bullseye weakness.

But then it was gone, replaced by a smile so wide and phony that, for a moment, she looked like a movie star. "Oh, that'll be great. About time you come out of your shell, New Girl."

"Yeah," Jordyn said, playing it cool. "Bobby says the same thing."

"So, what role did you get?"

A bitch move to remind her of the pecking order. Jordyn smiled anyway. "Tituba."

"Aw, that's great," Brianna said.

"Congratulations," crowed Bethanee, Brianna's shorter and less beautiful doppelgänger.

"Thanks," Jordyn said.

Bobby leaned in and whispered into her ear, "See? They do whatever I say."

Jordyn kept smiling.

LUNCH for the popular kids at Belmont meant getting your food and meeting in the quad, a spacious open area outside, filled with benches, basketball courts, and enough space for the Army to practice lacrosse. It reminded Jordyn more of a park than a school. Her old campus in South Florida was nothing like this. It had a Commons Area — a giant square carpeted stage between the cafeteria and auditorium — with no seating or activities.

Not wanting to be the only person to bring a bagged lunch, Jordyn bought a slice of pizza and a Diet Coke from the cafeteria. Brianna and the other girls apparently didn't eat carbs. It was salad or nothing.

They were standing and sitting in a loose group of about nine people along two benches, joking around, laughing louder than necessary, and picking songs to play on their phones. A trio of guys tossed a football between them.

Jordyn nibbled her piece of pizza, watching Bobby joke around with two of his teammates, Adam Ramirez and Nate Thomas.

It was weird seeing Bobby in his natural environment. For one, he couldn't sit around these people — at all. He was like a little kid amped on sugar, trying to be the center of attention. The opposite of the laid back, sensitive guy she knew from when they were alone. The guy who could talk for hours about books, plays, and musicals. Around his friends, he seemed to be playing the macho jock.

Standing next to Nate, who stood maybe 6' 6", Adam looked like a kid. He was 5' 10" and the team's wiry running back. What Adam lacked in stature, he made up for in volume. Everything was either "dope" or "gay," and he used the N-word like children use ketchup. Well, he didn't say *nigger*, so much as nigga, referring to Nate as nigga several times.

Though it was said in affection, and Jordyn didn't think Adam meant to be hurtful, she wondered why Nate tolerated it. She wasn't sure how many other black friends were in their group, including people who weren't around right now. Maybe it was something that nobody even thought about.

Jordyn, growing up with a black father and a white mother, had been teased by kids of every color over the years, putting her in a limbo of emotions whenever stuff like this popped up.

She pretended to laugh and wondered if she was as complicit as Nate in letting Adam go unchecked. Despite his homophobia and racism, there were times that Adam had her genuinely laughing, like when he chased Nate with a fallen wasp that he'd found on the ground.

Nate was a big defensive linebacker, not exactly someone you'd think would be afraid of a dead bug, but he practically screamed like a girl as he ran away.

She finished her lunch, while Bobby's pizza got cold on the bench beside her with barely a bite missing. She took her plate and half-full Diet Coke to the trash and tossed them inside.

She was about to go to the bathroom to wash up and check her teeth when Calum Kozack appeared.

"Where the hell you been?" Adam asked.

"Your mom didn't want me to leave," Calum teased. When everyone stopped laughing he added, "I had to meet with Coach Williams about something. That something being Adam's mom."

Everyone laughed again.

Brianna greeted Calum with a big kiss on the lips. He cupped her ass as she walked away. Then Calum noticed Jordyn.

"And who might you be?" He approached Jordyn and spread his arms wide for a hug.

"Jordyn Parish," she said, returning the hug uncomfortably.

"Jordyn's new to the school," Bobby said. "We're in drama together."

"Ah, so she's your beard?"

"Beard?" Jordyn repeated, confused by the term.

"It's nothing," Bobby said. "Just Calum's way of saying that because I'm into drama, I must be gay."

"Ah," Jordyn said, not sure how to respond.

"Not that there's anything wrong with it," Calum said, smiling his pretty-boy smile. "Just as long as you can keep catching my passes, you can wear a dress and suck five guys off on stage for all I care. To each their own."

Charming.

Seeming to sense her discomfort, Calum said, "I'm just fucking with him. Bobby is my bro from way back." He pulled Bobby into a hug and play punched him in the gut before letting him go. "We go back to what, first grade?"

"Yeah," Bobby said. "I was new here, just like you, and Calum showed me the ropes. He got me into football."

"That's cool," Jordyn said.

Shit, did I just say, 'That's cool?'

Jordyn could feel everyone staring, as if she was in some sort of initiation. She probably had something in her teeth.

"So," Calum said, "how long you two been going out?"

"Um ..." Jordyn looked at Bobby, his eyes wide.

"Oh, shit. I'm sorry. I just thought you two were ... Never mind. So, um, did you turn him down or what?"

"Dude, stop," Bobby said.

"What? Oh, wait, you didn't ask her out, did you? Shit, I'm sorry, Jordyn. Bobby's a bit shy when it comes to girls he likes. So, let me ask for him. Do you want to go out with my man, Bobby, star wide receiver for the Belmont Wildcats?"

Nate stood behind Bobby, shaking his head, "Yo, if you don't ask her, I am." He flashed his most winsome smile.

"She ain't gonna go out with someone afraid of bugs, you big bitch." Then Adam threw the wasp at Nate, and Nate ran away screaming.

Jordyn laughed. She'd never seen someone so big and heavy move so fast.

Brianna said, "You don't have to answer. Calum can be soooo obnoxious. Leave Bobby and his friend alone."

Calum shot Brianna a glance, hard enough to startle Jordyn. It looked like he was about to tell her to back the fuck up. Maybe even smack her. But then he smiled, making Jordyn wonder if he was genuinely pissed, or acting for comedic effect.

"You're right, dear," Callum said, then turned to Jordyn, "I'm sorry. I didn't mean to pry. But, seriously, you couldn't ask for a nicer guy. Even if he might be a bit gay for drama."

Bobby punched Calum in the arm, and they laughed.

"Great to meet you, Jordyn," Calum said, extending his hand. "I'm gonna give you two some space."

They shook.

Calum turned, with a bit of comedic flourish and to the others said, "Come, bitches. I'm starving."

Everyone followed him except Bobby.

He turned to Jordyn, blushing. "I'm sorry. He can be a real dick. So, um, aren't you glad you came to lunch?" He croaked an uncomfortable laugh.

"It was fine. Your friends are … funny." Jordyn realized her pause and didn't want Bobby to think she was judging them. "Nate and Adam are hilarious. I can't believe Nate is so scared of bugs. He's, like, ginormous!"

"Yeah, he's a bulldog on the field, but a teddy bear out of uniform."

Jordyn was thinking the same thing about Bobby. Gruff and crude around the guys, but sweet as a Gummy Bear once alone.

But she didn't dare say that. While Jordyn had no experience with boys herself, she'd read enough books and watched enough TV shows to know that if you came off too desperate, or too nice to a guy, they would lose interest immediately.

She kept her cool and played coy, though Jordyn wasn't sure how long one was supposed to act disinterested, or if she might scare him away anyway if she didn't try harder.

"Since we've established that you don't have a boyfriend that you meet for lunch every day," Bobby said, "Is it safe to assume that you don't have a date for the fall dance?"

Jordyn laugh-snorted.

Oh. My. God!

"Did you just snort?"

Jordyn wanted to teleport away and never see Bobby again. He burst out laughing.

Her cheeks burned. She turned away.

"No, it was cute," he said.

"Snorting is *not* cute!"

"It is when *you* do it."

A moment of silence passed. She stared into the bushes, ignoring him.

"So, will you go to the dance with me?"

Jordyn couldn't believe he was asking her to the dance. She never thought any boy would *ever* ask her to the dance, let alone one of the sweetest, most handsome, most popular guys at school.

"I don't really dance. My dancing is worse than my snorting."

"Me neither. It's just an excuse to be with you on a special night. I like you, Jordyn."

A million butterflies took flight in her gut.

He is actually asking me!

Oh my God, what do I say?

Should I keep being coy? Make him work harder for a yes?

But her knees went weak when she saw his blue eyes, and Jordyn could only say, "Yes."

Chapter 10 - Mallory Black

MAL RECORDED KATIE'S STATEMENT, then Carrie Thompson took over.

They had a few options. They could relocate Katie and her mother to a women's shelter, or arrest Katie's father and let the women stay home. Or, they could do nothing; what all too many women did.

"Thank you, Katie. Mrs. Thompson is going to help you now, but I'll be checking up on you tomorrow." Mal hugged her and pulled a burner phone from her pocket. "My number is programmed into this phone. Call me any time, day or night."

Katie collected the phone, looking back a few times as she walked to the second floor, Victim Services offices. Mal wished she could stay with her, but she didn't have time. She had a case to investigate, and, thanks to Katie, new leads to follow.

~

Two hours later, Mal stared at a computer screen in Aanya's office in the Creek County Sheriff's Department.

Captain Wilson spoke first. "What the fuck is this crazy ass shit?"

Aanya said, "This, folks, is the /Killeveryone sub board of NonAMus Chan."

Mal stared at the thread of photos. Dead bodies including mutilated animals, men, women, children, and even babies, with commenter after commenter laughing or making jokes like, "Looks like Joey really lost his head this time LOL!"

"What the hell?" Mike wondered out loud. "Who are these people? How is this thing allowed to be online?"

"Someone ought to round these fuckers up and lock them away for good," Wilson said.

"Well, most of the stuff you'll find here is in poor taste, but it's not illegal to go on the internet and write stupid stuff," Aanya explained. "Even the actual illegal stuff posted on the site, it's hard to do anything about. This particular chan shuts down every few months then pops up somewhere else. Nobody knows who owns it, and it's hosted in places that aren't big on international law. As to who posts here, most of them do it for the LULZ."

"What the fuck is a LULZ?" Wilson asked.

"Like a plural of LOL, Laugh Out Loud. Most of them are trying to outdo one another in posting the most shocking or depraved images, or what they see as the funniest comments."

"What ever happened to good old fashioned 'your mama' jokes or bragging about your sexual conquests?" Wilson asked. "Man, what the fuck is wrong with these people? They don't give a damn about anything. Posting dead baby photos and *LULZING* and shit. Let me in a room alone with 'em for an hour. See if they're all *LULZ* then!"

Mal stifled a laugh. She enjoyed when Wilson got cranky with his *Get off my lawn!* bit, but the way his brows were furrowed as he stared daggers at the screen, she wouldn't be pressing any buttons today.

"Anyway," Aanya continued, clicking away from the thread and loading another bookmark, "this was posted by a user calling themselves Orestes666 right before the ball-park shooting."

I'm going to kill some people. Help me choose a target.

A photo accompanied the text of a gloved hand holding a Smith & Wesson Shield 45ACP. There were several suggestions under the comment.

Mike leaned in and read out loud, "*Go to a grocery store, find someone in the ten items or less lane. Shoot them in the fucking face if they have eleven or more.* Did you write that one, Wilson?"

He shot Mike a look: *Don't even start.*

Aanya scrolled down the screen, reading off a list that included popular stores, schools, and several suggested politicians, celebrities, and pretty much every race on the planet. After a while, it was hard to tell the jokes from the hate, people who truly wanted to watch the world burn.

An anonymous user eventually suggested a baseball game.

Orestes666 replied, "A baseball game it is."

About two hours later, Orestes666 posted a link to a LiveLyfe livestream.

Aanya said, "It's down now, but that was the URL of the killer's stream. I've contacted LiveLyfe; they're getting me everything tied to that account, including IP addresses used to access it."

"I'm guessing the killer used Kincaid's phone," Mal

said, updating them on the information she'd mined from Katie earlier. "Is there any way to get an IP address of this Orestes666?"

"No. I've sent messages to admin for the board, but they'll probably ignore them. But here's the interesting thing: Orestes666 is still posting. At first, he's bragging about the killing. Then he went radio silent. Until last night, long after Kincaid was dead. He posted this."

Mal clicked on an image of the coach's house with sheriff's deputies surrounding it. "Fuck. Do we know when this picture was taken?"

"Looks like it was when we were interviewing witnesses," Mike said. "See, there I am, talking to one of the neighbors."

Aanya said, "I wonder if you interviewed him."

Mal stared at the image, burning with rage, wondering if they had let the killer slip through their fingers. They got names and checked ID for most of their interviews, but maybe this guy was standing on the periphery, avoiding interaction.

Aanya refreshed the page. "Shit."

"What?" Wilson asked.

"Orestes666 posted again. It says, 'Round Two tomorrow. Be ready to play along.'"

Wilson exploded. "I want every photo from every goddamned phone there. The ones we took of the crowd, and ones from the looky-loos. I want everything the news crews took. And I mean *everything*. Call in any favors you've got. I want this bastard before he kills again!"

"Yes, sir," they all said.

"Alright, if there's nothing else, I'm going to go update the Sheriff so we can figure the best way to contain this. Is there any way this doesn't get to the press?"

"I don't know," Aanya shrugged. "With cuts to the

newsrooms, maybe they don't have anyone chasing this angle. But this case is attracting national attention, and I can't imagine that this post will stay hidden."

"Damn it. Any *good* news?"

"Nothing yet. We'll keep you in the loop," Aanya promised.

Wilson sighed as he left. Mal didn't envy him having to report all of this to Gloria. A serial killer was the last thing she needed during election season.

Mal asked Aanya to scroll back to the NonAMus thread where Orestes666 was posting.

"Why do some people have usernames while most are anonymous?"

"Anonymous is the default username for most image-boards. You can create an account. Most of the more prolific posters will do so that they can get credit."

"Did the user who suggested the baseball game have a username?"

Aanya scrolled. "No. Anonymous. Why?"

"I'm wondering if the killer was truly doing a random killing or if this was staged to cover up a targeted murder. Is it possible that Orestes666 *also* posted as the anonymous viewer who suggested the baseball game?"

"Definitely."

Mal nodded. "Great stuff, Aanya. Thank you. Keep an eye on this board and let us know if Orestes666 posts anything else. But I think we need to keep our focus on the victims, including Kincaid. See if anything links them."

Mike nodded.

Aanya refreshed the page. Commenters were already suggesting places for Orestes to strike. They ranged from random people and places to specific ones, with many far from Creek County.

"Do we think he's local?" Mike asked. "Or he just stopped by our town on some nationwide spree?"

"I think we need to consider this as a local thing until we have evidence otherwise," Mal said. "Meaning we need to keep on top of this and see if he lists any hard targets we can reach before he strikes. We also need to call the Feds, especially if this isn't local. Got to share everything we have so far."

Mike shook his head. "I'll go catch Wilson and give him the good news."

Mal laughed. "Yeah, he's gonna be pleased as punch."

As Mike left, Mal watched Aanya refresh the screen to reveal even more suggested targets.

Celebrities and politicians. People offering up their ex-girlfriends. People suggesting schools and little kids. It was all too much. The height of cowardice and disconnected-ness that seemed to be spreading like cancer. And seeing the comments coming in so fast made Mal feel powerless against a rising tide of hate and despair.

Chapter 11 - Mallory Black

MAL SAT in her cubicle pouring over photos and videos collected at the baseball field and the coach's house, searching for anyone or anything that might jump out at her. She'd didn't have the stomach for the child porn. Her cell rang.

"Hey Mike," she said, picking it up.

"We got a few hits from the partial tags. Five names, all local. Aanya rushed a request to the phone companies and got GPS data. We've narrowed it down to one name at the ball field on Saturday."

"Who?"

"Brendan Woods. Not on either list of interviews."

"Really?" Mal leaned forward. "Tell me more."

"I'm sending you details. He's a twenty-nine-year-old former IT consultant who lives at home with his parents since he lost a job when TeleCorp left town last year. No priors."

"What else do we have?"

"Some posts on LiveLyfe bitching about local politicians, mostly about how they're not doing enough to attract new industry, and how they're catering to 'old farts' who don't add to the economy. Nothing violent."

"Is he friends with any of the victims on LiveLyfe?"

"Coach Kincaid. But none of the others."

"So, not enough for a warrant?"

"Not yet. But once we get his internet history, we might have more to go on. I don't think we should interview him until we know more. We'll sit on him. If he leaves the house, we'll follow and contain him. What's going on over there?"

"Not much. Wilson pulled in Skippy and Graham to help chase down some leads. The feds are offering support, but not taking over the case or anything. They have their cyber people helping Aanya, so maybe we can find this fucker before he strikes again."

"How's Gloria doing?"

"So far, all is quiet. She's holding a press conference at 6 PM tomorrow which I need to be at. Unless you want to fill in?"

"Um, no thanks. Have fun with that. And try not to curse out any reporters."

"You take the fun out of everything. Alright, I'm gonna get some food. Keep me in the loop."

Mal hung up headed to the second floor to check up on Katie.

The Victims Services office was empty, as was most of the second floor on Sundays. Stevie was only there because Mal had asked her to help out.

Had Carrie finished up that quickly? Or were they on their way to Walmart to get Katie's mother?

Mal thought about calling but figured Stevie would update her with any relevant news.

Mal checked the clock. She couldn't believe it was 4:15 already. The day had gotten away from her, and she hadn't eaten anything since the banana she grabbed on her way to meet Katie.

She got in her car, drove to a Wendy's, ordered a burger, fries, and Diet Coke. Then she sat in the parking lot eating while listening to the local NPR station's weekly local show.

The hosts were talking with a roundtable of "experts" about the rise of gun violence while speculating on the killer's motives. They also discussed the coach, and what little information they'd received from the Sheriff's Office.

The conversation was mostly calm until they cut to Harold "Harry" Conlan, a city councilman who was trying to undermine the Sheriff so he could sneak his candidate of choice, former Sheriff Claude Barry, into the November seat.

Conlan replied, "The only thing I need to know is that we didn't have these kinds of shootings under the former sheriff."

One of the guests on the panel, a reporter named Trinity Watkins, who operated a local online news site, responded. "No, you just had cops shooting unarmed black folks. This is an isolated incident, and for all we know, the suspect is dead."

Conlan didn't squander his opportunity. "The numbers don't lie. Violent crime is on the rise since Gloria Bell took office. Robbery is up 34 percent, sexual assaults up 19 percent, and murder is up 240 percent! I'm sorry, I don't think this is the change we were hoping for when voters elected Ms. Bell."

"That's *Sheriff* Bell, Councilman Conlan," Trinity corrected the man. "And we all know that those numbers are wrong—"

She killed the radio.

Sometimes Mal wished that she'd taken a job at a

police department, instead of the sheriff's office. There was only one other department in the county, the tiny understaffed Butler PD, and she didn't want to move or spend half her life commuting. Plus, Creek offered better pay than the neighboring counties when Mal was coming up.

Still, reporting to a boss that was voted in every four years was like building houses on sand. Not only did the sheriff have her hands tied by the political realities of being an elected official, but there was also always a tug-of-war in the rank and file, people looking to undermine the current power system in hopes of earning a promotion or getting "their guy" in.

With the election only seven months away, it would only get tougher. Murders, especially high profile or serial cases, tended to make or break a career. Even if the sheriff closed a case, people hated to feel vulnerable. When bodies dropped, people voted for the stronger opponent, even if it was a corrupt racist who was run out of office. All because they want to *feel* safe, even if they weren't really any safer under him.

Mal shoved her burger wrapper and fries box into the bag, crushed them up, got out of her car, and crossed the lot to toss them in the overflowing garbage.

She glanced into the restaurant. Her heart stopped when she saw Jessi Price standing in line beside her mother.

It had been six months since Paul Dodd had kidnapped the little girl and killed her father. Six months since Mal, with the help of the Mystery Man, had saved her life. The girl was smiling, somehow going on with life, even after all of Dodd's atrocities. He may have taken her innocence, but he couldn't claim her life.

It had been four months since Mal had seen Jessi.

She'd checked in a few times, and had taken statements from the girl and her family. Mal had also helped them navigate their interactions with the press. Additionally, she'd anonymously paid for a top therapist to help Jessi and her family cope, to give them the best possible chance of surviving their hell.

Mal watched Jessi smile as her mother handed her the tray. They looked for a table. She thought again how much the girl reminded her of Ashley, whose life Dodd had taken. Who Mal couldn't find, much less help, despite being a detective. A girl who died at the hands of a monster.

Mal was surprised to find herself pushing through the front door.

She wanted, no, *needed*, to see Jessi. To ask how she was, to hear her laughter and feel her presence — it might be the only thing to soothe her sudden, aching pain.

It wasn't seeing Ashley, but it was the next best thing, seeing the girl whose life Dodd tried to take, alive despite the monster's attempts to snuff her out.

Jessi and her mother sat at a table in the back, next to the door leading to the restaurant's colorful ball pit and playground. Mom looked like she'd just gotten off work. Jessi was in her school uniform of beige pants and a white shirt.

Mal had expected a big smile. Maybe the girl running up to hug her as she had in a few of their earlier meetings.

But they stared at Mal with a look of pained confusion.

"Hello, Officer Black," her mother said. "Is there something wrong?"

"Oh, no," Mal said, feeling like shit for interrupting their fun time, for wiping that smile off Jessi's face. "I was just getting some food when I saw you two. Hi, Jessi."

The girl looked like she was about to cry. She waved a weak "hi."

"I'm sorry, I shouldn't have interrupted," Mal said, turning to leave. "Have a good day."

She left before the mother could awkwardly apologize or utter another word. She pushed through the door, trying to reach her car as quickly as possible.

A horn blasted as she stepped into the path of a blue Toyota just leaving the drive-thru. A young woman with giant owl-sized glasses, yelled, "What the hell, lady?"

"Sorry, sorry," Mal said, throwing her hands up, then running away.

She got in her car, closed the door, and sobbed.

Chapter 12 - Jordyn Parish

JORDYN WONDERED if she looked as ridiculous in her dress as she feared.

It was strapless, rose gold, above the knee, and three inches shorter than her father would have liked. She'd bought it while shopping with Brianna and Bethanee at Missguided last week. She'd spent a lot of money on it, too. The hardest part was acting like it wasn't gutting her savings. The dress was way more than she'd ever spent on herself, but Jordyn didn't dare mention that in front of the rich girls that had become her new friends in the month since Bobby had asked her out. For the first time, she wanted to fit in.

It was a weird feeling, especially after the last few years cultivating an attitude of not giving a crap what anyone thought.

But now, staring in the mirror, and seeing how well the dress flattered her, Jordyn had to admit that maybe she did like fitting in just a little.

She wasn't trying to get in with the cool kids, at least not exactly. She really did like Bobby, and he happened to be part of this group. And now, so was she. In a way. But Jordyn hadn't changed to fit in. Not really. Or all that much. And it wasn't like buying an expensive dress made you anyone different. Sometimes, a girl just wanted to look nice. Was there any harm in that?

Jordyn eyed her hair and makeup. Her hair looked intentionally messy, and her makeup looked simple, despite the hours it took to get there.

She wished her mother could see her. This was her first dance that a boy had asked her to. A big deal that every girl should have a mom to share with.

Sharing it with Dad wasn't the same. He had more or less been pretending it wasn't even happening. He joked around, saying he knew that Bobby liked her. But as the big day approached, he seemed to be withdrawing. Again.

He was drinking, feeling down on himself.

Maybe he misses Mom, too.

Jordyn wondered what her mom would say if she were there now. No doubt she'd be telling Jordyn how gorgeous she was. Probably crying, saying things about how her little girl was growing up so fast.

She looked at the clock: 6:20 PM. Bobby was due in about ten minutes.

She checked her hair and makeup one final time, figuring her hair looked good, and it was too late to do anything about her makeup, even if it was a little too much.

She headed downstairs, wondering what her father would say, or if he'd be as blown away by her dress as her mom probably would have been.

But her father wasn't in the living room.

She went into his study where he'd been spending most of his time, either working out, watching TV, or reading the news — stuff she figured retired dads did to mine meaning from life when they didn't have a wife or hobby to swallow their days.

She knocked on the door. "Daddy?"

"Yeah?" he said, his voice slurred.

She shook her head, sighing as she heard his footsteps on the other side of the door.

He opened it.

Her dad was a mess, wearing sweats and a stained black shirt. He had dark circles under his bloodshot eyes. The stench of alcohol bled from his pores.

"Wow. You look bee-yuu-tee-ful."

"Really, Dad? *Tonight* you get drunk? Bobby is gonna be here any minute!"

She turned away and started toward the door. "I'm waiting outside."

"What? I embarrass you? Hey, honey, she's embarrassed by me. How's that for gratitude?"

Great. Dad was talking to her dead mother again. "Can we not do this now?"

"What?"

"This, all of this. Getting drunk, talking to mom like she's here. When's the last time you took your pills, Dad?"

"That's none of your *bidness*," he slurred as he stumbled towards her. "You don't need to worry about me. I'm fine."

"No, you're not fine. You're really fucking far from fine!"

"Hey, watch your mouth!" He turned to the ghost that wasn't there, and argued, "What do you mean *my* mouth? I don't talk like that in front of her."

"Please, stop!" Jordyn screamed. "Bobby will be here to pick me up, and I do not want him seeing you like ... like this!"

"Well, excuuuuuse me. Sorry to be so embarrassing to

my own flesh and blood. You know, you used to be sweet. But now look atchya, with your fancy friends and your ..."

Jordyn had to leave before she started crying.

She heard the car pull up outside.

Her father's eyebrows arched up. "Uh-oh, *heeeee's here.*"

He started toward the door.

"No! You are not going out there like this."

He smiled. "Like what?"

"What the hell is wrong with you? Why are you so wasted, tonight of all nights?"

He looked confused.

Jordyn fought her welling tears.

Any moment, Bobby, and maybe his friends, would be approaching the door. The sheer thought of him, or any his friends like Brianna, seeing her father in this condition terrified the hell out of her.

Just like that, any respect gained in the last few weeks would vanish. She'd be the daughter of a drunk. Worse, maybe he'd start talking to ghosts and make her the daughter of a crazy drunk.

She could almost hear Brianna and her friends laughing behind her back.

Jordyn grabbed her father by the shoulders and looked him in the eye. "Daddy, I love you, but please, *pleeeeease* do not do this to me tonight."

"Do what? I'm fine."

She heard the car door close outside.

She could almost feel Bobby approaching. She had to do something quickly, or her entire night, if not life at this school, would be shot.

She turned to where her father had been talking to her mother. "Mom, please, talk some sense into him."

Her father looked at Jordyn, eyebrows knitted: *You can see her too?*

Then he turned to the empty spot as if listening to someone.

Is this actually working?

Her father broke down in tears, turned to Jordyn, and said, "I'm sorry, baby girl. I didn't mean to."

"It's okay," she said, hugging him. "I need to go now. Will you be okay?"

He turned to the ghost, then back to Jordyn. "Yes, I'll be fine. You go, have a good time."

She sighed, then opened the front door.

Bobby came up the sidewalk alone, dressed in a simple tux and holding a corsage. He looked so sweet, so handsome. Jordyn did her best to pretend she wasn't on the verge of tears.

She said goodbye to her father, then stepped outside to greet her date. As she closed the door, she heard him say, "You look beautiful, baby."

She met Bobby's bright blue eyes, his nervous-looking smile.

"You look great."

"So do you," Jordyn said, blushing.

"Are you okay? You look like you've been crying."

"Allergies," she lied, wiping at her eyes.

"You sure? We don't have to go."

She looked past Bobby to the limo. The sunroof was open, and Calum and Brianna stood, holding up glasses. Calum shouted. "Come on, lovebirds, let's get a move on!"

Jordyn followed Bobby to the car. He held the door open. She climbed inside; saw the back seat crowded with Calum and Brianna, Adam and Bethanee, and Nate with a girl with brown curly hair and an adorable smile.

"This is Sammi," he said. "She's on the dance squad."

"Nice to meet you," Jordyn said, with the obligatory hug.

Bobby got in and closed the door.

As the car drove off, Calum passed Jordyn a glass of whatever he was drinking. "Here. Drink this."

"What is it?" She looked down at the clear and sparkling drink.

Champagne?

Jordyn had never drunk anything stronger than a Shirley Temple, but after everything with her father, she needed *something* to calm her nerves.

She took a drink.

Chapter 13 - Mallory Black

MAL WOKE to her phone singing the theme song to *COPS* — the ringtone she'd given Mike's number as a joke.

"Yeah?" she answered.

"Orestes is on the move. He gave a countdown of four hours."

"Fuck!" Mal sat up and glanced at the nightstand clock: *6:05 AM.*

"Bastard can't wait for a decent hour to announce a killing spree? Anything else? Any news on Brendan Woods?"

"Nothing. Aanya got his internet history but didn't see anything unusual. That doesn't mean he's not routing traffic through a proxy or using another device we don't know about. Maybe another stolen phone."

"He's still in his house?"

"Hasn't left."

"Okay, I'm getting up."

~

MAL PULLED into the Sheriff's Office parking lot, news vans out front.

Shit. Someone must've found out about the threat.

She drove past the main lot, pulled up to the security gate which closed off the rear portion, checked in, and headed toward the back, away from the news crews and their electronic eyes.

Looking for a spot, Mal spied several cars, far more than were usually there this early in the morning. Additionally, there were several FDLE and unmarked sedans practically screaming FBI.

Mal immediately wished she'd stopped for coffee. She'd need caffeine to get through this morning.

MAL TOOK a chair next to Mike in the Situation Room, which had eleven tables forming a giant upside-down U, three across and four down each leg. At the top sat Sheriff Bell, Public Information Officer Felicia Day, FBI Special Agent in Charge Terry McDaniels, Florida Department of Law Enforcement Captain Don Bailey, and Chief Stephen Price from the Creek County Fire Department. Everyone else sat at the other tables, including Mike and key personnel from each of the agencies, all forming the Orestes Task Force.

Every table had several laptops, outlets for additional ones, and enough cables to power a small city.

Gloria and McDaniels stood in front of a wall monitor with a chart displaying all the info they'd gathered so far and delivered a status update on the current situation.

The killer planned to strike at ten in the morning. Patrols were beefed up at all the local parks with uniformed and plainclothes officers stationed with FBI agents. Meanwhile, the press had found the posting on the chan site and were asking a battery of questions. Same for the hundreds of residents calling in, demanding to know what was being done to keep them safe. Parents were keeping their kids home from school.

The task force's suspect, Brendan Woods, hadn't left his parents' house, nor did they have enough evidence for a search warrant. Approaching him without enough to arrest him could leave them high and dry. Far better to catch him with evidence or in the act of planning a crime's execution. As long as they kept their eyes on him and he didn't escape surveillance, the threat was likely contained — assuming they had the right guy, and that he was working alone.

They had to plan for both assumptions being wrong and to prepare for an attack.

Gloria turned to McDaniels. "What about your cyber crimes division? They have anything on Orestes yet?"

"No. We've run into the same roadblocks that you have. Once you have a suspect in custody, we'll have our best cyber forensics team on hand."

A large screen displayed information behind Gloria and McDaniels.

"Wait. The killer just posted something new." Aanya brought up the page on the monitor and broadcast the location.

Mal stared in disbelief.

Chapter 14 - Orestes666

ORESTES666 STOOD on the street outside the Morningstar Diner holding the stolen phone.

He opened a livestream on the LiveLyfe page he'd swiped, though he'd yet to start the broadcast. He copied the link, logged into NonAMus, and began a thread on /KillEveryone.

He wrote: *It's show time*, followed by a link to the livestream.

He closed out the NonAMus window, raised the phone, and began broadcasting, aiming his camera at the diner, careful not to keep its signage from the shots.

He spoke, his voice altered by an app he downloaded onto the phone.

"Okay, kiddies. Time to play. And this one is gonna be bloody! Which one of these fuckers should I shoot first?"

He walked closer, slowly panning across the windows, revealing faces of diners in booths. Old people, young people, and a handful of families. Among them, his true target, taking an order from an elderly couple.

She had no idea that her morning was already spiraling

into hell. No idea that her worthless existence was already over.

He liked that feeling of knowing that someone's life was over before they did. That was true power. Not the kind that most people clung to, with position, wealth, or authority. The ability to spare life or deliver death was the ultimate power, and *he* held them.

Immediately, people called out their targets of choice. Some suggested killing the old fucks. Other suggested women and children first. And some people challenged him to *kill 'em all.*

Orestes666 smiled as he read the comments.

"Kill 'em all? Sounds like a plan."

He lowered his ski mask, slid the GoPro headband over it, then entered the diner, an AR-15 tucked under his trench coat.

Chapter 15 - Mallory Black

"THAT'S THE MORNING STAR DINER!" Mal practically yelled.

The command room turned to chaos with each person getting on the phone and ordering their people into positions near the diner. EMT, SWAT, and patrol officers all directed, in addition to the FDLE SWAT unit also on hand.

Wilson grabbed his coffee, barking at Mike and Mal. "Let's get over there! Mal, pull up that livestream on your phone."

Mal turned to Gloria, "We need to find out whose LiveLyfe account he's using, and get to their house. Make sure we don't have a repeat of Kincaid."

Gloria nodded, getting on the phone.

Mal and Mike followed Wilson toward the parking lot. They reached his department-issue Chevy Tahoe, and he threw his keys at Mike.

"You drive!"

Mike and Mal traded glances.

Wilson raced to the passenger side door and climbed inside.

Mike hopped into the driver's seat. Mal got into the back.

"Get a move on!" Wilson yelled, flicking on the siren and light bar.

Mike gunned the engine, gravel spitting as he tore out of the lot, past the security gate and toward SR 110.

Wilson dialed someone on his phone, for the third time since they left the station, anxiously waiting through the ringing.

When they were getting into his truck, Mal wasn't sure why he was in such a hurry. Detectives weren't usually first responders. They handled the investigations *after* bodies hit the ground. Maybe he missed the chase.

But then Mal realized that he knew someone at the diner.

Wilson looked back at Mal. "Is he inside yet?"

"No. He's approaching."

"Fuck! Come on, Trey, pick up the fucking phone."

Trey, Wilson's son. He worked as a cook at the diner.

Trey finally answered.

Wilson didn't wait for him to say anything. "Get out of there! *Now*. Take anyone in the kitchen and run out the back door. There's a gunman about to go in there."

Mal watched in horror as Orestes666 burst through the diner's front door and opened fire. "No!"

Mike pushed the SUV to go even faster, though they wouldn't arrive at the scene before the other officers, still roughly three minutes away.

Wilson's eyes were wide. "Trey? You there? Trey?"

He stared back at Mal, then down at her phone, watching the carnage unfold.

Chapter 16 - Orestes666

CHAOS ERUPTED as he strolled through the diner, firing indiscriminately.

Well, that wasn't entirely true. He tried to avoid children. Everyone else was fair fucking game. Aside from the kids, this diner held no innocents.

Shattered glass crunched underfoot; bloodied people cried for help and coughed up blood; others screamed in agony as they bled out. All of it, music to his ears.

He kept his eyes out for two things: another person with a gun, and the bitch he'd come here to kill.

As his first magazine emptied, he ducked behind a wall separating one row of booths from another and reloaded.

He saw the woman he'd come for: Lynn Macklin, co-owner of the diner along with her brother, Stewart.

She cowered beneath a booth, probably thinking she'd somehow avoid detection.

He let go of the rifle, hanging by a strap around his shoulder, grabbed his pistol, then seized Lynn by the hair, yanking her out hard.

"No, please!" She stumbled forward and fell at his feet. Then she looked up, her eyes wide and terrified. *"Please!"*

Lynn was in a simple blouse and a fitted pair of jeans that on a younger woman might have been flattering. But at forty-one her best years were behind her, and no amount of plastic surgery would help her keep pace with the younger, hotter women that worked for her.

He was tempted to remove his mask so she could see his face, and know who was pulling the trigger. That would give him immeasurable pleasure. Hell, it almost aroused him. If he had time, he might even have fucked her first, just because he knew how much she'd hate being taken by the man she'd ridiculed so much.

But, with sirens wailing, there wasn't time to hang around. The place would be crawling with cops any second, and he was only done when Lynn was dead.

He pulled her up roughly, barking, "Stand!"

She did.

He put the gun to her head, then leaned in and whispered, "You shouldn't have interfered."

"Interfered in what? Who are you?"

He reached around, grabbing her tit and squeezing it hard.

She cried out, spinning around as if she were going to strike him.

He put the gun on her face.

That shut her the fuck up.

"Who am I?" He smiled under the mask. "You wanna know who I am?"

She nodded, unable to speak.

He killed the audio on his GoPro and told her.

Then he said, "And all of these people are dead because of what you did."

Recognition dawned, followed by a look of anger, then

contempt. Like Lynn was about to become the megabitch he always knew her to be. Like she was going to grab his gun. As if she hadn't just witnessed him destroy her precious diner. As if he wasn't holding the ultimate power.

Before she could say or do anything, he pulled the trigger and wiped that bitch look off her fucking face.

Then, with sirens ever closer, he ran.

Chapter 17 - Mallory Black

"WE'RE TOO LATE!" Mallory said, watching the livestream die. "He's on the run."

"How's Trey? Did you see him?"

"No," Mal told Wilson, even though they were watching the same stream. With all the madness of people running and screaming, the camera's jerky movements, and the killer cutting the feed after he killed the woman he seemed to have taken the most interest in, it was difficult to tell how many people had been shot, much less if Trey was among them. Plus, bullets could have ripped through walls into the rear of the diner.

All Mallory knew was that there were many bodies, maybe the most in Creek County's history and that the killer was getting away.

Mike turned up the radio as dispatch updated them on the position of the killer's car, a black, late model Dodge Charger, last seen going west on SR110.

Several officers responded, saying they were en route. Other officers and EMTs were already on scene.

"Is that him?" Mike pointed at a black Charger racing toward them on the opposite side of the street.

Mike slammed on the brakes, screeching to a stop as the killer raced by without a cop in sight.

Mike cranked the wheel hard and jumped the median, turning onto the westbound street, and floored the pedal.

Wilson got on the radio to update dispatch that they were in pursuit, filling them in with as much info as he could, hoping for a roadblock with spike strips farther up the road.

There was surely a part of Wilson that probably wanted to circle back to the diner and see if his son was okay, but a deputy's duty was to chase an escaping killer first. Besides, they'd know soon enough once information started trickling in.

Cars flew by on either side as Mike weaved through traffic, about ten car lengths behind the Charger.

Mal wished they were driving one of the department-issued Chargers. The truck was slower and its handling was all over the place. The odds of a Tahoe winning this pursuit were nil. Their only hope was that the killer made a mistake, without murdering more people, or that another unit could get a spike strip in place.

The Charger was approaching a major intersection and a red light.

This was their chance.

But the car didn't slow.

It blew through the light, narrowly missing oncoming traffic.

A pickup slid to avoid the Charger, spun out, and slammed into another car in the westbound lane.

Wilson called it in as Mike kept driving.

They slowed approaching the intersection, cars stopping for the siren.

Mike went through it at about 50 MPH, Mal bracing for an unseen collision.

They made it through unscathed, but The Charger was gaining, approaching the railroad tracks.

And, of course, the crossing gates were falling, red lights blinking.

"Shit!" Mike yelled.

They had about thirty seconds before the train appeared.

Traffic stopped for the gates.

The Charger swerved to the right, and for a moment, it seemed as if it was going to turn along a side road. But then it gunned the engine, bursting through the gate to cross the tracks.

"Fuck!" Mike yelled, gunning the engine, pushing the SUV to its limits.

They were about ninety yards away.

The train was in sight, maybe a hundred yards.

The Charger made it, with nobody to stop it if they failed to catch up.

"Hold tight!" Mike said, eyes narrowing on the road as he swerved left of the traffic, heading straight into the train's path.

"Cortez!" Wilson yelled, eyes wide.

Mal's heart was a jackhammer, glancing at the space ahead, at the Charger in the distance, then at the train.

Quick spatial reasoning said there was no way they could avoid the train.

Mike was going to crash.

At best, it would be the slimmest of margins.

They closed in fast.

Mal closed her eyes, bracing for an explosion.

Mike screeched to a sudden stop.

She opened her eyes and saw the train, inches from the

SUV, speeding by, deafening, a wall of wind blasting their truck.

"Fuck!" Mike screamed, punching the steering wheel with both fists.

Wilson called into dispatch: *they'd lost the Charger.*

Mal hoped that there were other officers en route from a different direction, or maybe they'd managed to get a chopper in the air, but her gut knew what her mind wasn't yet willing to accept.

The killer got away.

Chapter 18 - Jordyn Parish

THE SCHOOL GYMNASIUM usually smelled like sweaty boys. But somehow, whoever put the dance together expunged the place of its reek, and decorated it so that it barely looked like a gym.

Jordyn was stuck in the *Circle of Calum*, as Bobby called it behind his back, for the first half of the dance. The Circle was essentially Calum holding court with his friends, his girlfriend and her friends, and everyone else who wanted to be in their group. They kissed his ass, laughed at his off-color jokes, and acted like the adults held hostage in that Twilight Zone episode with the creepy kid who uses his powers to harm anyone who doesn't amuse him.

Jordyn was enjoying a happy buzz, not yet tipsy or pukey.

After listening to Calum and Nate bust balls back and forth while the girls laughed at every punchline, Bobby finally managed to break them free and ask Jordyn to dance. Slow pop with a female singer, a song she vaguely recognized from hearing people playing it on their phones, but it wasn't her style — which mostly consisted of 90s

British music from, as her father called them, "effeminate men singing moody music."

Jordyn had never danced with a boy, so her heart galloped as she took his hand.

He met her eyes and held her gaze.

They stared into each other's eyes, Jordan trying not to trip or worse. Maybe she shouldn't look so hard. Was he going to think she was a creeper?

She glanced around. Most of the girls were resting their heads on, pressed to their partner's chest.

Jordyn did the same.

Bobby wore a light, sweet cologne. She loved it on him.

His hands closed tighter around her waist, brought her closer to him.

Her heart kept racing. She wondered if he could feel it against his chest. She tried to listen to his heart, to see if it was also beating fast, but the music was too loud.

Oh, that wouldn't seem weird at all.

"You look beautiful tonight," he whispered in her ear.

Just the kind of thing she'd make fun of if a guy said it in a movie or TV show, but it worked well enough on Jordyn — melted her stomach and weakened her knees.

She could feel her big, goofy smile.

"Thank you," she said.

He leaned forward and kissed Jordyn gently on the lips.

Oh, my God!

She didn't know what to do. Open her mouth? Put her tongue in his mouth? What if she kissed like a fish?

Jordyn closed her eyes and went with what felt right, hoping she didn't mess up.

His tongue slid into her mouth, just a little, and then the kiss was over.

She opened her eyes and found him staring into hers, smiling.

From his pleasure or her inexperience, Jordyn didn't know.

Mercifully, the song was over. The lights brightened, and a faster song started to play.

Brianna and Calum ran over. "Come on!" Brianna said, her voice slurred and eyes red. "Time for Second Party!"

"Second Party?" Jordyn asked.

Calum said, "We got a suite at the Parke Grande."

"A hotel?"

Brianna laughed, "Oh, honey, you thought *this* was the point of tonight?"

"I dunno. My dad is expecting me home by midnight."

"Don't worry," Bobby said, "I'll have you home at 11:59 PM."

Suddenly, Nate, Adam, Bethanee, and everyone else in the Circle of Calum were there, looking at Jordyn, their judgment on her like a stink. She could practically feel them thinking, *Who doesn't want to go to the after party? What kind of dork is she? She's not one of us!*

She *had* heard of parties after dances, particularly proms, and while Jordyn hadn't been to any, she knew a few girls who had. And according to them, they were typically alcohol and drug-fueled orgies. The sorts of places that Jordyn always thought she was too smart to go.

As her father had said plenty of times, the best way to stay out of trouble was to stay away from people who found it.

She'd always been good about that. It was easy to avoid those kinds of people when they didn't want anything to do with you, and you traveled in different circles. But now she was going out with one of the most popular boys in school. She was part of the very sort of group that she'd always judged but had never taken the time to know.

While they seemed like bitches and assholes collectively, individually they were perfectly nice. Most of them, anyway. She genuinely liked Bobby, a lot.

And while they engaged in the sorts of things that got most people in trouble, Calum and his group never seemed to suffer a single consequence. They somehow floated above it all, immune to the pitfalls that befell so many kids.

"Well," Calum said, "is Cinderella coming with or heading home to her pumpkin?"

Jordyn drew a deep breath, digging deep for the bravery required to bloom from the shy, introverted wall-flower to the young, strong woman she yearned to be.

"Yes."

Calum, Brianna, Bobby, and the others all cheered, then pushed her like a wave to the exit, and into the waiting limo.

THE HOTEL SUITE was out of this world.

It felt like a rich person's home. The bathroom was all marble, and the tub looked like it could have held a half-dozen people. Twice that for the gorgeous shower, practically sparkling with thousands of tiny tiles. Pillow-top king-sized beds, Jordyn wasn't even sure how many — she thought the place had four bedrooms. The living room was twice the size of Jordyn's, and the city sprawled below like peasants at the foot of a mountain. Jordyn knew that Calum came from money — everyone had seen his Teslas — but this hotel was unbelievable.

There were eight of them at the after party. Four guys, four girls. Calum and Brianna, Bobby and Jordyn, Adam and Bethanee, and Nate and Sammi.

Music blasted as the group gathered around the bar and Bobby rolled joints with admirable skill.

Jordyn found a spot on a couch, away from the group, anxious as she fondled a Corona that Adam had handed her. Two sips and she knew the drink was disgusting, but Jordyn smiled as she sipped. Better to nurse a bottle than call attention to herself by saying no.

How long before the loud music attracted hotel staff? How long before police showed up to break up the party?

Jordyn would never live it down if she got busted at a party like this. Dad would guilt trip her, and likely forbid her from going out with Bobby — not that they were officially dating.

Are we?

She wasn't sure what the criteria were. They hung out a lot, and he asked her to the dance. He'd kissed her.

But that didn't make them a couple, did it? Did guys even ask girls to be their girlfriends? Or did people just slide right into a relationship?

Jordyn wished her mom was still around. Sure, she hadn't been a kid in about twenty years, but she probably knew how to navigate these waters better than Dad.

She sat alone on the sofa, watching the group, trying to figure out how each of the couples ended up together. Nate was drinking a Corona while flicking through Snapchat, critiquing each girl's shortcomings in clinical detail. Brianna and Bethanee occasionally cut in, either laughing at the unfortunate girl if she didn't fit their standard of beauty or calling the girl a whore if she did.

Calum sat back in a seat beside Bobby, smoking the first rolled joint, handed it to Nate, who took a drag, coughed, then passed it to Sammi.

Just as Jordyn was starting to wonder how long before someone would urge her to smoke, Brianna, Bethanee, and Sammi all approached her, Brianna holding the joint.

"Why are you sitting here by yourself? Here." She passed the joint to Jordyn.

Jordyn held it in her fingers, staring at it like a snake that might strike her.

Brianna laughed, "Please tell me this isn't your first smoke?"

Jordyn shrugged her shoulders. "Um ..."

Brianna laughed harder.

"You don't have to if you don't want to." Sammi held out her hand, offering to take the joint.

"No," Calum said, getting up from his spot beside Bobby. "She *does* have to. You don't party with us and not *party* with us."

He approached Jordyn, stone faced, like she'd personally insulted him.

Everyone was quiet, watching her.

She couldn't see past Calum to gauge Bobby's reaction.

"I'm sorry. I just never smoked before. I'm not judging you."

He stared at her. The room was silent.

Her heart raced. She'd committed a horrible faux pas and didn't even know it. And his eyes were so angry.

Everyone stared.

Then he burst out laughing, and so did everyone else.

"Nah, I'm just fucking with you, girl." He took the joint and deeply inhaled.

Jordyn sighed as Bobby walked up behind Calum and punched him in the arm. "Man, don't be messing with my girl like that."

"Oh, so now she's your girl? Glad to see my boy's balls dropped and he asked you out."

Jordyn didn't correct Calum.

Brianna handed Jordyn a drink she'd made at the bar. It was red and frosty, with a little umbrella sticking out of the top.

"Okay, you don't have to smoke, but you do have to drink. You need to loosen up, Jore."

Jore? Nobody's ever called me Jore before.

She didn't entirely hate it.

Suddenly, everyone, Bobby included, began to chant, "Drink, drink, drink, drink!"

Jordyn tasted it. The drink was fruity, and though the alcohol was strong, its bite wasn't awful.

"I'll make sure you're okay," Sammi said. She was always so nice, and her honest smile was easy to trust.

Jordyn took a bigger drink.

Chapter 19 - Jasper Parish

JASPER WAITED IN THE DARKNESS, stewing in anger.

He'd called Jordyn six times. Each call went to voicemail. What the hell was the point in buying her an expensive phone if she never fucking answered?

"You need to calm down," Carissa said. "She's a big girl. She can take care of herself."

"Big girl? She's *seventeen*, not thirty-seven. I think you forget what teenage boys are like."

"You raised her well. *We* raised her well. You're not giving her enough credit."

"And you're not giving that boyfriend of hers enough skepticism."

"He's fine."

"Yeah, you know that from the few times he's been in this house? Damn, every boy is on his best behavior in front of a girl's father. Look at *me* when I was courting you."

"Yeah, and don't think my Daddy wasn't on to you, too. He warned me, but I went out with you anyway. And I think I handled myself pretty well."

"Well, I'm not Bobby."

"No, but you need to have faith in your daughter. You've got to trust her."

"I'd trust her a hell of a lot more if it wasn't one in the morning, Carissa. You're not worried that she's late? I told her to be home by midnight."

"How many times has she stayed out late? Come on, Jasper, it's a special night."

"Well, it better not be *too* special is all I'm saying."

"Tell me, Jasper, how well do you know this Bobby kid?"

"Not well enough, and that's the problem."

"And yet, she's been hanging out with him for more than a month, and you knew she liked him. You didn't make the time to invite him over for dinner or do anything to get to know him?"

"I'm busy."

"Busy doing what? You're retired."

"Don't start on me, Carissa."

"Lie to yourself all you want, but don't expect me to join the chorus."

He glared at her.

A flash of light cut through the curtains.

He stood, ready to give Bobby a piece of his mind, but Carissa grabbed his arm. "Don't do it, Jasper. Don't you embarrass that poor girl."

He looked at Carissa, smiling as if Jordyn wasn't an hour late. As if she wasn't with some boy that Jasper barely even trusted.

He listened to Jordyn fumble with her keys, trying to unlock the door, his anger rolling to a boil.

The door opened.

In the background, he watched a limousine shrink down the street.

Jordyn reeked of weed and alcohol.

He felt as if someone had taken a sledgehammer to the pedestal holding his girl, reducing his child to another drink and drug using punk.

"I'm so sorry," she said, stumbling.

Jordyn fell forward.

Jasper moved quickly, grabbing her in an awkward catch before she tumbled face first to the ground.

He helped her to her feet.

She looked up at him, and laughed.

Jasper exploded. "You think this is funny?"

Her eyes widened.

"I'll tell you what's funny: you're not seeing Bobby ever again. How's that for laughs?"

"You can't do that!"

"I can, I will, and look, I just did."

She shook her head. "No, you can't stop me."

"What?"

"I'm seventeen; I'm old enough to go on a date!"

"Oh, yeah, you really know how to take care of yourself! Look at you. You're drunk, you're high, and your makeup is a mess."

And even though he didn't want to go there, he couldn't help himself once the idea popped into his head.

"Did he take advantage of you?"

"What?"

"Did he take advantage of you? That's what guys like him do, you know."

"First off, you don't even know the first thing about him! Second of all, what I do with my body is my business!"

"Not while you're living under my roof!"

"What? Do you even hear yourself?"

Jordyn got in his face.

He couldn't understand what was going on. His daughter had never acted like this. Yes, she was occasionally moody, but nothing like this.

"What happened tonight?"

Jordyn started to walk away.

He grabbed her by the shoulders and spun her around. "Don't you walk away from me when I'm talking to you!"

She laughed in his face, her eyes cruel and full of loathing.

Where is this coming from?

She inched closer. "No, you don't get to play now, Dad. You've spent the last six years barely acknowledging me! Hell, you spend more time talking to a fucking ghost than you do me!"

"Don't you talk like that about your mother!"

She laughed again. "She's dead, Dad! Maybe if you took your pills once in a while, or, I don't know, maybe stopped drinking, you'd see things straight for a change!"

He slapped her across the face.

Jordyn's eyes welled with tears. Something else had swallowed the loathing, a betrayal he never imagined seeing in his daughter's eyes.

She ran up the stairs, sobbing.

Jasper stared down at his trembling hands.

He'd *never* laid a hand on a woman. Not his wife, whom he barely even fought with, nor his daughter, even in punishment.

Jasper had always told himself he'd never be like his alcoholic, abusive father. And in one white hot instant, the lie gave way to a horrible truth. He had failed.

Upstairs, he heard Jordyn puking.

Carissa appeared beside him at the bottom of the stairs, looking at him with disappointment all over her face.

"Go up there. She needs you."

"She hates me."

"No, she doesn't. You're her father. She loves you. She just needs to know that you still love her."

He started up the stairs, then stopped on the fourth step.

He couldn't go any farther.

"What are you doing?" Carissa asked.

"I can't."

"Why?"

"I don't know. I … I just can't."

Chapter 20 - Mallory Black

ELEVEN DEAD BODIES, including a six-year-old boy and a nine-year-old girl. The worst mass shooting in Creek County history, and still no suspect. The one they did have was sitting in his parents' house when the shooting went down, and they had nothing tying him to the killer.

Mal stood outside the diner, interviewing witnesses while FBI agents — as part of the task force headed by McDaniels — processed the crime scene.

She typically enjoyed being lead on the case — walking the crime scene, determining next steps, helping evidence techs sort between collection and documentation. But a part of Mal was glad that she didn't have to enter the diner.

She saw these people die in the video, watched this maniac butcher them, fueled by the cheering of anonymous cowards online.

It was all she could do to bury her burning rage at this murderer. They almost had this man in their grasp but failed to catch him.

She kept wondering what would have happened if they

had not stopped for the train. What if they kept going? Sure, maybe they would've been killed in the pursuit, but they *might* have caught him and prevented the next massacre.

As Mal talked to a crying woman named Louise, she looked up and saw Wilson standing next to his son, Trey, whom he'd hugged for nearly five minutes straight once they arrived on the scene. It was odd seeing Wilson's softer side. She was glad that he didn't have to discover what it felt like to lose a child to a serial killer.

After thanking Louise for her information, though she offered nothing helpful, Mal took a moment before moving on to the next witness.

She stared into the diner's broken windows, shattered by gunfire, trying to comprehend what could make one person kill so many.

Her phone rang. Mal answered.

Katie was crying. "He's going to kill her."

"What? Your dad?"

"Yes, they've been fighting all day."

"What's happening?"

"I don't know. My dad just showed up, pissed and yelling. I thought he was in jail."

Daryl probably made bail, was given a temporary injunction for the protection of domestic violence, and was told to get a deputy escort to his house, to pick up his shit and get the hell out until the judge could see both Daryl and Sue.

That was the typical procedure, and the husband or boyfriend usually obeyed.

Daryl was ignoring a court order, and that made the situation volatile. Mal had to get someone over there before Daryl snapped.

"What's going on right now?" Mal asked.

"They're fighting."

"Where are you?"

"Hiding in my room, under my bed."

"You need to stay put and call the police. Can you do that?"

"Yes."

Mal heard Katie's father screaming. It was a punch to the gut. There was nothing she hated more than seeing someone in trouble and being unable to help, especially a child.

"Katie? Stay on the line. I'm calling dispatch."

Mal called dispatch with Katie on the line, relaying details while looking around for a car to use. Her car, like Mike's, was back at the Sheriff's department.

The dispatcher, a woman named Wanda Green, asked Katie questions, coaching her through the ordeal, explaining that an officer was on the way.

Mal found Skippy interviewing witnesses. She pulled him aside and asked if he had a ride she could borrow. Something in her face or voice must've been screaming. He reached into his pocket and handed her his keys with a sympathetic smile and not a single word behind it.

"That one." He pointed toward the end of the parking lot, just inside the crime scene zone.

Mal ran toward it. "Stay with me, Katie. I'm coming right now, just a few minutes away!" She hopped into Skippy's car, adjusted the seat, and peeled out of the parking lot.

A loud *POP!* came through the phone.

Katie cried out, "Oh, my God. Oh, my God."

"What is it?" Mal flipped on the siren bar and lights.

"I ... I think he shot her."

"I'm on the way, Katie. Do *not* do anything."

"I have to help her!"

"No, Katie! Stay put. I'll be there. Ambulances are on the way, too! *They* will help her, but I need you to stay put so he doesn't hurt you."

"I ... I can't hear her." Katie cried.

"Katie?"

No answer.

Mal's gut sank. Katie must've gone into the other room to try and save her mother.

No, no, no.

Mal was approaching a red light.

A big Target truck was crawling through the intersection, probably not seeing her approaching until it was too late to stop.

She swerved, pumping her brakes, and managed to avoid the truck.

She was a block away.

"Katie?" Mal said, same as the dispatcher.

Neither got a response.

She made it through the intersection and turned into Katie's neighborhood, now four streets away.

Come on, come on.

Katie's father screamed in the background. "This is your fault, you little whore!"

Katie cried out, "Mom!"

Mal yelled at the phone, though she didn't think Katie could hear her. "Do not engage him, Katie! Do NOT engage him!"

Two streets away.

Mal narrowly avoided a pair of bicyclists, making a hard turn onto Katie's street.

Four houses away and it seemed like a mile.

Just hang in there, Katie. Hang in—

Another gunshot.

"Katie!" Mal screamed as she floored the pedal, then

braked as her car hopped the curb and rolled right into the front yard, stopping just inches from Katie's front door.

Mal jumped out, gun drawn.

The front window curtains were wide open.

Daryl stood staring at Mal with stunned disbelief on his red face, a shotgun loosely slung over his shoulder.

"Put the gun down!" she yelled, aiming her pistol at him.

Mal was too far away to see the ground, but she had to assume that he was standing over his wife and daughter.

"I didn't mean to! It was an accident!"

"Put the gun down!" Mal repeated, stepping closer to the window, and finally getting a better look.

And then she saw them.

Katie's mother was lying face down in a pool of blood behind him.

Katie was lying beside her, hands clutching at a gunshot wound to her gut.

Her eyes were wide open, but she wasn't moving. Mal had to get in there to try and save her, assuming she wasn't already gone.

She yelled again. "Put the fucking gun down!"

Daryl didn't.

He lowered his shotgun, aiming at Mal.

Mal fired first.

Four times.

Chapter 21 - Mallory Black

MAL WATCHED raindrops slide down the window. A world of grays had seeped into her soul, a darkness no amount of rainfall would rinse away.

Katie was in a hospital bed next to Mal, hooked to machines monitoring her vitals and helping her breathe. She looked so pale and fragile; Mal felt a sickening certainty that the girl would die before morning.

After coding twice, once in the ambulance, and the other on the operating table, Katie was now in the ICU following a three-hour surgery. She was expected to survive her wounds, but she'd lost a lot of blood and had slipped into a coma.

The surgeon had said it was too soon to tell if she'd come out of the coma. Mal had seen this story enough times to keep a positive attitude. Usually the younger or more innocent a person, the more likely they were to die.

If Mal believed in God, this would be more evidence that He was a cruel bastard. Mal had lost count of how many good people she'd seen die over the years.

A knock on the door. The nurse peeked in.

"You've got a visitor. Mike Cortez?"

Mal stood and squeezed Katie's hand. "I'll be right back. Okay?"

Mal stepped out of the room and saw Mike holding a large cup of Dunkin' Donuts coffee.

He handed it to her.

"Thanks," she said, taking it in her hands and feeling its warmth through the foam cup, the anchor of routine rewinding the day and inviting it closer to normal. She sipped, savoring the heat.

Mike asked, "How's she doing?"

"She pulled through surgery okay. But she's in a coma. So, I dunno."

"Any family show up yet?"

Mal shook her head. "Her parents were all she had."

"Shit."

"Shit, indeed," Mal said.

"So, how long you on administrative leave?"

"I don't know. Could be a few days, could be a few weeks of desk duty."

"I'm sure IA won't hold it up too long. One, we need all hands on deck. And two, it *was* a clean shooting. The dude had just shot his wife and daughter."

Mike said it as a fact, but Mal felt like he was asking.

But that was the sort of question a good partner knew better than to ask. The kind that could haunt you during an Internal Affairs investigation.

"Yes, it *was* a clean shooting. He was aiming at me."

But it wasn't as easy as that. If Mal were honest, she would tell Mike that a small part of her had decided to shoot him the moment she saw Katie and her mother bleeding beneath him. A part of her wanted him to pay.

Fortunately, he had aimed at her.

But what if he hadn't?

She didn't dare present the question to Mike. It wasn't the sort of baggage anyone but she should carry.

What would I have done if he hadn't aimed at me?

She felt no joy in killing him. Hell, she was pissed that he forced her to pull the trigger. She wanted him to sit in a prison cell and pay for what he'd done, for many years. And if he had to die, then it should be an execution by the state, not at her hands.

"Ain't no way they'll try and jam you up on this, Mal. I wouldn't sweat it."

"Any updates on our serial killer?"

"No. Two more dead, though. An elderly couple. Woman died en route to the hospital. Her husband died from a heart attack a few minutes later."

Mal shook her head. "Nothing on the killer?"

"Nothing. It's like he vanished."

"Brendan Woods?"

"We talked to him, but no, I don't think he's involved."

"What about the woman whose LiveLyfe account he used. Was she dead?"

"No, not this time. It was a waitress who worked at the diner. And she had her phone. Someone had logged in using her account."

"Interesting. And have you gotten anything on that yet?"

"Aanya's working it, but I doubt the killer used his own phone. Might have been a burner."

"And we're sure this waitress isn't connected to the killer?"

"Doubt it."

Mal paced in the hallway, looking out the windows to the parking lot below. Thunder rumbled as rain pelted the windows.

"What about the victim?"

"Which one?"

"The last one he killed. He spent most of his time talking to her. They need to be looking at her, finding out if she's any relation to any of the victims at the ball field, specifically Chip Halverson. Maybe talk to the guy's daughter, see if she knows the woman. Or Coach Kincaid."

"So, you still don't think this is random?"

"If it's random, then why does he spend more time with these two people? And why does he cut the audio?"

"Good point."

"What are the Behavior Analysis people saying?"

"They think this is random."

Mal shook her head. "They saw the same videos I saw, right? How could they not have noticed him talking to the victims?"

"There was some discussion, but the consensus is that he was savoring the moment because they were his last kills. But I'm sure they're considering every possible angle. They've brought some of their top people from the Jacksonville field office and a couple more from Quantico."

Mal stared out the window, taking a long sip of coffee.

Mike was quiet until she finally spoke again. "What if we don't catch this guy?"

"We will. There's no way he vanishes with this much heat."

"It's happened before. Not here, but hell, there are plenty of unsolved serial killings."

"Two in a few days? This doesn't seem like someone looking to lay low. I think he's only going to ramp up."

"Me too. And may your God help whatever crowd he walks into next."

Mike joined her in staring out the window. "You need a ride home?"

"No, I'm staying the night."

"What?"

"She doesn't have anyone else. I feel responsible. I pushed her to Victims Services, which set off a whole chain of events."

"Yeah, but you couldn't have seen that coming."

"She said her dad would kill them. I didn't think he'd do it."

"Still, you can't blame yourself."

"It doesn't matter who is to blame. Me, her father, Fate, whatever. All I know is that there's a kid all alone in a coma, and she needs someone by her side. Someone to hold her hand, and talk to her. A reason to hang on."

Mike nodded. "How about dinner? Want me to bring you anything?"

"Nah, go home to your wife. Kiss her and tell her how you almost got us all killed by a train today."

Mike laughed, then hugged her goodbye. "Call me if you need anything."

"Thanks, Mike."

Mal returned to Katie's room, sat in the chair, and held her hand.

She wasn't sure what to say. She'd read a book on coma patients when a former informant of hers, Karen Kelton, had gone into a coma following an overdose. Recent science said that it was important to talk, let the patient know that she isn't alone. It was thought to help people survive, and sometimes even wake from their comas.

She'd never tested the theory on Karen, who had died before Mal had a chance to see her.

She looked at Katie and shook her head, vowing not to repeat that mistake. "Is there anything you'd like me to talk about? A story you'd like me to read?"

She squeezed Katie's hand, but the girl didn't even flutter her eyelids.

Only the sounds of the ventilator and the rhythmic beeps of the heart monitor filled the room.

"Okay, I'll tell you about how I got into law enforcement. Maybe I'll throw in some stories about the dumbest criminals I've ever arrested. Sound interesting?"

No response.

Mal told her story anyway.

Chapter 22 - Jasper Parish

JASPER STARED at the large storefront of Fixed Fitness, a trendy gym where Bobby worked the front desk after school.

Bobby joked and laughed as he checked in a steady stream of muscular men and fit women in tight workout clothes. He was hoping to see him flirting with the girls, as evidence that he wasn't interested in Jordyn as much as any hot girl that came along.

But the boy didn't seem to be flirting with *any* of the women or leering as they passed his desk — surprising given his age. What high school boy wasn't leering at half-naked women in a gym?

"Don't do it," Carissa said from the passenger seat.

He squeezed it as he struggled to decide whether to go in or leave.

It had been a week since Jordyn's curfew breaking debauchery. A week since he punished her for a month, saying she could only go to school and straight home, that she couldn't hang with Bobby outside of school.

A week since their Cold War began

She hadn't given him more than a few icy words. Their tentative friendship had now been replaced by a standoff in which neither would show the flaw of apology.

She'd answer his questions in short, clipped sentences, but other than that, Jordyn didn't utter a word or laugh at his attempts to joke around.

She hated him.

The day after the dance, when he'd sat her down to dish the punishment's excruciating details, he'd forbidden her from dating Bobby. According to Jordyn, they weren't even dating. Bobby had asked her to the dance, and that was it.

When Jasper tried to broach the subject of whether or not anything sexual had happened, without being too judgmental or accusing the boy of taking advantage of her, Jordyn ignored his questions.

Which only reinforced his opinion that something *had* happened. He wanted to tell her it wasn't her fault, and that she could talk to him, but he couldn't get the words out in a way that didn't piss her off.

He finally dropped it.

Carissa asked, "What are you going to say to him?"

"I don't know."

"Well, *that* sounds like a terrific plan!"

"You have something better?"

"Yeah, go home and forget this."

"Not an option. Besides, I'm sure he already saw me."

Carissa shook her head. "Why are you here, Jasper?"

"I want to know what happened. I want to know why that boy got our daughter drunk."

"Okay, let's just say it was for nefarious reasons. Do you expect him to tell you? 'Oh, yeah, Mr. Parish, I got your daughter drunk so she'd sleep with me! She was out cold, but I had fun!'"

Jasper glared at Carissa. "That's not funny."

"I'm just trying to show you how ridiculous this is. What boy is going to be honest with the father of the girl they like?"

"So, you agree, he's only after one thing?"

"I didn't say that. But he is a teenage boy, and all teenage boys are after that, but that isn't exclusive of being in love. Think about when you were a kid. You wanted to get laid. But you also felt like you were in love, right?"

"I was stupid then. I didn't know what love was."

"You're acting like love is this one thing, that it doesn't change. When we're younger, love is impulsive, but is it any less of an emotion? No. You can't discount what either of them feels just because they're kids."

"Stop it."

"Stop what? Making sense?" She leaned toward him, smiling at Jasper like she did when she was right and he was about to swallow a mouthful of crow. Her eyes sparkled. He wished he could reach over and touch her, hold her close again. This time he'd never let her go.

"Fine. You're right," he said, opening the car door.

She called out after him, "If I'm right, where are you going?"

"I still want to talk to him."

He slammed the door and walked toward the gym.

Bobby looked up from his monitor as Jasper entered. His eyes widened with surprise, but he quickly recovered, smiling as he stepped out from behind the desk to greet Jordyn's father with a handshake.

"Hello, Mr. Parish," he said from behind his firm shake.

Jasper stared him in the eyes, wanting to put the kid on blast for getting his little girl drunk. He resisted, for now.

Bobby spoke. "Listen, before you say anything, I just

want to apologize. Jordyn told me that you were upset with her coming home drunk, and that's all my fault."

A good start. Jasper kept his mouth shut, waiting for Bobby to say more.

Bobby asked Jasper if he wanted to go outside and discuss it. He nodded. Bobby asked one of the girls he worked with to watch the desk for a few minutes. They went outside, circling the parking lot as Bobby talked.

"Believe me, that's not a normal thing, us getting drunk. Well, not for me, anyway. Some of the other kids, well, they're a different story. In truth, I was nervous as hell going to the dance with Jordyn. I like her a lot and thought maybe a bit of drinking might calm my nerves, make me more confident. But before too long, a bit was too much. I shouldn't have ever offered her any. It was a terrible decision, and I'm sorry."

"What about the weed? She smelled like a Phish concert."

"Neither of us were smoking, I swear. Hell, I'll take a drug test if you want. But some of the other kids were, and it's kinda hard not to smell like it when you're around. But I don't smoke, and neither did Jordyn."

They'd walked toward the side of the shopping plaza, out of earshot to anyone that would matter to either of them.

Jasper stopped. "What happened?"

"What do you mean?"

"I'm asking if you took advantage of my daughter."

He held Bobby's gaze. The boy seemed scared, but he didn't flinch or look away.

"No. Nothing happened, I swear."

As a cop, Jasper's bullshit detector was rarely wrong. He could smell a lie, no matter what a person might say or do to try and hide it.

And while he didn't think Bobby was telling him everything, he believed him on two counts: Jordyn didn't smoke, and nothing sexual happened between them.

Jasper nodded, then reached up, pinching a nerve in Bobby's shoulder to render him temporarily paralyzed. "Okay, here's the deal, Bobby. Jordyn is all I have left in this world. Her mother died of cancer, and I'm what they call overprotective. I'm not happy with what happened after the dance. *At all.* But I won't tell my daughter who she can and can't see. However, I'm telling you right now, man to man, that if you ever get my daughter drunk, or high, or bring her home in that sort of condition again, I *will* kill you. I'm not exaggerating. I mean that I will murder you and nobody will ever find your body. Are we clear?"

Bobby swallowed hard and Jasper released his hold.

"Yes, sir."

"Good," Jasper said, then offered his hand.

Bobby shook it, barely.

Jasper shook his hand hard, leaning in just close enough to look Bobby right in the eye to prove that his threat was stone cold serious.

He left Bobby standing alone, hopefully needing a clean pair of underwear.

Chapter 23 - Mallory Black

MAL WOKE in the darkness to an obnoxious bleating.

Startled, heart racing, she sat up in the chair, hand reaching for her gun only to remember that she'd turned it in after the shooting and had yet to get issued a new one. Her personal firearm was back at the hotel. But a weapon wasn't needed — it was the emergency broadcast system coming through the hospital room TV.

She found the remote, lowered the volume, then checked on Katie, still alive but unconscious.

She picked up her phone from where it was charging on a portable table next to Katie's bed and glanced at the clock. 3:15 AM.

She set the phone down, then turned the TV back up as a familiar face appeared on-screen — Calum Kozack.

"Authorities are searching for any information on the whereabouts of nineteen-year old Calum Kozack, son of Oliver Kozack, CEO of White Label Empire. Calum was last seen three days ago at Vibes night club in Coral Cove."

She watched as a reporter interviewed Calum's mother, Marilyn Kozack, on-screen.

"It's not like him to leave for so long. If anyone knows anything, please call. We're offering a reward for any information leading to his whereabouts."

The camera cut back to the overnight TV15 news anchor, Jillian Harris, who reminded viewers that Calum Kozack was recently involved in a scandal involving the alleged rape of an underaged girl.

Mal stared at the screen, at the smiling, good-looking young man. She wondered how many others could see through to the darkness inside him.

Kozack only got off was because his father pressured the DA, Lyle Dobson, to not file charges.

Maybe karma finally caught up with him.

Mal wondered which detective got saddled with the case. Mike would've called if it were him. She felt sorry for whoever it was — no doubt the Kozacks would be at the station daily to bitch, trying to find out why their precious prince hadn't been found.

They were likely too oblivious to see, or too sociopathic to care, that the sheriff's office had its hands full with a serial murderer.

Mal remembered a few years back when Calum had been a person of interest in one of the department's suicide cases. The girl's father had insisted that Kozack and a few other kids were to blame. He accused Calum of some nasty stuff, but with the victim dead and the evidence almost nonexistent, the DA argued that there wasn't enough to bring the case to trial. Calum walked. His involvement never made the press.

And a few months ago, he walked from yet another case, though this time the girl was very much alive, and the story leaked in all its ugly glory.

Mal wondered if this was a case of revenge. Maybe the father, brother, or a friend of the raped girl took the law into his own hands. Maybe—

Katie's arm moved.

Mal dropped her phone, went to the bed, waiting for another movement.

But the girl was still.

Mal pressed a button and called the nurse, told her what she'd seen. Then the nurse called a doctor who came in to check on Katie.

Mal waited outside the room, pacing, hoping for good news. But that wasn't what she got when the doctor finally emerged.

Katie's movement was a common occurrence. It could be a good sign, but then again it might be nothing.

After the nurse and doctor left, Mal returned to her chair, held Katie's hand, and told her more stories — this time about Ashley.

Chapter 24 - Jordyn Parish

JORDYN WAS LYING in bed reading a book when something hit her window.

She hopped to the floor, killed the light, parted her curtains and looked outside to see Bobby on the lawn.

Shit! What is he doing here at nearly two in the morning?

She opened her window and whisper-shouted, "What are you doing?"

"I need to talk to you," he said, too loud.

Jordyn shushed him, praying that her father didn't wake from his drunken slumber in front of the living room TV.

It had been nearly a month since her punishment. She was on winter break, and it had been a *loooong* week since she'd heard from Bobby. A *loooong* week at home with her father. Christmas was in two days, and the house didn't have a tree or a single colored light.

Bobby was a salve for her eyes.

But if Dad saw him on their lawn at this hour, he'd probably punish Jordyn for another month. Maybe forbid her from ever seeing Bobby again.

He ran toward her window, looking for a way to climb up.

"No," she whispered.

"Then come down, Rapunzel," he said, still too loud.

Jordyn sighed, long and deep, then told him to hold on.

She left the window, went to her bathroom and flicked on the light for a once-over. She was in sweats and an oversized black Fallout tee.

She opened her door slowly, listening for her father. To her surprise, the sound machine purred from behind his closed bedroom door. He hadn't fallen asleep on the couch.

She closed her door, went downstairs, and slipped on her sneakers. She disarmed the alarm, opened the door, and went outside.

But Bobby wasn't on the lawn.

He's trying to climb up to my window!

She was about to run onto the lawn when he leaped out from behind her.

Jordyn yelped.

He covered her mouth, laughing.

She laughed.

He kept his hand over her mouth, staring at her.

Bobby looked tipsy, or maybe high. Jordyn didn't smell any alcohol, but he was definitely sweaty.

"I missed you so much," he said, his hand still on her mouth. He moved it and kissed her, surprising Jordyn with an unexpected intensity.

His hands slid over her back, then down, squeezing her ass.

Bobby's hardness pressed against her belly.

It was the first time she'd ever felt a penis. It shocked and aroused her.

He kissed her harder, his tongue darting around hers as his hands swam to her front then climbed to her breasts.

Jordyn backed away. "If my dad sees us, he will kill you."

"I know," he said, smiling. "He told me."

"What?"

"Oh, he didn't tell you?"

"Tell me what?"

"Nothing. Forget I mentioned it."

"Tell me, Bobby." Jordyn crossed her arms.

"He came by my work and said that he couldn't stop you from seeing me, but that if I brought you home intoxicated again, he'd kill me."

"Oh my God, he is so lame. I'm so sorry."

"No, he's right," Bobby said, his voice slurred. "He's your dad. He loves you. If you were my daughter, I'd kill anyone who brought you home in that condition."

It was touching that Bobby would be protective, even if he was a bit wasted. "Why are you here? It's too late."

"I missed you."

"I'm sure Calum and your bros keep you from getting too bored."

"Yeah, we've been hanging out a lot, but it's not the same as being with you."

She smiled. "It's only been one week, did you all already run out of Your Mama jokes?"

"Ran out after two days. Now we're on to Your Sister jokes, but it's not the same when we don't have sisters."

"Sorry, that's a shame. I wish you all had sisters so you could make sexual jokes at their expense."

Bobby laughed. "Ha-ha, smart ass. See, *that's* what I miss."

He started toward her again, putting his hands on her hips, pulling her to him, trying to kiss her.

She pulled out of his grasp.

"No. Not now."

"Why?"

"Because it's two in the morning and you're wasted. Speaking of which, why are you driving?"

She looked around but didn't see his car.

"Wait. Where's your car?"

"At home. I walked."

"You walked? You live like three miles from here!"

"I wanted to see you."

"That's nice and all, but it's too late. And if you ever want to see me again, you need to leave before my dad wakes up."

"Which window is his?"

"All of them. He's like the Eye of Sauron."

"Fine. I'll leave. But I just wanted to tell you something."

"What?" she asked.

Suddenly, Bobby was looking down, his hands in his pocket. Like some shy dorky kid, rather than one of her high school's brightest stars.

"I just … I really missed you."

There was something there, something in his voice, maybe in his eyes, something sad.

"Are you okay?"

"Yeah, I'm fine. Well, a little high, but otherwise okay."

"You sure?"

"I just realized how much I missed you, and that I'd never properly asked you out."

Jordyn wondered if her cheeks were as flushed as they felt.

"So, you decided that getting high, walking to my house at two in the morning, and throwing rocks at my window was the way to go about it?"

"Well, when you put it like *that* it doesn't sound nearly as romantic."

Jordyn laughed.

"So, is that a yes?"

"Will you get off my lawn?"

"Only if you say yes."

"My punishment ends on Friday. Come to my house, preferably in the afternoon, before my dad's had too much to drink, and ask me out then."

"You sure?"

"If you want to go out with me, you'll have to pass through the gauntlet."

He nodded. "Okay, it's a deal. Can I kiss you goodbye?"

She shook her head. "Not until you pass through the gauntlet."

He laughed. "Okay, Jordyn Parish, I'll see you, and your father, on Friday. Oh, yeah, one other thing."

He reached into his pocket and pulled out a small gift. "Merry Christmas."

"Thank you," she said, taking the box. "I didn't get you anything yet."

"Don't worry about it," he said.

"Oh, you want me to open it now?"

"Yeah."

She ripped off the paper, then opened the small black velvet box.

Inside was a silver ring with a sparkling heart that looked like diamonds, but she didn't know jewelry well enough to be certain. But it was certainly beautiful, and it made the moonlight dance.

"Thank you," she said, sliding it on.

"Does it fit? I wasn't sure on your ring size."

"Perfect." It was the first time a boy had bought her

jewelry. And while she didn't have expensive tastes, Jordyn loved the ring and would wear it always — well, after she was off punishment and could say that Bobby gave it to her at a reasonable time.

"Thank you." She gave him one last kiss then pulled away.

He smiled, walking backward. "Merry Christmas, Jordyn."

"Merry Christmas, Bobby."

He jogged away, and Jordyn stood smiling at him from her porch. Maybe things might be okay after all.

Chapter 25 - Mallory Black

IT HAD BEEN one week since Katie fell into her coma. A week since the diner massacre, and Orestes666's disappearance. He'd gone underground. Hadn't commented online or threatened new attacks, at least so far as the authorities knew.

The FBI, despite its massive resources, had no luck finding Orestes666 or getting anything from the NonAMus site owners — or the Russian company that hosted it. There was some debate over whether they should try to shut the site down, but it was decided that having a way to monitor Orestes666 was best, even if they had yet to catch him in time. At least that was better than having him slink off to some other anonymous image board that they weren't aware of.

Mal worked on her laptop in the hospital room next to Katie, studying a spreadsheet with the saved LiveLyfe profiles from both Peter Kincaid and Lynn Macklin for the hundredth time — at least — clicking on names, looking at public profiles, searching for connections that nobody else had found.

She cross-referenced shared friends, hoping something would pop out. Kincaid seemed to be friends with half the damned county, and the diner's owner was beloved, so they had hundreds of shared friends between them.

Since she knew their killer was male, she moved the men into a separate list, which reduced the number of common friends to 321.

She searched memorial posts about both victims. Lynn's posts were mostly about how she was such a wonderful woman and would be deeply missed. The coach's postings were a mix of people who were shocked about the child porn found on his computer and accusations of abuse from former players. There were also others — including former players — vigorously defending Kincaid, insisting that the media was railroading the coach as part of a conspiracy to sway attention from the murders.

Mal shook her head, scrolling through page after page of hate and stupidity. She couldn't stand social media. It gave every moron with an internet connection a platform to abuse and spread ignorance. Still, there was no arguing that it made investigations so much easier. It never ceased to surprise her how many people posted incriminating stuff for all the world to see. Angry people who thought nothing of posting death threats; ex-cons posting pictures of themselves doing drugs or brandishing guns; people claiming they were nowhere near a crime scene only to have their Twitter or LiveLyfe log them in at the *exact* location they claimed not to have been at.

Unfortunately, this killer was smarter than the average LiveLyfe user, though that bar was practically in the dirt.

Mal closed her computer, slipped it into her backpack, and touched Katie's hand. "I'm going to get some lunch. I'll be back in a bit, okay?"

"Okay," the girl said.

Mal jumped back, startled.

"Katie?"

The girl's eyes were closed.

She didn't seem to be conscious.

Mal squeezed her hand, "Katie?"

And then her eyes opened.

~

MAL PACED OUTSIDE the room while the doctor and nurses tended to Katie.

She was out of her coma, and, from what Mal could see while still in the room, the girl was going to be okay.

Mal's phone rang. A number marked PRIVATE. "Hello?"

"He's not done."

A chill ran through her. Mal recognized the voice immediately. The mystery man that had saved her and Jessi Price, and insisted that she kill Paul Dodd.

"*Who's* not done?" she asked, her heart racing, thinking that he had some information about Dodd.

"The man who shot up the diner. The man who killed those people on the baseball field. He's going to do it again. Tomorrow."

"Where? And who is he?"

"I don't know. But I sort of know where he's going to strike."

"Where?"

"A strip club. I don't know which one, but it's definitely a strip club."

"What else can you tell me? Any details to help me figure out which one?"

"I dunno. It's dark, and there are topless women. But I've never been to wherever it is."

"How do you know this?"

"I told you before that I can't tell you how. I just know things."

"Why don't you come in and we can talk? Maybe you can help us catch this bastard."

Her Mystery Man was a vigilante. In addition to the murder of Dodd's childhood abuser Wes Richardson, which he'd more or less copped to, Mal had found four more cold case deaths that she suspected her Mystery Man — the Hunter — might be behind.

"Hello?" she said.

Silence.

The call had been disconnected.

MAL CALLED Mike and told him about the tip, deleting a major detail.

Mal didn't want the Feds or the press digging up her daughter's case or revisiting Jessi Price's looking for a link between the Mystery Man and Orestes666. It wouldn't help them find Orestes and it certainly wouldn't help Jessi's parents.

But Mal also had selfish reasons for keeping the source of the tip anonymous. She didn't want the Feds taking the vigilante case. It was *hers*, a back burner that wasn't attracting any attention, and she wanted to keep it that way. Mal wanted to bring in the vigilante.

"So, you don't know who the tip was from? Could it have been the killer?"

"I don't know," Mal said, instantly realizing that lying to Mike, and everyone else, might unnecessarily complicate the case. They might start thinking that if it wasn't the killer that called, but an accomplice instead.

The door to Katie's room opened, and the doctor stepped into the hall. It was too late for Mal to recover the lie.

"I've gotta go. Katie's out of the coma."

"Thanks," Mike said, hanging up.

Mal dropped the phone in her pocket, hoping that she wasn't ruining everything.

Chapter 26 - Jordyn Parish

"So, what do you think?" Bobby asked as Jordyn bit into her $54 filet.

"It's good," she said, still not sure what the big fuss was, or how this steak was so different from the steaks she'd had from places that weren't even a quarter as fancy.

It was their first date, on New Year's Eve. Bobby delayed plans with his friends to take her out for a special night at Prime, a fancy restaurant with stone floors, high vaulted ceilings with thick wooden chandeliers, rich leather upholstered chairs and dark wood tables. Bobby had to wear a blazer, and even though she was dressed in her nicest dress, she still felt shabby compared to some of the beautiful women she saw sitting at the other tables. Even the hostess, in a dark burgundy gown, looked like a model.

But Bobby's mom worked at a construction firm. No big deal. Maybe his father had left him some money. Or maybe he did better than she imagined working at the gym. In any event, Jordyn appreciated the effort. And while she wasn't used to being spoiled, she did enjoy dressing up and feeling fancy, even if only for a night.

Bobby looked handsome in an Oxford and tie. Jordyn was even more enamored after he'd gone down the menu, discussing all the different foods with delight and authority.

They fell into silence once food was set on the table until Bobby asked Jordyn about her steak. She didn't want to tell him the truth, that she wasn't the biggest fan, so she changed the conversation. "Where did you learn so much about food?"

"My mom is a really good cook. She taught me how to appreciate, and cook, good food."

"Do you enjoy cooking? Like is it something that you wanna do?"

"I dunno. It might be something to fall back on if I don't get a football scholarship."

"What's your favorite thing to make?"

"Ricotta strawberry French toast."

"Ricotta? Like the lasagna cheese?"

"Sure," he said. "It's amazing. The ricotta makes it creamy. Goes great with the honey and mint."

That sounded a lot better than steak.

Jordyn took a bite of garlic mash as Bobby finished off his meal. She'd barely touched her steak, and she felt bad as he looked down at her plate.

"Wow," he laughed. "You don't like it, do you?"

"Well, yeah, it's *good*. I'm just not that big into steaks, I guess."

"Then why did you order it?"

"Um, you only spent the whole week telling me that I just *haaaad* to try the steak here."

"Well, not if you don't like steak! You can't possibly appreciate how good it is if you're a steak philistine."

She laughed. "Sorry."

"Do you want to try something else? I can see if they have chicken nuggets or something."

"Ha-ha. I don't even like chicken nuggets."

"Okay, so what *is* your favorite food?" He stabbed a piece of her filet with his fork and popped it into his mouth. "I'll finish it if you're not going to."

She pushed the plate toward him. "It's all yours."

"So, what do you like?"

"Pasta."

"Okay, like what kind of pasta? Linguine and clams? Chicken Tetrazzini? Capellini with zucchini and tomato sauce? Tagliolini with truffle sauce?"

"No, just spaghetti and meatballs."

He laughed again. "Wow. I'm going out with a ten-year-old."

"Hey!" Jordyn threw her napkin at Bobby.

He laughed, then tossed it back.

She went to return the volley but accidentally knocked over her water. Bobby caught the glass before it hit the ground, but ice and water still splashed them both.

White hot embarrassment. Eyes like lasers from all the adults. A deep sigh from a table across the way. An older man with an angry face, a bad toupee, and a shiny suit. He, and the young woman he was dining with, had been giving them dirty looks whenever Jordyn or Bobby laughed too loud or looked like they might be having too much fun. Now the guy wouldn't stop glaring.

"Hi, buddy! Like the hair!" Bobby waved at the man, giving him a giant shit eating grin.

The man rolled his eyes and looked back at his date.

Jordyn laughed, then covered her giggle. "Aw, you stuck up for me."

"Fuck that guy," Bobby said, way too loud.

Strangely, Jordyn liked seeing Bobby's aggressive side.

A busboy came and swept up the ice cubes from the ground, along with some crumbs from the table.

"Sorry," Jordyn said.

"No problem," the busboy nodded.

The waiter appeared with more water.

"Do you all have chicken nuggets?" Bobby asked.

The waiter looked confused. "I'm sorry?"

"Never mind," Bobby said, "just an inside joke. We're ready for the check."

"Of course," the waiter said.

He returned a few minutes later and set a black leather folder onto the table. Bobby looked inside, added some cash, then set it back on the table.

"Thank you," Jordyn said as they stood.

"Next time I'll take you to a nice Italian restaurant. It's the best. I'm not sure if Generosità does *sketti* and meatballs, but they do have other pasta."

She laughed.

They stepped outside and onto The Boardwalk, home to several seaside restaurants, shops, and trendy spots. Jordyn had never been to The Boardwalk at night. It was a different place, almost beautiful with strings of lights, a salty breeze, and the moon hanging like a lantern in the sky.

"Wanna walk around?" Bobby looked at his watch. "We've got another hour before you've gotta be home."

"Okay," she said as Bobby took her under his arm.

"Thanks for coming by and talking to my dad the other day. I think he appreciated it."

"No problem. Sorry I missed him earlier."

"Yeah, he wasn't feeling well."

After a long pause, Bobby said, "So, what's his deal?"

"What do you mean?"

"Well, I don't wanna stick my nose where it doesn't belong, but I think you said he drinks a lot."

"Yes. He took my mom's death hard. I think part of it

was regret. He worked a lot when she was alive. We didn't see him all that much."

"What did he do?"

"He was a cop."

"Oh, shit. So I *really* shouldn't mess up."

"You don't need to be afraid of him as much as you need to be afraid of me," she teased. "Anyway, things got bad. He started drinking a lot after she died, then eventually went off his meds. Eventually, I ran away."

"Oh, shit. Really?"

"Yeah, two years ago."

"Where did you go?"

"To my friend, Lisa's. He found me within an hour."

"Oh, not very dramatic, then?"

"Well, I did leave a note. And I told him how I couldn't live like that anymore. He needed to get some help and get back on his meds."

"Meds for what?"

Jordyn paused, not sure how much to share. She liked Bobby a lot, but she knew there were still things she shouldn't share outside of her family. But she wasn't just protecting her father. A part of Jordyn worried that he'd think she was crazy, too, since so many mental disorders were genetic.

"Anxiety," she said, figuring that lie was close enough to the truth. "He got some help. Got back on his meds and stopped drinking. The final step was to leave my childhood home, the house where my mother was still such a heavy presence."

"Wow, that must've been tough."

"It was, but we needed a new beginning. Anyway, it took a while to sell the house, but then we came here, and voila, new school year and a fresh start for me."

She said this last part sarcastically.

"What happened? Did he fall off the wagon?"

"Yeah, it didn't take long for old habits to return."

"Shit. I'm sorry," he said hugging her.

It had been a long time since Jordyn felt as safe as she did in Bobby's embrace.

"You wanna go on the pier?"

"Sure," she said.

They paid a fee to get on the pier, walked past some people hanging out and others fishing, to a spot near the end away from anyone else.

Jordyn shivered.

Bobby doffed his jacket and wrapped it around her.

"Thank you," she said.

"So, how bad is it?"

"How bad is what?"

"Is he abusive?"

"Oh, God no. Dad would never hurt me. He gets moody, and we argue a lot more than ever before, but he's not abusive or anything. He's different. And a lot of times, it just feels like he's not there. Like he's living in the past. Sometimes I think he resents me."

"Resents you, why?"

"I don't know. Maybe I remind him of her. Maybe he feels bad that the connection between him and me isn't as strong as it was between my mother and me."

"What was her name?"

"Carissa."

"What was she like? Do you remember?"

"Yeah, though sometimes I wonder how much of what I remember is accurate."

"What do you mean?"

"Well, they say that memories aren't concrete. That each time we remember something, we can't help but alter the actual memory. We fill in the fuzzy details, and before too long memory might be more made up than fact. There are times I remember her as being vibrant, funny, and just super into being a mom — going to school and volunteering, making projects with me, reading to me, teaching me to paint like her. Then, other times, I remember her as quiet and withdrawn. Tired, especially towards the end."

"Well, can't both be true?"

"Yeah, but sometimes I feel like her last days rob the color of those earlier memories. Fortunately, I have a few videos she recorded, and they help me anchor the reality."

"I don't have much video of my dad. And no videos with the both of us."

"I'm sorry. Do you think about him a lot?"

"Yeah."

"Did you get along?"

"Yeah. Like your dad, he worked a lot, so I didn't see him that much. But every summer we did something special. Sometimes he took weekends off. He was a good guy."

She looked at Bobby's face as he stared up at the moon — the smile lit by the mention of his father seemed so terribly sweet.

"What was his name?"

"Robert."

"So, you're Bobby Junior?"

He smiled, "Yeah. When I was a kid, people called me RJ, BJ, or just Junior."

"Aww, *Junior*," she teased.

He kissed her, then pulled away, looking at her.

"What?" she asked.

"Just admiring your beauty."

She laughed, turning away. "Oh, stop."

"You are beautiful."

"Thank you," she said, meeting his eyes. "Thank you for blowing off your friends to take me out."

"I can see them anytime. And, besides, I missed you. It's been a long month."

They only had drama class together, and during the weeks leading up to the Christmas break, Bobby was running lines with Brianna and a few others with bigger roles, so Jordyn didn't get to talk with him as much.

"Besides," he said, "I'm sure I'll hang out with the others after I drop you off."

"What are they doing? Big New Year's Eve party?"

"Calum rented another hotel room. Invited a ton of people. Gonna be a huge party. His Cousin Perry is even coming. That guy's a handful."

He was playing it down, but she could tell that he was looking forward to going. It was difficult to reconcile the sweet, quiet Bobby she knew with the one who liked partying.

"Ah," she said, feeling a bit envious that she wouldn't be there. A part of her wondered if there would be single girls, looking to hook up. She'd seen the way Bobby was eyed in the hallway, and because they weren't officially dating, Jordyn always felt like they thought he was fair game to flirt with.

She wondered how their school dynamic would change, now that they'd been on a date. Would they walk through the hallways arm-in-arm? Would everyone know they were going out? Would he officially be off the market?

Or did guys like him date multiple girls? Keep their options open?

Again, she wished her mom were alive. She didn't want to presume anything or be played for a fool.

"What's wrong?" Bobby asked, as if sensing Jordyn's insecurity.

"Nothing," she lied, trying to think of some way to ask him about their status. Were they officially dating? Was it an exclusive situation?

Just as she was about to ask, and maybe say something stupid, someone yelled, "Asshole!"

They turned to see Calum approaching. Jordyn whispered, "What's he doing here?"

"I dunno. I thought he was hanging with the gang."

"Hey, there," Calum said. "Long time, no see. I thought your ass was put in a dungeon!"

He hugged Jordyn, then kissed her on the cheek.

"Yeah, I just got out."

"Awesome! You coming to the party tonight?"

"No, no more parties for me, at least not for a while."

"Shit. Well, don't worry, I'll make sure your boy doesn't kiss anyone else at midnight."

Calum punched Bobby in the gut. It looked harder than it needed to be.

Bobby laughed uncomfortably, then said, "Where's everyone else? I thought you were all hanging out at the hotel pool?"

"I needed to go for a walk. Brianna is driving me fucking crazy."

"What's going on?" Bobby asked.

"You know how she gets. Just in a super bitchy mood. Must be that time of the month." He laughed, then turned to Jordyn, "You know what I'm talking 'bout, right?"

Jordyn wasn't sure if he was asking if she could relate because she was a girl and had PMS or that yes, she knew Brianna could be a real bitch.

"Happens to the best of us."

"I dunno," Calum said, looking Jordyn up and down. "Some girls it happens to more than others. I mean, Brianna gets *really* bitchy. Admit it, you don't like her, right?

I heard the shit she said about you when you first started hanging around with us."

Jordyn felt acutely uncomfortable. Was Calum trying to create drama?

"Yeah, I like her," she said, the insincerity probably clear in her voice.

"What did she say?" Bobby sounded pissed.

"Oh, you know, just the catty shit that she always says when she's full of herself. Don't worry. She stopped that shit when she saw you were one of us."

Jordyn nodded. She wasn't about to say anything bad about Brianna, even if Brianna talked shit about her every day. Sure, Calum was pissed, but that would pass in a day or two, and whatever Jordyn said would be all that anyone would remember. It was best to say nothing.

This was just the sort of high school drama that Jordyn tried so hard to avoid.

Calum put his arm around her. "So, is my boy treating you okay?"

"Yes, he's very sweet."

Calum laughed. "You two make a cute couple. And, Bobby, you'd better hold onto this one, or else I might have to take her. You should've seen the sluts he dated before you. Might want to get him checked for STDs."

Calum laughed, his arm still around her.

Jordyn tried not to take offense. After all, Calum and the guys busted each other's balls. This was how guys showed affection, and that was probably Calum telling her that she was now one of them.

Still, Jordyn felt a weird undercurrent, one that she couldn't quite put her finger on. Something that made Calum's words seem more like veiled threats.

"Don't listen to him," Bobby said. "I don't have any

STDs. And Calum has no room to talk about being a slut. Dude's slept with half the cheerleaders."

"And three teachers," he said, smiling.

"Really?" Jordyn asked shocked.

Calum nodded.

Bobby said, "And two of them were female."

"Fuck you," Calum said, letting go of Jordyn and rushing Bobby, the two of them trading a few playful punches.

They went back and forth, taking jabs, a few connecting.

And again, Jordyn felt an odd undercurrent, this one decidedly violent. Like at any moment they might go from playing to an all-out fistfight.

Was this how most guys played?

Calum grabbed Bobby in a choke hold, squeezing tight.

"Let go!" Bobby said, his face red and hair a mess.

"Tell me you're my bitch."

"Fuck you," Bobby said.

Calum squeezed tighter, his face twisted into an angry red knot. "Say it, bitch."

"Fuck you," Bobby spoke through gritted teeth, twisting and managing to slide out of the choke hold.

He slipped out of the hold and managed to slap Calum in the face. It was loud, almost echoing in the night.

Surprised, Calum glared at Bobby, raising his fists.

They circled each other.

"Okay, bitch, it's on," Calum said, taking a swing.

Bobby barely managed to evade it.

Jordyn's stomach lurched. This was it — whatever was brewing beneath the surface would now spill over into an ugly fight.

Calum broke into a laugh and pulled Bobby into a hug. "I'm just fucking with you, bro."

Jordyn sighed with relief. Calum had his arm around Bobby as they walked back over to her.

"Okay, you two, it's been fun, but I'm gonna get back to Brianna before she starts whining and ruining everyone's night."

"Good luck with that," Bobby said.

"Seriously," Calum said to Jordyn. "I'm glad to see you two together finally. Bobby needs a nice girl like you."

"Thanks," she said.

Calum grinned, looking at Bobby. "Is it true what they say about nice girls?"

"What's that?" Bobby asked.

"How they're the dirty ones when the lights go out?"

"Fuck you," Bobby said, punching him playfully.

Calum winked at Jordyn. "So, that's a *yes*. Awesome."

He gave her a thumbs up then left them alone.

Once out of earshot, Bobby said, "Sorry about all that."

"What was that?"

"Sometimes he gets jealous when other people seem happy."

"Why?"

"I dunno. I think he feels trapped with Brianna. They're like a fucking power couple or something. Been dating for two years, which is like a twenty-year marriage in high school. It's complicated."

"I guess so." After a long pause Jordyn said, "Why do you let him treat you like that?"

"Like what?"

"The little insults. The grabbing you in a choke hold. If I didn't know better, I'd think you two were enemies."

"Nah, that's just how he is. You just gotta know him

like I do. It's not a big deal. Are you okay? I'm sure he wasn't trying to insult you."

"I'm okay. Why is he such a …"

"A dick?"

Jordyn laughed.

"Let's just say that even though his dad is like the most powerful man in town, he isn't a nice man. Sometimes Calum takes it out on other people, but he means well."

"What's his dad like?"

"Well," he said, looking down at his watch. "Shit, I need to get you home."

"Okay," she said. Bobby was clearly changing the subject.

Jordyn changed the subject as they walked back to the car, teasing him for his borderline fetishistic love for steak, while he ribbed her for her inability to appreciate the finer things in life.

She considered bringing Calum up on the ride home, but didn't want to end New Year's Eve, and such a wonderful date, on a sour note. Besides, maybe Calum's personal life wasn't her business. She couldn't expect Bobby to surrender his best friend's secrets.

Chapter 27 - Mallory Black

KATIE HAD BEEN out of the coma for nearly thirty-five minutes before the doctor came out of the room to update Mal.

Katie needed to stay in the hospital a few days for observation but seemed well on her way to recovery. Swelling had receded, so barring any unforeseen situations, she was on the mend and would be okay.

Mal entered Katie's room. The girl was off the machines and sitting up, holding a styrofoam cup with ice chips.

Mal smiled.

Katie's eyes were red and puffy.

"They told me that she's dead."

Mal nodded.

"And my father, too. You shot him?"

"Yes," Mal said, approaching the bed. "I'm sorry."

She was saying sorry for the loss of her mother, not her father, but allowed Katie to interpret it as needed.

Katie shook her head, staring down at her ice cup.

"I wish I never met you."

Mal said nothing. She expected the girl to have some anger. It was good to vent those feelings. And she'd been told by the doctor not to upset Katie in any way.

She looked up at Mal, eyes tearing, "Why did you have to get involved?"

"Your father was abusing you. Both of you."

"Yeah, but it wasn't that bad. We could deal with it. It was better than having my mother dead."

"I'm sorry, Katie. I wish I had gotten there sooner."

"Now I don't have anyone. My family is gone. Peter is gone. I don't have any friends. What am I going to do?"

"Someone will come by to discuss your options. But the most important thing is that you're okay. You survived."

Katie looked up at Mal, met her eyes. "Is it? Is *that* the important thing? Or is the important thing that you get me to give you info on Coach Kincaid so you could use it to find another bad guy? Or give you info on my father so you could take him away from me? Take my family away? You don't care about me, Ms. Black, so please don't pretend otherwise."

"I *do* care. I sat with you, waiting for you to come out of your coma."

"You did that because you felt guilty. If you cared about me you wouldn't have pushed me to report my father. I told you that he'd hurt us, but you didn't care."

Katie closed her eyes, tears now pouring down both sides of her face.

Mal got up, grabbed a box of napkins, and handed it to her.

Katie looked up, her eyes dark and vacant, ringed in red. Her mouth open, as if she didn't have the strength to shut it.

"Please, just leave."

"You just said that you don't have anyone. I'm here to look after you until I can get someone to see you tomorrow."

"I don't want you here. All I see when I look at you is my mother's eyes looking back at me, bleeding out in my arms. You should've just let me die. At least then we'd be together."

Mal stepped back, tears brewing as she tried to think of something that might make things better, or maybe heal the girl. But what could you say to someone who lost the only three people who cared about her?

She didn't have a single word to change the facts. Katie was all alone. Life was about to get even harder than it had been. She'd likely end up in the foster care system. That could either be the best or worst thing for a child. A roll of the dice and there was nothing a kid could do to twist the odds in their favor. Losing meant ending up in the home of people looking to cash in on some kids, or worse, in the homes of predators waiting for prey.

It was a vicious cycle that took kids, broke them down, and turned them into husks, more likely to abuse others once they left childhood behind.

Mal started to say something, but Katie bellowed, "*Leave!*"

The scream was so loud and sudden that Mal jumped back, startled.

"I'm sorry."

"Leave!" Katie said, pressing the button on the device beside her bed. "Can someone get her out of here?"

Mal grabbed her backpack and her purse.

She rushed past a nurse in the hallway, ignoring the woman as she asked Mal if she was okay, then ducked into the restroom.

She went into a stall, closed the door, and sat on the toilet, shaking and crying.

She unzipped the backpack, reached into the middle pouch, and grabbed her bottle of painkillers.

She unscrewed the cap. The bottle trembled in her hand.

She dropped a pill into her palm.

It fell, bouncing on the tile floor, under the barrier, and into the neighboring next stall.

Mal stood, opened the door, and went into the next stall, bent down, and grabbed the pill.

She was about to pop it in her mouth, damn the germs and hail the relief.

179 days off the pills.

She *had* to calm her racing brain.

Six months without the pills — an accomplishment. Hell, the days weren't even as hard anymore.

Six very long months.

Mal's entire body was shaking. Her chest was tight. Panic crawled up her chest and into her throat, threatening to choke her.

She would surely crack without relief.

Just one pill.

She needed something for the pain, something to heal her aching heart. The pills were made to dim the aching.

Just one to numb the swelling chaos. One to make her feel something, anything, other than the unending agony.

Just one pill would make it all go away, for a little while.

She could start over tomorrow.

Start her streak all over again. A new run at sobriety.

Just one pill.

She popped it into her mouth, felt it on her tongue.

All she had to do was swallow, and the shaking, sweating, and pain would fade.

She started to swallow, then stopped.

She opened the stall door, leaned over the toilet and spit it out.

She flushed, then fell to the floor sobbing.

Chapter 28 - Jeffrey Brown

JEFFREY BROWN SAT in the tiny dark bedroom of his crappy little apartment, clicking on his shitty laptop to view the LiveLyfe account of his bitch ex-wife, Sandra.

The newest post included a photo she'd taken of her and Lynn Macklin at last year's Christmas party. Shit, he could post a few photos to show what total sluts they were. Lynn was the whore who got them involved in that swinger's club in the first place.

She'd posted several paragraphs under the photo detailing her grief over her "best friend's" death, then even *more* paragraphs about how fucked up the world was, with lunatics walking around with such dangerous weapons.

Jeff laughed at that particular choice of word. *Lunatic.* The same word she'd used to describe him once after a particularly nasty fight that *she* had started. The one where he'd hurled a wrought iron bar chair through the sliding glass door of a gorgeous home they once shared. The McMansion he'd worked his ass off for, where she now lived with one of his former co-workers. Eugene, the back-stabber who stole his promotion.

Jeff re-read the post, delighting in Sandra's ability to turn any situation, even the death of her so-called best friend into a spot on her soapbox. But everything always came back to bite her.

"Best friend, eh? You bitched about her *all the fucking time* when we were married." He laughed at the screen. "You said she was white trash who *lucked* into that diner. You are such a fucking hypocritical cunt!"

Jeff stood to pace, wishing he'd recorded some of the things Sandra had said about her friends, about her enemies, about everyone. Hell, she'd once called Eugene a "shifty fucking Jew." He wondered how *that* would go over with him and her new friends.

Judging from her recent pro-Israeli LiveLyfe political posts, you'd think she was the next Golda Meir or something. She had this way of taking shit from other people and making it her own. Culture, stories, money. She didn't care.

Jeff stared at the 51 hearts and 120 thumbs up her "tribute" post had received.

Jesus, she has these fuckers so fooled. They have no clue what she really is. None!

All these people saying how sorry they were for *her* loss as if she'd suffered a tragedy or something!

"Fuuuuuuck you!"

He'd wanted to rattle her. To take down everyone in her inner circle. Everyone who had betrayed him. Destroy all of their lives before finishing her.

But she wasn't frail or getting scared. The bitch was using the tragedies, first Chip Halverson, and now Lynn Macklin, to shine the spotlight on herself.

"You are a fucking vampire!"

The immigrant asshole in the apartment next to his banged on the wall. "Shut the fuck up!"

Jeff grabbed the AR-15, shoved it up against the wall, and wrapped his finger around the trigger.

He hated the fucker next door. Some old asshole who did nothing but sit home all day bitching whenever Jeff cranked his music, or watched TV too loud, or yelled at his wife's LiveLyfe page.

Jeff wasn't sure if the dude was Greek or from one of those *Muslimistan* countries, but he definitely looked like he should be on a fucking watch list. He had olive-colored skin, big bushy eyebrows, and beady dark eyes that glared at Jeff every time they passed in the hallway. Jeff had never done shit to the guy, had even gone out of his way to invite the fucker over for drinks when he moved into the complex last year.

Jeff continued to hold the gun against the wall, finger twitching on the trigger. It would be so easy to let her rip. Turn the guy into Big League Chew. Then maybe peek through the holes and spit on his corpse.

He laughed.

The old man had no idea what Jeff was capable of.

Nobody did.

They all thought he was some fucking loser cuck who got fucked over by his ex and former co-worker. He could feel their stares, hear their whispers when he ran into them around town. He could see their judging glances the few times he'd shopped in the store.

He could hear them laughing behind his back.

And every time he ran into someone from his past who even looked at him wrong, he added them to The List.

They'd pay.

They'd all pay.

He leaned his rifle against the wall, then sat back at his desk, scrolled down the screen, and saw that Eugene had left a comment on Sandra's post.

We all know how much she meant to you. I'm so sorry.

"She didn't mean shit to her! For fuck's sake! And that's some bland shit to write to someone you live with!"

BANG! BANG!

"Shut up!"

"Fuck you!" Jeff yelled back, getting up and punching the wall repeatedly. "Shut the fuck up!"

"No, *you* shut up!" The man pounded the wall even harder.

Jeff glanced at the rifle, then at his nightstand and the Beretta M9.

He grabbed it and stormed out of his room.

He went to his door, unlocked and opened it, then marched toward his neighbor's apartment.

They were on the third floor, on the short end of an L-shaped building, with only one other apartment, unrented, on the other side of Orestes.

Gun in hand, he marched toward the old man's door, then stopped at the sound of giggling coming down the steps behind him.

He slipped the gun into his front waistband, covered it with his long black tee, and kept walking past the old man's door, and to the rail running the long side of the complex. He leaned against it as if he'd just come out to gaze at the weather.

More giggling.

He turned to see a set of twins, a brother and sister, around eight-years-old, chasing each other with squirt guns.

They raced past him, then back toward the stairs where their mother was descending the steps.

She was an attractive blonde, wearing tight pink sweat pants like usual. They hugged her ass ever so perfectly. She was also wearing a loose-fitting Nirvana tee, her braless nipples pointing through the worn cotton. She was carrying a laundry basket on her hip, probably because the fourth-floor machine was out of order.

"Hi," she said, giving him an awkward wave as she passed with her kids in tow.

"Hi," he said, just as awkwardly.

When he'd first moved in, he'd ended up on the elevator with her one evening while coming home from work. She was alone, arms loaded with groceries. He tried to make conversation. But he was in his Pizza Shack uniform. Sweaty and greasy, reeking of dough and despair.

The conversation was short, and he could practically feel her disdain.

Another time when she and her kids had passed him, Jeff was certain that she'd rolled her eyes.

Rolled her fucking eyes at me! What the fuck did I do to her?

He wondered how she'd treat him if he'd had his old job as a front-end manager at Mac's Food Mart. It wasn't glamorous, like being a doctor, athlete, or lawyer, but it had paid well. He had no shortage of women — hot women, too — wanting to sleep with him when he had that job, including several college-aged cashiers. But he'd always said no because he loved his wife.

Fucking idiot.

Now he couldn't even get a single mother of two, a woman who might be a Six on a scale of One to Ten, to give him the time of day.

If I had that management job, she'd show a little fucking respect. Women always respect money and security.

And he would've landed that management job if Eugene hadn't stabbed him in the back and completely fucked a relationship with one of their biggest vendors, which somehow became Jeff's fault.

Work being what it was in his town, he'd had to take a

job as a delivery driver to make ends meet until he could find another decent paying gig. But fuck if he knew when that would be.

Meanwhile, Jeff lost it all — his job, his wife and son, and finally his house. All of it gone, months swept away by an avalanche of shit luck.

As the hot mother passed, her son turned around and aimed his squirt gun at Jeff. "POW!"

He didn't fire the water gun, but he obviously wanted to.

Jeff laughed as he considered pulling out *his* gun.

Pow yourself, you little shit!

He wouldn't shoot the kid. He might be a lunatic, but he wasn't a monster. And he hadn't meant to kill the kids in the diner, either. But he would have no problem killing their stuck-up cunt of a mom.

As he watched the mother's ass walk away, he heard the door open behind him.

Fucking Old Man.

He turned.

The old man, in his thick whatever accent, said, "What?"

Jeff thought about shooting him right there between his bushy fucking eyebrows. Send his brains all over the back of his door.

Fuck you, that's what!

He ignored him instead, went back into his apartment and slammed the door.

He had to control his emotions. At least until Sandra was dead.

He returned to the computer and saw someone had posted on Eugene's wall.

"Can't wait for the bachelor party this weekend at The Purple Pole."

Surely thinking himself witty, Eugene responded with, *Shh, don't tell my wife.*

"Fuck you, Eugene," Jeff said under his breath, thinking of a way to make Eugene's bachelor party especially memorable.

Chapter 29 - Jasper Parish

JASPER WOKE to the sound of a man crying.

He opened his eyes and saw someone standing in the corner of his room. He was tall, broad built, with a dark crew cut, for some reason reminding Jasper of a pre-Depression era boxer. He was wearing shorts and a white tank top, his chest heaving as he sobbed, staring at the ground.

Jasper reached for the pistol on his nightstand, grabbed it then trained it on the man, all in a second. "Down on the floor!"

"How could you?" the man asked, still staring down, ignoring Jasper.

Is this fucker on drugs?

Jasper climbed out of bed, gun still trained on the man, hand searching for his cell to phone the sheriff's office. His heart raced as his fingers fumbled for a phone that wasn't there. He didn't dare turn to look for it.

The man was holding something behind him.

Then he brought it forward — a machete.

"Woah, put it down!" Jasper commanded.

The man didn't respond. He looked up and stared to Jasper's left.

Jasper turned toward a light bleeding from a wide open bathroom that didn't exist on the left side of the room.

Where the hell am I?

Nothing was making sense, his head swimming in fear and confusion.

He wasn't in his room.

Or in his house.

Nor was he alone with the man.

Appearing from nowhere, a dark-haired woman in her mid-thirties clutched a crying dark haired boy who couldn't have been older than three.

"Put the machete down!" Jasper demanded, stepping between the woman and child then child and man.

"Please, Tony, don't!"

"I'm sorry," he cried, walking toward them, machete raised.

Jasper lifted the pistol and fired.

The bullet went through the man as if he were a ghost. And then the man passed right through Jasper.

What the hell?

He turned to see the woman scream, defensively raising a hand while clutching the child tight.

There was nothing she could do as Tony lowered the blade, lopping off her arm before plunging the machete straight into the back of the child's head.

Jasper woke screaming, soaked in a cold sweat, gun in his hand, back in his own room.

His bedroom door flew open.

Jasper raised the gun and readied himself for Tony, as if the man had crossed over from the dream, or vision, into Jasper's reality.

But it was Jordyn.

"Don't shoot!" she yelled, dropping to the ground.

Head spinning, Jasper dropped the gun. "It's okay," he said, getting out of bed.

Jordyn, in her pajamas, stared at him, terrified. "What happened?"

He stared past her and through the hole he'd fired through his bedroom door. Sleepwalking was one thing, but sleep*shooting?* He could have killed her.

"Oh my God, I'm … I don't know."

She stared at him, terror parting the sea to concern. "Was someone in here?"

"Um … no. It was just a bad dream."

She shook her head, her concern now wilting to annoyance. "When was the last time you took your medicine?"

He shook his head. "Please, don't start."

Carissa appeared. "She's right, you know."

"Not you, too," he said.

Jordyn looked at Carissa.

"Do you see her?" Jasper asked, hopeful.

"Come on, Dad. You know that she's not there."

Jasper sighed, long and deep.

Carissa said, "You're the only one, Jass."

Jordyn went to the door. "You could've killed me!"

"I'm not going to kill you!" he argued, despite that he was thinking the same thing.

She glared at him, then dove for the gun. She held it in her hand.

"What the hell are you doing? Put that down!" Jasper wasn't worried about her hurting herself or him. He'd taken her to the gun range ever since she was ten — any child of his would know how to use a gun and how to respect it.

"No. You don't get this back until you're better."

"Jordyn, give me the gun."

"No," she said, backing toward the door.

"I'll take my meds."

"I don't believe you."

Carissa shook her head. "Me either."

Jasper sighed again. "Come on. I don't need the meds."

"You almost shot me!"

"No, I did not almost shoot you. It's …" he looked at the clock on his nightstand. "It's one in the morning. You were in bed."

"What if you shot through the wall toward my room? Or what if I was walking to the bathroom? Huh?"

Silence.

"What were you even shooting at?"

"Nothing."

"I wanna know."

"I think I had a vision."

"A vision?" she asked, surprised. "What did you see?"

"It doesn't matter."

"I wanna know."

"A guy … he killed his wife and kid, I think."

"Oh my God. Really?"

"I don't know. Maybe it was a vivid nightmare. But this isn't about me not taking my—"

"Please, Dad. You're not healthy, and something's wrong. We both know it. When was the last time you took your meds?"

"I don't know."

"Last week?"

He shook his head, "I don't know."

"Last month?"

"I don't know."

She started towards his bathroom.

"What are you doing?"

"Checking," she said.

She flipped on the light, set the gun on the sink, and opened the mirrored drug cabinet.

From his angle, Jasper couldn't see what she was looking at, but he knew — rows of full pill containers.

"What the hell, Dad?" she asked, picking up one bottle after another, reading the labels.

"You haven't taken any of these in like six months!" Her eyes began to water. "Why aren't you taking your medicine?"

"You wouldn't understand."

"Try me," she said, stepping out of the bathroom, rattling a bottle, gun still on the counter behind her.

"I … I miss her. I don't see her when I'm on them."

"But you're not really seeing her. She isn't here. It's all in your head. Please tell me that you're not so far gone that you don't know that?"

"I know," Jasper said, though he wasn't being entirely honest. Lines blurred. There were times when he believed that maybe he was somehow seeing her ghost. He was psychic, after all. Why wouldn't he have other senses that most people didn't?

"What happened? I thought we were going to start fresh. I thought things were going to be better — for both of us."

It was hard to see your child cry and not surrender to tears of your own, but Jasper did his best to trap the sorrow inside. Succumb, and he might just collapse to the ground. No child should have to witness their father's break down, especially when there was nothing they can do to help.

"I missed her. I wanted to see her again."

"I miss her too, but you know who I miss more? *You.*

You're not the same off the pills. You're mean. You get drunk. And even when you're nice, you're just not all there."

Jasper bit his lip to keep it from trembling.

"You need to take your pills."

Carissa gave him a disapproving look and said, "She's right."

"You don't understand. It's not just that I won't see her anymore. The pills dull the visions."

"What do you mean?"

"I was on pills for three years leading up to your mother's cancer diagnosis. If I hadn't been taking them, I would've had a vision. We would've known. We could have saved her."

Carissa stared at him, wiping at her tears. "You think it's your fault?"

Jordyn, as if somehow channeling her mother, said, "It wasn't your fault."

"Yes, it was! We could've saved her." He turned away, squeezing his eyes shut tight to keep the tears inside.

"You said before that you couldn't control the visions. Remember that time I asked you why you didn't use your visions to stop Hamster from running away?"

"Yeah," he said, smiling as he remembered the big teddy bear looking dog that they'd saved from the shelter when Jordyn was four or five. Named Hamster because Jordyn's hamster, also named Hamster, had died a month before.

Jordyn had only known about his visions for the past year. She asked him three questions at the time: Why he didn't use his visions to get rich, why he didn't know that Hamster was going to run away, and why he didn't see where Hamster had gone.

He thought it odd at the time that she hadn't asked

about her mother. But maybe it was something she *couldn't* ask, so she used Hamster as a proxy to discover the same thing — why couldn't he do more to prevent loss?

Jasper looked at Carissa but spoke to Jordyn. "I need the visions. It's the only way I know to keep you safe. I figure if something bad were going to happen to you, I'd get *something*. I've had visions about you a few times, which I think might have saved your life."

"What do you mean?"

"Remember when you wanted to go to that summer camp and you were all set to go, but we had to cancel at the last minute?"

"Yeah, you said that we'd missed the registration deadline."

"That was a lie. I had a vision about that. I saw you getting hit by lightning. Your mother thought I was paranoid. You were only seven, and she figured I was an overprotective father. I'd never told her about my visions. I just acted really, really worried until she finally gave in."

"So, how do you know you saved me?"

Jasper, tears now dried, turned to Jordyn, "Because a kid at the camp *did* get hit by lightning that summer. And he died."

Jordyn's eyes went wide. "Really? How come I never heard about that?"

"You didn't know him. And besides, what kind of father would tell their kid terrible things that they couldn't do anything about?"

"Okay, that was one time. But you can't not take your pills on the off chance that you *might* get some vision about me. You're suffering. You think you see Mom. And it's not healthy."

"I don't care."

"Well, I do," she said, approaching him, "You need to

take your medicine. I'm going to tell your doctor if you don't. And I'll tell her that I don't feel safe in the house, which means someone will probably come and put me in a foster home. Is that what you want, to lose me?"

"No."

"Well, then you need to choose. Do you want to hold onto a ghost or me?"

Jasper turned to see Carissa, now just inches away from them, as if she was about to hug both of them. She met his eyes, and without saying a word, Carissa conveyed a bottomless well of love and encouragement.

She nodded.

"Okay," Jasper said, taking the bottle from Jordyn. He unscrewed the cap, spilled a tiny pill into his palm, popped it in his mouth, and swallowed.

Then he opened his mouth to prove it was gone.

"Thank you," she said, hugging him. "I'm going to make sure you take these pills every day. Okay?"

"Okay," he said, hugging Jordyn as he looked at Carissa, wondering how many hours or days until she finally left him forever.

AFTER JORDYN WENT TO BED, Jasper put his gun in a lock box in the bottom of his nightstand, then slipped the key into the top drawer.

It was an extra step that he hated, but it was the responsible thing until he could trust himself not to shoot up the house.

Carissa talked to him a bit after Jordyn went to bed, telling her how proud she was of him.

Then she vanished, which she often did at odd times.

He wondered if that would be the last time they'd see each other.

And that made him anxious.

He went downstairs, made a peanut butter and grape jelly sandwich, pounded a tall glass of milk, then sat in the living room and turned on the TV.

It automatically went to the local news where the weather girl was discussing the dry climate and the burn ban in effect. Then the anchor cut to a reporter standing outside a house, fronting a battery of sheriff deputy vans and vehicles.

"We're coming to you live from Creek County where a man is in critical condition following a shocking crime. Authorities are calling this a home invasion gone bad. It all began earlier this evening when intruders broke into a house on Coventry Road and robbed Anthony Alvarez and his family at gunpoint before murdering his wife and son with a machete, then stabbing him and leaving him for dead. Suspects are described as two African American males wearing black hoodies."

Jasper was paralyzed, staring at the television, a creeping dread washing over him.

No, no. It has to be a coincidence.

Jasper had been having visions all his life, but not of murders. That would have been helpful if he hadn't been medicated during his years on the force. He wanted to deny that this was a vision. Yes, the man was named Anthony. Yes, mother and child were murdered.

But that could be a coincidence.

Carissa laughed.

He was relieved to see that she hadn't left yet.

"So, you're willing to believe that I'm here talking to you, but you try and deny that this was a vision? Wow, Jass, the mental gymnastics you must go through to stay in denial." She glanced at the TV. "Uh-oh, you may not want to look."

He did. And Jasper saw the last thing he wanted to see — confirmation that he wasn't dreaming, a photo of Anthony Alvarez, his wife, and son.

"No, no, no," he said, shaking his head. "Fuck. Why the hell did I see that? I can't do anything about a murder that's already happened."

"Well, you're taking the meds now, so maybe you won't have anymore."

He stared at the television with an overwhelming sense of loss and helplessness. He's seen the murder as it happened, or maybe just before. Hell, or right after. No time for him to intervene, even if he'd been able to get a name and address.

This was even worse than the helplessness he sometimes felt as a cop. At least then, on a good day, Jasper had a chance to prevent a murder. Failing that, he could at least help to put the killer away and stop future atrocities. But there was nothing he could do here.

"So, the sheriff's department thinks Tony is a victim?"

"Hard to say," Jasper said. "He must've staged the scene and cleaned it well. But I'm sure they're still looking at him as a potential suspect. The husband is *always* a suspect in crimes like these."

"What if they don't? What if he gets off? Maybe you should call the sheriff's office and tell them what you saw?"

Jasper turned to her, laughing. "And say what? That I had a *vision*? That I'm *psychic*? Um, no thanks. I'm not getting involved. The evidence is there. Most people don't know half the things that'll trip them up in a murder investigation. There's no way he's getting off on this."

"I dunno, they're putting out a description of two black

males in hoodies. Sounds like they're at least entertaining the idea."

"Well, there's nothing I can do about it now."

Jasper kept staring at the TV, listening to the report repeating itself.

He looked to see if Carissa had anything else to say, but his wife was already gone.

Chapter 30 - Mallory Black

MIKE ASKED Mal a question before she even said hello.

"You ready to come back to work?"

"That depends. Is it sitting at a desk or out in the field?"

"Out in the field. Riding with me. If I'm without a partner too long, they'll probably put Skippy with me again."

She laughed.

"Orestes has another countdown. Five hours."

"So, what's the play?"

"We've got undercover deputies and FBI agents at all three strip clubs in town."

"Why do you need me? I'm *not* going undercover as a dancer."

Mike laughed. "Oh, come on. *I* would do it."

"Yeah, I'm sure *you* would."

"No, nothing as exciting as undercover work. Just ride with me, do whatever the Feds tell need doing."

"Did Gloria clear me to come back?"

"I wouldn't be calling if not. She wants you here. So

does Wilson. And no, the investigation into your shooting isn't over, but ... special circumstances and all. No point in sitting this out."

"Yeah, I'll come in," Mal said, glad to have some distraction to prevent her from wallowing in the misery of what happened with Katie. Less time alone meant the less likely she was to turn to pills.

~

THE SITUATION ROOM was abuzz with activity as the clock ticked down toward Orestes666's strike. An hour to go.

The FBI and Creek County PIO were fielding questions from media organizations from across the country as well as concerned residents and business owners who were scared shitless that they could be at a place where the killer might strike. Many of the stores and restaurants were planning to close early.

Everyone in the room was either consulting with one another or on phones coordinating efforts between the various organizations. The situation seemed to be escalating into something just shy of a military offensive.

Mal needed to get out of the room. She needed to be up, not sitting. Even if it was only to pace. Being cooped up in a busy room only made her that much more removed from the case.

She needed to be out in the field, at a crime scene that didn't exist yet.

It was an odd feeling to want the murderer's next strike behind them, so that they could get on to the next step, whether that meant capturing him before he could kill, or processing the crime scene.

Anything was better than sitting around waiting.

Mal stepped out, to the adjoining break room, hitting the vending machine for a Diet Coke.

Wilson and Mike were standing in front of the coffee machine shooting the shit.

Wilson looked up at her as she approached.

"You hear what they're calling this fucker?" he asked, pointing to the TV which was tuned to TV 15.

A reporter Mal hadn't seen yet, a young blonde named Stephanie Ryan, stood outside the Sheriff's Office in a charcoal and blue dress, talking about the looming deadline. Beneath her a graphic read, *ANON KILLER TO STRIKE TONIGHT?*

"Anon Killer?" Mal said. "Who gave him that name? And who told the press?"

"As of about an hour ago, that's all anyone's calling him. It's like the media all got together and decided, *Hey, this Orestes666 thing isn't scaring people enough, what could we call this fucker to get people to watch? Oh, I got it, Anon Killer.*" Mike laughed. "Well, the story ends tonight. As to who told them, who knows?"

Wilson refilled his coffee cup. "If our tip pays off. But maybe the tip was to throw us off?"

He looked at Mal, looking for her to weigh in. "You don't have any idea who called?"

Mal had already talked to Terry McDaniels and the sheriff, telling them everything she could, without revealing the Mystery Man's involvement.

"No idea."

"So why are we even listening to this? What's to keep him from sending us all to strip clubs while he shoots up a church?"

"Because at the moment, we've got a room full of experts but no actionable anything. We have to hope that either the killer is trying to turn himself in, or it's someone who knows the killer but is too afraid to come forward publicly."

Wilson shook his head. "Well, I hope you're right. Because this shit needs to end tonight."

"Yeah, so I've heard," Mal said. "Gloria is freaking out, but at least the Feds are in town to take some of the heat off her. She's doing everything she can. I don't think anyone can use this against her in the election."

Wilson laughed. "Ah, the naïveté of youth. You think this won't be used to hurt her?"

"I don't know. I'd like to hope that her competitors wouldn't use a tragedy this big to score political points. That's just so cynical."

Wilson laughed again.

Mal nodded. "Yeah, you're right. Which is all the more reason to hope that tonight goes well."

Mal stared at the TV, then at the clock.

Twenty-five minutes to go.

Chapter 31 - Jeffrey Brown

JEFF IMAGINED himself strolling into The Purple Pole strip club, blowing away the bevy of whores, drunk assholes, steroid case bouncers, and anyone else who got in his way.

He imagined finding Eugene, probably in the back room getting a lap dance, maybe some head — the last he'd ever get if his marriage to the bitch was anything like Jeff's.

It would also be the last head he got on the count of the bullet holes in the back of his cranium.

Maybe he'd even kill the stripper choking on Eugene's tiny cock.

He smiled at that image.

Jeff had never had the time to stage a crime scene, what with the public nature of his sprees. When he was fifteen, he found true crime books in the library. He was stunned by some of their graphic content, explicitly detailing graphic and sometimes sadistic sexual mutilations. Sometimes he'd take the books home and read them in bed, furiously masturbating and imagining some of the more sexually violent scenarios.

He'd tried to introduce some violent sex play into his marriage, but even the slightest hint at a slap and Sandra freaked out, always asking what the hell was wrong with him.

Judgmental cunt.

What kind of woman judged her husband for sexual fantasies? It wasn't like he *really* wanted to hurt her. It was a fantasy, just enough to get his heart pumping harder. He loved her, like a blind fucking fool, until she dumped him.

Now he'd love to hurt her. Hell, maybe he would rape her first. Let every sick fantasy off of the leash.

He imagined her recoiling at his touch. That only made him want her more.

He still couldn't understand how the hell a bitch could just up and leave her husband. Wasn't it supposed to be until death do you part?

He hadn't fucking died, so why should she be allowed to part?

Times like this, he wished they lived in a part of the world where a woman couldn't leave her husband without getting stoned to death.

He laughed at the thought of Sandra crying, begging for him to take her back in front of a swarm of men clutching rocks.

"Okay, I'll spare you if you suck every one of us off."

And then when she was done, they'd stone her anyway, for being a slut.

He thought about all the whores in the club. He'd been to The Purple Pole a few times. The women were fake as hell, but a lot prettier than the ones at that shitty little club in Butler, filled with trailer trash whose tattoos battled with their meth acne in a war for which could occupy the most room on their skin.

A blonde there who had milked him for drinks and tips

working him up to getting a private dance. He must've spent $150 on her before he even got the lap dance, and then when it came time to go back to the "champagne room" she wouldn't even grind on him to get him off. When he'd put his hands on her hips to guide her, she pulled away and waved her finger, saying, "uh uh uh" like he was some fucking child putting his hand in a cookie jar. Like he wasn't a man who'd just dropped $150 for her to do what whores did.

He wished he could freeze time while in the strip club. He'd find that bitch, assuming she hadn't died of an overdose. He'd find her, and he'd get what she owed him — dead or alive.

He imagined forcing himself on her. Maybe he'd leave her alive long enough to hate what he made her do. Then maybe he'd slit her throat while he came in her. Or maybe put his gun in her mouth and pull the trigger as he finished.

He was aroused just thinking about it. He reached down and adjusted his dick, squeezing the end of it hard as he imagined the filthy things he'd see.

Maybe he could take a minute to bust a nut before leaving. If not, at least he'd have the footage of his spree. He could watch that later, imagining scenarios.

Red and blue lights filled his cabin.

He looked in the rearview mirror to see a Creek County Sheriff's car behind him.

Shit.

He looked down at his speedometer and saw that he was going two miles per hour over the stated 45 speed limit.

He swallowed. The traffic stop played out in his head. They'd pull him over; maybe it was one of their random stops, maybe they'd want to search the vehicle. Not only did he have the AR-15 sitting beneath a blanket between the seats, but his trunk was full of more weapons he planned to use tonight.

But he was likely fucked even before then. The moment they ran the stolen plates, then tried to match them to the stolen white Toyota Camry, he'd be fucked.

He had a choice to make. Stop and hope they didn't run his plates, or make a run in a car that wasn't nearly as suited to a high-speed pursuit as the Dodge had been.

He watched, hoping the patrol car would peel away and follow somebody else.

But when he didn't pull to the side of the road the officer blurted the siren twice to get his attention.

Shit.

Fuck.

Cunt.

Jeff pulled over. He was along one of the few deserted stretches of beachside road in Creek County with a few homes to the left and nothing but a few dozen feet of sand and ocean to the right.

Not another soul in sight.

His plans to murder Eugene were on hold. But that didn't mean he couldn't give his followers a show.

He wouldn't be able to livestream this one. There wasn't enough time to set everything up. But he could record and post it later.

Jeff took the stolen phone, connected it to the GoPro mounted camera already strapped to his chest, and slid on his ski mask.

He stepped out of his car, AR-15 in hand.

Before the officers even had a chance to ready their weapons, he fired into the windshield.

Bullets ripped through the windshield, then into the officers' heads.

They never had a chance.

Dogs barked, the closest a block or two back in the residential neighborhood.

A light went bright in the second story of a house directly in front of him, a nice home with a red tiled roof and a beautifully landscaped yard. Well-lit. The house probably cost at least a million.

Jeff saw a shadow appear in the window, looking down at him.

It quickly vanished.

He ran toward the house, went to the front door and looked up. Through the window, he saw a man in his early forties yelling at his wife to get up and hide as he picked up his phone.

Too late.

Jeff shot through the window, hitting the man in his chest, causing him to drop phone. The woman screamed and ran toward an open patio door in the back of the house. Jeff raised his gun and fired, hitting her in the back.

She stumbled forward and splashed into the pool.

Jeff considered reaching in through the broken window, opening the door, and making sure both people were dead, but he didn't have time — especially if the officers had called in his plate.

It was time to go.

He looked back and saw a red Lexus sitting in the driveway.

Maybe I should go inside after all.

He turned his camera off and headed inside the house to get the keys.

He saw a blue Southwest-style plate atop a wooden shelf just inside the doorway, holding a wallet and two sets of keys.

He grabbed the keys and was about to leave when he spotted the framed photo on the wall of the man and woman he'd just killed. With them, a young boy, around eleven.

Shit! I don't have time for this.

He searched the house, going room to room to find the kid. Seconds turned to minutes. The clock moved faster. The kid could be hiding somewhere in the house and calling 9-1-1. Someone, maybe another sheriff's car, could pass by and see the dead pigs outside.

Why the fuck did I come in here?

"Fuck you, kid!" Jeff yelled as he headed outside, keys in hand.

JEFF WAS PLEASANTLY surprised not to find sheriff's deputies standing with guns raised as he left the house, got into the Lexus and pulled up to the murder scene on the road. He was also pleasantly surprised that the dead pigs had yet to attract any attention.

He parked the Lexus in front of the car he was driving, got out, and grabbed his stuff from the trunk. He turned his camera back on, making sure not to get a shot of the Lexus in the video. Then he reached into the trunk, retrieved a canister of gasoline, poured it all over the patrol car, mostly on the hood before splashing a generous amount on the deputies, and finishing with a trail of gas leading back to the Toyota.

Jeff reached into the bag of weapons, grabbed a flare gun and walked backward to his Lexus.

A car approached.

Shit.

It turned onto a side road before it got close.

Jeff sighed, then fired the flare at the ground between the vehicles.

Flames erupted, spreading fast in both directions.

Jeff wanted to watch the pigs roast, but he had to get going. He clicked the camera off, removed his ski mask, and was about to turn back to the Lexus when a dog barked on the other side of the street.

He froze, hand reaching into his jacket for his pistol, and turned to see a child standing there with a German Shepherd.

Not just any child, but the one from the house he'd just turned into a second murder scene.

Fuck.

Chapter 32 - Mallory Black

10 PM CAME and went without a post from Orestes666, and the command room began to get antsy. Gloria got a phone call, then went to Aanya and whispered something.

Aanya typed in the web address on her computer and then mirrored it to the screen at the front of the room. Wilson and McDaniels turned, and a hush fell over the entire room as the YouTube video began to play.

Gasps as Orestes fired at the deputies.

Then audible cries as he poured gas over both cars and shot a flare.

This monster killing their brothers in blue, and them helpless to do anything but watch as the flames swallowed the deputies.

The video went black.

Silence smothered the room.

Then robotic cackling startled them, drawing their attention to text spelling out on the screen: *More in Three Days.*

"Motherfucker!" Wilson yelled. "What the hell is this? This isn't a strip club."

Gloria cut in. "According to Chief Franks, the deputies had pulled someone over for a busted taillight and were running the license when they lost contact with dispatchers. Judging from his location, he may have been on his way to The Purple Pole."

Wilson shook his head.

McDaniels ordered his people to send a forensics team and investigators.

Mal stared at the screen as Aanya played it again in hopes that someone might see something that yielded a clue.

But Mal wasn't holding out much hope.

MAL LEFT the Situation Room and went to her cubicle, where she felt more comfortable.

She thought about the Hunter, resuming her search on LiveLyfe, looking at the threads of everyone on her list, searching for any lead at all. She wondered how her vigilante knew about the strip club. He didn't know the name, or maybe wasn't volunteering it. She figured if he did know, he would've told her.

So how did he know the little he did? Was he on some website she didn't know about, one where Orestes was posting additional details? That seemed like a good assumption.

She went to her browser and searched for keywords such as murder, shoot, massacre, Anon, along with "Purple Pole" hoping to find something.

But there was nothing.

There were all sorts of secret forums, chat rooms, and websites that a monster like Orestes could be outlining his plans with other sick fucks, none of them indexed by Google or any other search engine.

She wondered if her vigilante had infiltrated Orestes's inner circle.

It made sense, even if she couldn't figure out how he'd done it.

She wished that he'd call again. Maybe she could yell at him about giving her a shit tip and guilt him into giving her something she could use.

She checked her phone to see how much of a charge it had. Seeing fifteen percent, she plugged it into the power strip on her desk, then resumed her LiveLyfe search.

It was almost one in the morning when Mike walked in carrying his computer bag in one hand and a cold can of Diet Coke in the other. He handed her the drink.

"Thanks," she said. "On your way home?"

"Yeah, you going to stay all night?"

"I dunno. I've been eying that couch in the break room. It looks like a cozy sleep."

"Yeah, if you could somehow get all the farts out of it."

"Thanks," she said, scrunching up her nose at the thought of some of the more disgusting deputies, over-grown and mentally underdeveloped frat boys who considered farting a lost art in search of mastery.

"What you looking for?"

"Just looking through LiveLyfe on the off chance that Orestes will post a confession or something."

"Good luck with that!" he said on his way toward the door. "See ya' in the morning."

"Ugh," she said, looking at the clock.

Mal was about to close shop and head home herself when she spied a link to a new "In Memory Of..." page devoted to Lynn Macklin created by her brother, Stewart.

She clicked, then read through the comments on that page, including several new names which weren't listed as her friends.

One lengthy post stuck out more than the others, a mournful outpouring from a woman named Sandra Brown, detailing her close friendship with Lynn, and how even though they'd not talked in some time, she still loved her like a sister and would miss her every day.

She ended with: *I'm so sorry I let him come between us.*

Aside from the post's length, something else stuck out to Mal — the fact that there were fifteen thumbs down on the post from people in Lynn's circle of friends. This resulted in a few more posts from Sandra, sniping at people being cruel and how they ought to mind their own business.

Mal clicked through to Sandra's profile and saw that the woman always posted several times a day, often long sad or angry posts, with a few on Peter Kincaid, also on her friends list, and whom she defended from the media reports about the investigation into him possibly sleeping with girls he'd coached.

Going through the woman's entries, Mal slowly pieced together a profile. Sandra appeared to be a divorced, materialistic, possibly manic-depressive woman whose posts were a blend of nice places she was traveling to, things she wanted to buy, and things her fiancé had bought her. She sprinkled in vapid pseudo-political reposts of memes, posts about how awesome her third grade son was at pretty much everything that he already had or wanted to try, and depressing posts indicative of someone off their meds. It was these latter posts that Mal read while cringing.

Sandra had written at least ten posts about Lynn and Chip, about how close they were, how their losses would affect her profoundly and were making her take stock of her own life.

They seemed like desperate attempts to insert herself into an online conversation involving some very public deaths. The posts she wrote about Lynn turned into arguments about how she had no right to act like she was close to the woman after all the shit she put her through.

The posts where she talked about the coach only earned her condemnation from the many people who had jumped on the bandwagon to call him a child molester.

While the Sheriff's Department had only mentioned one confirmed assault, you'd think he molested the entire town judging from the comments and accusations in response to Sandra's posts. She followed a pattern of viciously attacking anyone who disagreed with her before vanishing, then no longer responding to posts or closing them off altogether.

Mal continued scrolling through the woman's older posts, most of them vapid, happy entries stretching back several months.

But then Mal found another depressing and cryptic one which read:

I'm sorry to everyone about my husband. You were right. And I'm finally free of the monster.

She clicked and saw several responses congratulating her.

One name hit her like a brick.

Chip Halverson — the man that Orestes had killed last at the baseball field — wrote, *Sorry to hear, but can't say I'm surprised.*

Sandra didn't respond. Nor was she friends with him on LiveLyfe, but that made three people connected to Sandra who were now dead.

Sure, a lot of people in Creek County knew one another. If you picked any four people, there was a good chance that three of them might have some connection. But something stirred in her gut. Mal knew when she was onto something.

She kept clicking through Sandra's post, learning that she'd been married to a man named Jeff and, while she didn't go into specific details, Mal didn't need her badge to connect the dots and determine that things had ended badly.

Mal couldn't find a profile for Jeff, at least one that had a photo or wasn't marked PRIVATE.

She grabbed her pen and made a chart with the names of the three victims whom the killer had seemed to single out.

Chip Halverson

Peter Kincaid

Lynn Macklin

And beneath that she wrote two names:

Sandra Brown

Jeff Brown

And under that, a big question mark, circled several times in red ink.

Her phone rang. Captain Wilson.

"I just got a call that they found a witness."

"Who?" Mal asked.

"A house right near the road. Deputies went to talk to neighbors and noticed a window busted. Inside they found a mother, father, and dog shot to death, and a boy tied up."

"He didn't kill the boy?"

"Nope."

"Where is the kid now?"

"At the hospital. We've got a deputy with him until Carrie Thompson shows up."

"I want to talk to him. I think I've got an ID on Orestes."

"Really?" Wilson asked.

"Let's see if this kid recognizes him."

Chapter 33 - Jordyn Parish

2014

THE CROWD MURMURED. She wondered if her father was part of the bustle. He'd been taking his pills for nearly a month and was doing much better. He was still moody from time to time, and still drank more often than not, but he seemed to be in better general spirits.

Neither of them had spoken much about the night he nearly shot her. Like the time she'd come home drunk, they'd pretend it didn't happen until they could finally forget.

Still, there was a slight iciness between them. The kind that comes when a person's worst is put on display.

But things were better. He even let Bobby come over for dinner a couple of times. And he'd let Jordyn go on dates — weekends only, with a midnight curfew. Still, it was progress.

Jordyn looked at the wall clock — five minutes until the play.

That felt like five seconds. Suddenly, despite six months of prep, and running lines with Bobby and others in Drama class, and two rehearsals last weekend, Jordyn wasn't sure if she could do it.

She imagined the hot, bright stage lights burning her body.

A theater packed with students, teachers, and parents. Hundreds of faces, all of them staring at her.

Jordyn was only with the Popular Crowd by association. She hadn't earned her spot. And while most people were nice to Jordyn's face, she heard at least some of the whispers.

He's going out with her?

Oh, that won't last.

I don't know why they're friends with her. She's just a loser emo kid.

And then there were the racist comments.

Why's he dating a nigger?

Can't he get white girls anymore?

It was 2014, and yet some people still had a problem with blacks and whites dating. Funny that some of the same kids who liked hanging with Nate and other black kids on the football team still had a problem with Bobby and her.

It wasn't like this in South Florida, where the schools were more diverse. Kids down there had been exposed to other cultures longer. Up here the majority had lived in Creek County for generations, and most of the families were white. Outsiders, no matter their color, were eyed with suspicion.

She stared at the curtains, her stomach tumbling.

"You okay?" Bobby asked.

He looked adorable in his period costume as John Proctor.

Brianna, behind him, said, "You don't need to go on, honey. That's what understudies are for. Want me to—"

"No, I've got this," she said, working to convince herself more than Brianna. But the world swayed underfoot. She leaned on Bobby and wiped sweat from her brow.

Brianna's eyes widened like they did when she was being dramatic. "Well, good luck. And if you do puke, try not to get any on me, okay?" She smiled then walked away.

Under normal circumstances, Jordyn might have laughed. Brianna was still a bitch to most people, but nice enough to Jordyn that she rarely took offense.

Bobby looked at Jordyn. "You sure you're okay? You look like you're about to faint or something."

"I'll be fine," she said, then felt it coming a split second before the vomit sprayed from her mouth.

Bobby dodged the worst of it, but everyone was looking at Jordyn.

"Jordyn, are you okay?" Ms. Franks asked, running over.

"Just nerves," Jordyn said, feeling every eye upon her.

Bobby raced away, then returned with a wet rag and wiped at Jordyn's mouth. "Hey," he said, trying to grab her attention.

She met his eyes.

"What the hell is this?"

"What?" she asked, confused by his anger.

"This fear thing. What do you have to be scared of?"

"I might fuck up my lines, and everyone will laugh at me."

"So what, let 'em laugh. But you know what?"

"No. What?" she said, smiling at the unintended word play.

"You know your lines better than anyone. You're a better actress than anyone on stage."

Brianna wasn't more than ten feet away, talking to Bethanee. Jordyn wondered if she had overheard. She'd probably give him no end of shit later if so. Or she'd whine to Calum.

Bobby didn't seem to give a shit who heard him. And she kinda loved that about him.

"Listen, Jordyn; you are the real deal. You're going to stop overthinking this, you're going to get out there, and you're going to kick some fucking ass."

He hugged her, then smacked Jordyn on the ass as if she were one of the team. "What are you gonna do?"

"I'm going to—"

"I can't hear you!" he yelled. Everyone backstage was looking at them. Again, Bobby didn't give a damn. "What are you going to do?"

"I'm gonna kick some ass."

"What kind of ass?"

"Some fucking ass!" she yelled, surely blushing.

"Yes, you are!"

Kids started clapping, many coming up to Jordyn and wishing her well.

She felt, perhaps for the first time, like part of the cast.

She looked up to see Brianna, still standing back, glaring at her.

Bobby, noticing this too, leaned over and whispered in Jordyn's ear, "Don't worry about her, she's jealous."

Jordyn laughed.

The curtains parted.

~

As Jordyn bowed to the standing ovation alongside the cast, a rush rippled through her, unlike anything she'd ever felt. Christmas morning, meeting a new friend, the thrill of an unknown adventure — this was more intense.

The curtains closed. Bobby ran up to her and kissed her on the lips. "I'm so proud of you!"

"Thank you, though maybe let me brush my teeth before we kiss again?"

Bobby laughed. "Yeah, I didn't want to say anything, but that *would* be a good idea."

Jordyn went back to the dressing room, changed out of her costume, then put on her jeans, tee, and blue sweater. A few girls congratulated her for conquering the fear and complimented her on a job well done. Jordyn returned their accolades and even complimented Brianna.

But Brianna said, "Good job. You'll get better the more you do. I mean, if you want to do more."

What kind of bullshit is that? I compliment you, and you give me a passive aggressive backhanded compliment?

What a bitch!

Jordyn was in too good a mood to let pettiness ruin her night. She smiled, said "Thanks," then went to the bathroom and brushed her teeth.

She went into the theater where Bobby said he'd be waiting. Most of the cast was going to Frederico's after the play.

But he wasn't alone. Bobby was standing beside her father, who was holding a bouquet of roses.

"I wasn't sure if I was supposed to give these to you before, after, or what?" he said, handing them to her.

"I have no idea." She took the roses and hugged him. "Thank you, and thanks for coming."

"Oh, I wouldn't miss my baby's debut. You were *excellent*. Your mother would be so proud."

She smiled, feeling the tears.

"And you did great, Bobby. I'm very impressed."

"Thank you, Mr. Parish. I wouldn't remember any of my lines if not for Jordyn."

"So, what are you all doing now?"

"We're supposed to go to Frederico's."

"Oh, okay," he said, looking disappointed.

"Why?" she asked.

"Oh, I thought I'd take you and Bobby out to eat. But that's okay. I can't argue with cheap pizza and good company. You guys deserve to celebrate. We can do it another time."

"Are you sure?" As much as Jordyn didn't want to let her father down, she also wanted to enjoy the night. Hang out with the cast, get to know them better.

"Yeah, another time," he said, hugging her then shaking Bobby's hand. "You two have fun."

"Thank you, sir. And we'll be home by midnight."

Her father nodded, giving Bobby an almost smile before leaving.

Calum and Brianna started toward them. "What's up, bitches?"

He and Bobby exchanged bro-shakes, then Calum hugged Jordyn tightly. "Wow, you were so damned good. Bobby didn't tell me he was dating a star."

Brianna said, "You should've seen her before the show, a total wreck. Poor girl puked all over." Brianna was smiling, her eyes like a serpent's.

Shit. She heard what Bobby said. Now she'll be bitchy for weeks until we kiss her ass and make things better.

But Jordyn didn't feel like kissing anyone's ass tonight. She was happy and proud of the job she'd done. And she didn't need Brianna Bitchface trying to bring her down.

"For real?" Calum fell a step back. "You puked?"

He lowered his voice to a whisper. "My freshman year on the JV team? I puked before every single game."

223

"Really?" Jordyn said. She didn't think confidence was an issue with someone like Calum Fucking Kozack, as people — including Calum — called him.

"Oh, yeah. Don't sweat it. It's not the fear that defines you; it's what you do with it. Hell, I've been telling Brianna all year to audition for some advertisements, but she's too scared."

Brianna went bug-eyed. "I am *not* scared. I just didn't find any roles that I liked."

Calum laughed. "Okay, sorry, Sweetie. You're right." He hugged her, winking at Bobby and Jordyn while rolling his eyes.

"So, we ready to split?"

"You're going, too?" Jordyn asked.

"Yeah," Brianna said, her voice climbing several octaves. "We're allowed a plus one."

"I wish I would've known. I could have asked my dad."

Bobby looked toward the exit. "I don't see him, but maybe we could still catch him."

Jordyn looked at Calum and Brianna, a bitch and a manipulative schemer. She didn't want to sit her father at their table. He'd either call them on their bullshit or later express regret that Jordyn didn't stand up for herself in their company. He couldn't understand what it was like for her, here at this new school, navigating these social waters, and trying to fit in with kids you didn't fit in with.

"That's okay," she said, giving Bobby a kiss.

Chapter 34 - Jeffrey Brown

JEFF FLOORED THE LEXUS, cursing himself while punching the wheel.

"Fucking idiot. Stupid fucking idiot!"

He should've killed the kid.

But he fucking froze.

The boy looked like an older version of his son, Liam.

And while it would've made things so much easier, and while it would've only taken a few seconds to raise his pistol and fire, he couldn't bring himself to do it.

He looked at the boy and said, "Sorry."

Then he got into his car and drove off.

The boy had seen him.

They would have a sketch artist.

They'd have the make, model and license plate of his Lexus.

It wouldn't be long until his name was all over every fucking news channel in the state. Hell, this would probably go national.

He wasn't ready to stop.

There was no fucking way he would let Eugene and Sandra have their Happily Ever After.

No fucking way.

While his cover as Orestes666 was now almost officially blown, he wasn't without a fallback plan — a vacant house at the edge of town that had been empty for nearly a year. One of the hundreds of homes in the county foreclosed on following the market collapse in 2008.

It was also a singular home in a cul-de-sac, tucked into the woods with nothing around for an impressive stretch of winding road. A forgotten place, perfect for a man who wanted to be overlooked.

Chapter 35 - Mallory Black

MAL AND MIKE pulled up to the house tucked away on a quiet cul-de-sac in a nicer section of Pine Harbour.

It was six in the morning, still dark outside. Mike was barely functional with only four hours of sleep. Neither of them got a wink of *solid* shut-eye, having spent half the night in the hospital talking to the boy and confirming a photo ID. The kid said it was dark, but that he was fairly certain Jeffrey Brown was the man he saw standing in front of the burning cars.

The SWAT team moved in on Brown's apartment, but the guy was long gone. The FBI issued a Be On The Lookout for the tri-state area and interviewed neighbors.

Mal and Mike were in charge of questioning Sandra, who might be their last hope of finding the bastard.

They got out of the car and approached the front door with Mal in the lead. She knocked, hoping like hell that they weren't at another murder scene.

Mal exhaled when lights went on beyond the blinds.

A man: "Hello?"

Mal assumed he was looking out the peephole. She

held her badge so he could see. "Hello, sir, is Sandra Brown in?"

"What's this about?"

"We'd like to speak to her," Mal said, pulling her badge away, wondering if they'd seen the news.

The door opened to an overweight man in blue boxers, a gray T-shirt, with orange tufts of hair surrounding a prominent bald spot. He was wearing brown-framed glasses with thick lenses, eyes wide behind them as he looked from Mal to Mike, then back to Mal.

This definitely wasn't Jeffrey Brown.

"Is everything okay?" the man asked.

"We just need to speak to Sandra, please."

"Hold on," he said leaving the door open as he went toward the kitchen.

From her spot on the porch, Mal saw a small blond boy, maybe four-years-old, sitting on an L-shaped couch in the dark watching TV and eating what looked like a Pop-tart.

He looked at Mal and Mike curiously, but didn't say anything, or stand. After a minute, he turned his attention back to the TV.

Moments later, Sandra Brown followed the balding man to the front door. "Yes, can I help you?"

She was wearing blue yoga pants and a white tee. A headband pulled her long dirty blonde hair into a tidy pony tail.

"We'd like to talk to you about your ex-husband."

Her brow furrowed. She looked back at the boy. "Hey, Liam. Mommy will be right back. She just needs to talk to the police for a moment."

Sandra closed the door, leaving the bald man and her son inside.

Outside, she asked, "What did he do?"

"We're not sure yet. We wanted to talk to you first. Can you tell us about your split?"

At first, Sandra seemed suspicious. But after a minute or so, she was spilling all the secrets of their marriage. Jeff was a "fucking loser" who her mother had never liked. He never did anything around the house because he was always too tired even though they both worked, and he was prone to angry outbursts where he'd punch holes in the wall and sulk for days on end. Luckily for her, she finally met someone who appreciated her. Eugene, the man she was marrying on Sunday. Two days from now.

"Did he ever hit you or abuse you in any way?" Mal asked.

"A few times, yes," she said, her complexion paling. "And like the fool I was, I stayed, trying to 'fix him,' even as my friends all told me I was an idiot. The last straw was a time he spanked Liam for spilling juice on the carpet. I knew it was over. Why are you asking me all of these questions?"

"Just a few more," Mal said. "Did he ever threaten any of your friends? Or do anything violent to them?"

"Oh, God no. He would complain a lot, and he tried to control me, tell me who I could and couldn't see, but he never threatened them or did anything to them. But isn't that how cowards behave? They talk a big game behind closed doors, but then they're all smiles while out and about?"

Mal nodded. "So, is there anything else you can tell us about him?"

Sandra seemed about to say something, but then she just shook her head. "Nah, that doesn't matter."

"Please," Mal said, "every little bit helps."

"Well, he tried to get me to do some violent stuff in bed."

"Like what kind of stuff?"

"At first it seemed harmless. He asked if he could spank me. I said yes, but then he got a bit too rough, so I told him I didn't like it. Then he got weirder. He asked me to put on handcuffs. I said *hell no*. Then another time he started to choke me, but I put a stop to that fast. Why are you asking all these things?"

"When's the last time you spoke to him?"

"Oh, I dunno. He came to get Liam a few weeks ago for a weekend visit, but we didn't speak much. Maybe a few months before that where fought about child support he wasn't paying on time."

"Can you think of any reason he might want to hurt Chip Halverson?"

"Chip? Oh God, I haven't heard that name in forever. Um, he's a local painter that we knew for a while. But we haven't seen him in forever. Why are you asking about Chip?"

Her face went even paler as she put two and two together.

Mal went on. "How about Peter Kincaid or Lynn Macklin?"

She started to shake her head, tears welling up in her eyes. "No. No. Please, don't tell me he did *that*."

"We don't know yet," Mike said in his most calming voice, "which is why we're talking to you and some other people he knew, trying to get a feel for the man. Is there any reason you can think that he'd want to kill any of those people?"

"Yes," she said.

"Why?"

She shook her head. "I don't know how to say it."

Mal said, "Usually I find the best way is just to spill it out. Don't worry, Mrs. Brown; we've heard it all before."

"We were all part of a club."

"*Club?* What kind of club?"

"Things weren't going so well between us, and I didn't want to do the violent stuff that Jeff seemed to need, so a friend of mine, Lynn, suggested we go with her to a swinger's club in Jacksonville."

Mal never saw this coming. She wanted to turn back and see Mike's face, see if he could hide one of his priceless reactions to weird shit. But he held his attention on Sandra and said, "And what happened?"

"Well, that's where we met Chip and Peter. Peter used to come with a young college girl. And we all just hit it off and had fun together."

"All of you?" Mike asked.

"Well, yeah, it was a swinger's club."

"So, how long did you go there?"

"A few times. But then Jeff started getting jealous when he thought I was becoming too friendly with Chip and Peter. We were talking on LiveLyfe until he made me stop. We stopped going. This was right around the time he was getting angry all the time and having problems at work. Like I said, one day he just blew up at our son, and I said I couldn't take it. I went to stay with Eugene, filed for divorce, and have been happy ever since. Do you think he killed them?"

"We're looking into it," Mal said. "Your husband is a person of interest in the murders, as well as others."

Sandra looked ready to vomit.

Mal remembered something that Orestes had posted online, a threat for more death in three days — the exact day of Sandra's marriage to Eugene.

"I think your husband may be planning to do something at your wedding."

"What?"

Mal explained her theory, then asked if Eugene happened to have been at The Purple Pole last night.

"Yeah, for his bachelor party. I asked him to do it early, so he wasn't hung over for our wedding. Why?"

"Because I think your ex-husband was going to crash the party."

Chapter 36 - Jordyn Parish

As FAR AS Valentine's Day dinners went, Jordyn couldn't have asked for anything nicer.

Bobby took her to Generosità where she ordered spaghetti and meatballs. He surprised her by ordering the same thing and apologized for giving her so much shit for loving such a classic meal.

They talked about their lives and what they wanted to do in the future. He wanted to go to Florida State to play football but also wanted to get a degree in business management. He had some creative — and impressive — entrepreneurial ideas. Not only was he a sports star, a solid actor, and a sensitive guy, he knew business. Her father would be impressed by this side of Bobby. He'd never run a business but used to dream about it before retiring from the force.

Jordyn wasn't sure what she wanted to do and was a bit anxious when thinking about the future more than a year or two out. She wanted to be a writer, maybe paint a bit, but beyond that, she had no idea.

They talked about why she was anxious, which ultimately led to her mother's death. Then Bobby talked about his father, and they shared their coping stories.

It was some of the deepest conversations they'd ever had, and the more she talked to Bobby, the more he felt like the other side of her.

After dinner, he told Jordyn to close her eyes. Then he drove somewhere to surprise her, playing a mix of music he'd made for her including bands she'd never heard. Instrumentals by Ludovico Einaudi and Max Richter surrendered to a slow song by Broken Social Scene.

He stopped the car as it ended. "We're here."

"Can I open my eyes?"

"Yes," he said opening the door and getting out.

Jordyn opened her eyes and saw the front of an unfamiliar house. One story and small, but with plenty of acreage, unlike most newer homes in the area. A large wooden fence circled the yard.

"Where are we?" she asked as he opened her door.

"Come," he said, taking her hand.

Jordyn smoothed the front of her dress as they ascended the steps.

She hoped he wasn't taking her to some stupid house party. Hanging out with his bros and watching him get drunk or wasted would be the worst way to end what had been the most romantic evening of her life,

He inserted his keys and opened the door.

This is his house?

Despite knowing Bobby for most of the school year, and having dated him since January, she'd not yet met his mom or been to his house. She didn't think much about it because they didn't have much time together, and when they were together, he was usually coming to Jordyn's house or picking her up to take her somewhere else.

He led her inside where a short woman with a long

brown ponytail approached Jordyn with a big, genuine smile. Even her eyes were happy. She was older than Jordyn expected. Early fifties. She wore a long flowing layered tie-dyed dress with several beaded necklaces.

"Mom, this is Jordyn."

"It's *sooooo* nice to meet you, Jordyn," she said, giving her a giant hug. "Bobby's told me so much about you."

"Hi, Mrs. Hollingsworth. It's so nice to meet you."

"Call me Candy, short for Candace."

"Okay, Candy."

She ushered them into the dining room, which, like the rest of the home, was cozy. But every space — counter, shelf, or hutch — was stuffed with knick-knacks. Commemorative plates, thimbles, salt and pepper shakers from around the world, porcelain children and puppies, amid an endless array of adorable collectibles.

Like magic she appeared behind them, holding a plate. "I hope you didn't eat too much. I made fresh chocolate chip cookies."

The chocolate was still melting, and the scent was a beautiful beast.

Jordyn couldn't help but smile while watching the woman. She wasn't sure why, maybe because so many of the popular kids had parents who seemed the type, but she'd always pictured Bobby's mother as some trendy soccer mom, not this down-to-earth, sweet older woman.

She poured them both cold glasses of milk and asked about their date. Then she asked Jordyn about herself, how she'd met Bobby, and other questions which inevitably led to stories, *many* stories, about Bobby as a kid. The time he tried to pet a skunk and wound up having to take three baths in tomato juice; the time he caught his first fish, then reeled it in, saw it was a catfish, and it scared him so much he threw the fish, and the pole, into the lake. She told

Jordyn about his kindergarten trouble, for pushing Emily Reynolds, whom he had a huuuuuge crush on; and some sweet stories about him and his father. After the tales, she pulled out a stack of photo albums.

Jordyn and Bobby exchanged several glances as his mother endlessly rambled, clueless to his embarrassment.

"Do you all want some more milk?" she asked after an hour.

"I'll have some water, please," Jordyn said, if only to give Bobby a break.

As she went to the kitchen, Bobby whispered, "I'm soooo sorry. She doesn't get a lot of visitors, so when she does, look out, she will talk your ear off."

"She's cute." The woman was overwhelming, sure, but it was nice.

Bobby smiled. "She's not always this chatty."

"It's okay." Jordyn smiled.

This sure beat going home to a mortuary, and a father too drunk for dialogue. He was doing better and taking his meds, but there were still days where he was in a dark place. On those days, Jordyn kept to herself.

"Here you go," said Bobby's mom, handing Jordyn a tall glass of ice water.

After a few more stories, Candy yawned and said, "Okay, I'm gonna hit the hay, let you kids have some alone time."

She winked, and Jordyn blushed.

Bobby barely covered a laugh. "Goodnight, Ma."

"Goodnight, honey." She hugged Bobby and then kissed him on the head. She turned to Jordyn. "It's good to meet you, Sweetie. Bobby had better bring you around here more often."

"Yes, ma'am," Bobby said, his face going red. Then once they were alone, he apologized again. "I'm so sorry!"

"It's okay. She's awesome. And she gave me a hug and a kiss."

"Yeah, she kind of is," he admitted.

It was nice to see a high school boy who wasn't embarrassed by his mom, or rude to her. When Jordyn was in fourth grade she had a crush on a boy named Spider Gentry. He was a charmer to girls, but whenever he was around his mom and dad, Spider had been an insufferable jerk. Jordyn's mom said, "If you want someone who will treat you right, watch how they act towards their parents. That's how they'll eventually treat you."

"Hey," he said, "I want to show you something else."

"Oh?" Jordyn said, eyebrows arched, wondering if *this* was his plan.

They'd only kissed and fondled. While she was attracted to him and had imagined doing more, Jordyn was also terrified. She had no experience with boys and didn't really know what to do. And she didn't want to make any mistakes that would mess up their relationship. Things were great. Why risk ruining them?

"Come with me," Bobby said, leading her toward the back of the kitchen and through a door into the pitch-black back yard. "Wait." He ducked back inside and flipped a switch.

The yard was illuminated by lights, strung from one tree to the next in a canopy of color. Blues, reds, greens, and yellows spilled from the trees onto the garden. The strings converged on a large oak tree with a wooden tree house built right into its heart.

Jordyn gasped. "Is that an actual treehouse?"

"Yeah. My dad made it for me when I was a kid."

"Wow!" she said, approaching the tree, tracing her fingers over the wooden pieces of ladder nailed into the trunk.

"Can I go up? I've never been in a tree house before."

"You've never been in a tree house? Wow, that's just sad, Ms. Jordyn. Let's fix that glaring omission from your childhood now, shall we?"

Jordyn bounded up the trunk like a giddy child, then stepped inside the house, surprised by its size. She could easily stand without hitting the roof.

Bobby climbed in behind her. "Welcome. You are officially the first girl to ever come up here."

"I bet you say that to all the girls."

"Only the pretty ones." He sat on the floor, reached into a basket filled with cold sodas and snacks, and grabbed a can of Coke. "Want one?"

"No thanks." She sat beside Bobby and looked around.

The wooden walls were filled with writing in pen, from various kids claiming their presence, a few initials with hearts, some scratched out with a knife, and a few insults — exactly what she'd expect to find in a young boy's treehouse. It had a sleeping bag, a pillow, a small fridge, a fan, and a shelf with paperbacks and comics. There were also a few metal and plastic lunch boxes. It even had plexiglass windows which, Bobby explained, were fully functional.

"Wow, this is like the coolest treehouse ever. Do you still come up here?"

"Sometimes, when I want to get out of the house and relax. Read some good literature." He handed her a couple of 90s era comics in Mylar bags. "These were my dad's."

She opened one. *The New Mutants* number one. The art was awesome. "Cool." Jordyn carefully returned the comic to its bag then handed it to Bobby. She saw something behind him, written on the walls in big black marker: *Calum & Bobby: Blood Brothers For Life*

She laughed. "Oh, that's so adorable."

"Yeah, that's from last week," he joked.

238

"Blood brothers?"

"Yeah, got the scar and everything," he said, holding up his right palm.

She put her fingers on it, feeling for a scar that she couldn't see. "I don't feel anything."

He looked at his palm and shrugged. "Hmph, guess it faded."

"How long have you two been friends?"

"Since I was ten. I'd just moved here from Jersey one summer and didn't know anyone. And I didn't fit in, *at all.* I was like this city kid moved to the backwoods. I mean it was *really* Rednecksville when I first came here. Anyway, I immediately caught the attention of some assholes who started bullying me. And I was sort of a Mama's Boy, so I didn't fight back."

"Aw," Jordyn said, putting his hand in hers.

"Anyway, Calum was the shit back then too. We met one day down by the creek and just hit it off. And then when school started back up, all the kids who'd messed with me were suddenly kissing my ass."

"Because of Calum?"

"Yep. He saved my life."

"Wow." She traced her fingers over his, wanting to say something, but unsure of how to raise the question. "Do you feel like you owe him?" She couldn't make eye contact, and looked down instead at his hand in hers.

"What do you mean?"

"I dunno, it's just that he's a jerk to you sometimes, and I don't know why you don't tell him to knock it off."

His hand flinched, ever so slightly. What if she was wading into waters she wasn't prepared for? She'd heard stories from Brianna and the other girls about "bitches" trying to come between the guys over the years, and how they always found themselves outside looking in once the dust settled. Sometimes Jordyn felt like the girls shared these stories as not-so-subtle warnings.

Still, it was hard to sit by and watch Bobby take shit from Calum. It seemed to be worse than ever since the play. Calum's digs at Bobby had grown less subtle; he punched him in the arm hard and gave him hateful looks.

Brianna was a bit more subtle, still being nice to her face, but Jordyn could feel the girl's hate like heat from a furnace. In the past week, she had felt increasingly like an outsider. Jordyn couldn't help but feel like Bobby was slowly being phased out, and didn't even seem to notice.

"He's not bad. We bust each other's balls. It's a guy thing. We all do it."

Every instinct told Jordyn to quit. If Bobby didn't have an issue with the way Calum treated him, who was she to make it a problem?

"Yeah, but he seems to tease you more than the others. Don't you think?"

Bobby withdrew his hand.

Crap!

He looked at her, confused. "What do you mean?"

"Never mind."

"Obviously this is something you've been thinking about. What is it?"

"He's just kind of a dick to you, is all. But maybe you're right. Maybe it's just a guy thing, and I don't get it. Forget I said anything."

Bobby was quiet as he finished his Coke, staring out at the night sky.

Now she felt terrible.

Rain began to fall, tapping on the roof and hitting the plastic windows like rice at a wedding.

And just like that, a light rain became a deluge — trapping them in the treehouse at a most uncomfortable moment.

"I'm sorry," she said. "I just really love you, and I hate to see someone, anyone, be mean to you."

His eyes locked onto hers. "You *love* me?"

She couldn't read him. Her heart was racing. Before she could weigh the words, Jordyn said, "Yes."

Oh shit, did I just tell him I love him? LOVE?

Too late to take it back.

Yes, she did love him, at least Jordyn thought she did. That must be what it was when she couldn't think of anything else, and everything about him gave her butterflies. But it was way too soon to tell him.

He kissed her.

Her heart raced faster.

His hands explored, moving under her dress.

She was surprised when her hands didn't stop them.

Then everything happened.

And that felt right.

LATER SHE'D BE RIDDLED with worry: *Did I sleep with him too soon? Was the condom foolproof? What if I get pregnant?*

But for the moment, life was perfect.

She'd masturbated, but it was night and day, the difference between touching yourself and feeling someone inside you. She wanted to go again, but—

"What time is it?"

Jordyn fumbled for her purse.

Bobby grabbed his phone. "Eleven-forty."

"I need to get home."

Bobby was already standing. "Shit. Yeah. Sorry."

They quickly dressed, then headed down the ladder

planks, getting soaked in the rain. Instead of going through the house, where they might run into Bobby's mom, Bobby led Jordyn through the gate to the front yard.

On the way home he said, "Can I ask you a question?"

"Okay." Jordyn was nervous, wondering if Bobby's question might have something to do with the sex being bad for him.

"What's wrong with your dad?"

"What do you mean?"

"You don't have to tell me, but I noticed that time he came to visit me … it seemed like he was talking to someone when he walked away."

Shit.

Jordyn sighed.

"What?" he said.

Jordyn had spent years covering up her father's illness. He didn't want anyone to know, and she didn't want to share his secrets. And because of that, she stopped having friends over. She'd gotten tired of lying to them, saying her dad was just playing around, when he was, in reality, sick.

But she was also tired of lying. And she wanted to be honest with Bobby, especially after such a tender moment. It would feel good to have someone else shoulder the burden. "You promise not to tell anyone?"

"Of course," he said.

Jordyn told him everything.

Chapter 37 - Jordyn Parish

JORDYN DID *NOT* WANT to go to Calum's seventeenth birthday party but avoiding it wasn't an option.

Everyone who was anyone at their school would be there tonight. Their absence would be noticed. Things were icy between Bobby and Calum, and Jordyn knew people were whispering that she was the cause of it.

Things were fine between the boys before she *came along.*

On the drive to Calum's mansion, Bobby said, "Thank you for coming."

"Well, I'd never leave their shit list if I didn't."

"I think a lot of it is because we all don't spend a lot of time together. They don't know you like I do."

"So, they *do* hate me?"

"No. I mean, nobody's said anything to me."

"Well, I can't help it if my father doesn't let me party all night."

Bobby laughed. "Yeah, I don't know what his problem is — expecting you home before dawn, and sober. What a dick!"

Jordyn laughed.

"Well, not to worry, my dear. I will have you home before midnight tonight."

"Thanks. I'd hate to see my father kill you."

Jordyn didn't dare tell Bobby that her father wasn't even home. That he had business in South Florida for the weekend. Even though he still had his private PI's license, he barely ever worked. But an old friend needed him to help consult on something.

It was good to see him working again, and maybe get his life back together. He'd been on the pills for a few months now and rarely drank anymore. He was even waking up early, exercising every morning like he used to do almost fanatically back when he was a cop.

Not telling Bobby he was out of town meant two things: she would be home at a decent hour, and Bobby wouldn't get shit-faced.

As good as things were between her and Bobby when they were alone, he was always so different around his friends — especially Calum. He drank more, smoked weed, and acted like they did. Sometimes she wondered if he was two people, or putting on a show. And if it was an act, which one was true? The nice, sweet guy she knew or the obnoxious frat boy?

He reached over and held her hand. "We're gonna have fun tonight, I promise."

"Well, if you're in the mood for promises, make me one more?"

"Anything."

"Just don't leave me alone with Brianna and the others for too long? She *hates* me. And she only gets worse the more friends she has around."

"Well, she hates everyone, especially herself. And Calum likes you. So whatever shit Brianna might be trying to stir doesn't matter. You be you, and everything will be fine."

"Be me? So, if I want to tell Brianna that she's a two-faced bitch, I can do that?"

"Hell yeah," Bobby smiled. "Everyone will love it."

"Yeah, right!"

"And if that doesn't shut her up, punch her in the face. Break that expensive nose of hers."

"Wait, she had plastic surgery?"

"Oh, hell yeah. Got rid of a bump on her nose and got new tits when she was sixteen. Happy birthday."

"No way."

"Oh, yeah."

Jordyn shook her head, laughing. "Oh my God. That is insane. Who gets their kids implants before they're even out of high school? I thought that was something you only saw on those MTV shows."

"Up next on Real Teens of Creek County, can Brianna hide her baby bump for prom? Or will she need to get an abortion to fit into her slinky little dress?"

"She's *pregnant?*" Jordyn said, eyes wide, wondering what other bombshell Bobby was going to drop.

"Oh God no. I was only joking. Shit. I think Calum would shoot himself if he knocked *her* up!"

Jordyn laughed.

Bobby stared at her, smiling like a satisfied cat.

"What?"

"You act like you're above it all, but face it, you like gossip just as much as everyone else."

"No, I don't."

"You were smiling *soooooo* big when I said she was pregnant. It's okay to enjoy other people's misery, you know."

"I do not enjoy other people's misery," Jordyn said, crossing her arms over her chest and playfully pouting.

"Not even Brianna's?"

"Okay, maybe just a little," Jordyn smiled devilishly.

"See, you are one of us," he teased.

"Shut up and drive."

～

WITHIN MINUTES of arriving at Calum's mansion, Jordyn got a bad vibe. His parents were out of town. If this were a movie, it was exactly two scenes from mayhem. It seemed like every kid in school was there. The place was pounding from the bass. Pot hung in the air like a cloud. Red plastic cups peppered the yard, in hands and on the ground. The pool was filled with girls in bikinis and guys in their trunks, all of them horny and drunk. Alcohol was evident; pills were implied.

Jordyn wondered where Calum's parents were. Who leaves their kid alone on his birthday? Was that something that cool millionaire parents did all the time? Or were Calum's parents assholes, too? It took one to make one, so it was probably the latter.

Jordyn was sticking close to Bobby as Nate and Adam came up with bro-shakes and hugs.

Sammi hugged Jordyn. "*Soooo* glad you could make it!" Of all the girls in the group, Sammi was the only one who Jordyn believed genuinely liked her.

"I like your hair. You look so cute," Jordyn shouted over the music.

Sammi's hair was in short pigtails on top of her head. She was wearing a pink bikini top and surfer shorts.

"Thanks," she yelled, then ran off, returning with two cold bottles of beer. "Here!"

Bobby took one and started drinking.

"No thanks," Jordyn said.

"Okay." Sammi cracked off the top and started drinking herself. She pulled Jordyn from Bobby. "Come on, lemme show you around the house."

Bobby barely noticed, already joking around with his boys.

Jordyn reluctantly followed Sammi for a tour of "Casa del Douchebag."

Jordyn laughed. It felt good to hear someone other than her voice dissent over the ruling class. She might have worried that Brianna or someone might overhear, but it was so damned loud.

They were upstairs in front of two closed doors. "And this is where *Il Douche* was conceived."

Sammi was buzzed, and extra goofy.

Jordyn laughed again, looking around. The hall was otherwise empty. She whispered, "Please don't leave me alone."

Sammi laughed. "Oh, don't worry. They're harmless."

"No, I think the other girls hate me."

"They hate everyone. It took me three years to be accepted."

"Why would you even wait three years to be accepted by *them?*"

"Because four years is a long time to spend without any friends. I'd rather be friends with the popular bitches than have no one at all. Besides, when you get to know them one-on-one, most of them are okay. It's just Brianna who's awful. You get Bethanee alone, and she's nice."

"If you say so," Jordyn said with a shrug.

"Come on; I'll introduce you to some girls that *aren't* bitches."

They headed downstairs. Sammi introduced Jordyn to a bunch of kids she'd seen around the school but didn't know.

After about fifteen minutes, she found herself in a group of boys and girls where the talk was easy. They were all drinking, but no one was obnoxious.

As she chatted with her new friends, Jordyn peeked around, looking for Bobby. She didn't see him. Nor did she see Adam, Nate, Bethanee, Brianna, or Sammi. No Calum. They were probably all in the pool doing keggers and screaming stupid shit.

Just when Jordyn was starting to relax, she heard Brianna and Bethanee behind her singing, "There you are!"

She turned, finding her fake smile just in time. "Hi!"

The girls were wet, wearing bikinis. Jordyn couldn't help but smile, remembering what Bobby had said about Brianna's fake tits.

They all hugged. Brianna said, "Come, say hi to the birthday boy!"

The girls dragged her away from Sammi's group, leading her through the crowded kitchen and out onto the patio where teenagers were doing keggers and diving into the pool. Weed assaulted her nostrils.

She caught a glimpse of Bobby, drinking with Nate and a couple of guys she didn't know. They looked too old for high school, and a bit sketchy.

Jordyn could feel people looking at her as they cut through the crowd and headed toward the pool's edge. She felt painfully out of place, like a church girl entering a den of iniquity.

Sitting on a raft in the center, smoking a big cigar and holding a giant oversized beer stein, sat King Calum. He wore shades and a paper crown, surrounded by guys and girls in varying stages of sobriety. Some of the girls were topless.

"Jordyn, you came!"

He looked genuinely happy to see her. He was also shit-faced, so he was probably genuinely happy to see anyone.

"Happy birthday!" she said, waving to him.

"Indeed it is! Why don't you come in?"

"Um, I didn't bring a bathing suit."

"Get naked," Calum said.

Jordyn wasn't sure if he was joking. Before she could think of a response, Brianna said, "I have a suit you can wear if you want."

"Thanks," Jordyn said. "Maybe in a bit."

Calum said, "Has anyone gotten you a drink yet?"

"I'm good."

"No, it's my birthday, and I insist that you drink something. Brianna, get Jordyn something to drink!"

Brianna walked away, leaving Jordyn with Bethanee, smiling like a robot that didn't know what to do in the absence of its master.

A football whizzed toward Jordyn.

She caught it and tossed back a perfect spiral at the big oaf who'd thrown it.

Calum took off his shades. "Woah, nice arm, Parish! Bobby didn't tell me you play."

"I played a bit in middle school."

"Wow. I am impressed."

"If you want, I can give you some tips," she joked.

Bethanee laughed.

"I bet you could." Calum smiled.

She wasn't sure if he was still talking football or if he was sliding into perversion. Either way, she was relieved when Brianna returned with a drink.

"Here, made it myself," she said, raising a tall glass of neon blue drink with plenty of ice.

"What is it?"

"An aqua blue cruise."

"I dunno," Jordyn said, "I don't handle liquor well."

"It's a virgin. No alcohol."

Jordyn lifted it to her nose. It had a fruity smell and the burn of alcohol.

"It's not a virgin drink," Jordyn said handing it back.

Brianna laughed. "Come on; one drink won't kill you."

Calum chanted, "Drink, drink, drink!"

Everyone stared, then joined in the chant.

Where the hell is Bobby?

She looked around. The crowd was filled with drunken, wasted schoolmates, yelling at Jordyn to drink, but no Bobby.

She'd gone most of her life managing to avoid situations like this. Peer pressure had always seemed like one of those things that happened to other kids, those who cared what people thought. Jordyn had always considered herself above it all. Immune.

Time crawled. A cold panic crept across her body as everyone urged her to drink.

It was all so stupid, and she hated that she couldn't just walk away and ignore the crowd.

She brought the drink to her lips and took a sip. It was surprisingly good.

The crowd cheered.

She downed the drink just to get it over with, and prove that she wasn't some prude who couldn't have fun. That she was one of them.

JORDYN WOKE HUNCHED over the toilet.

Her head felt light, confused.

She got up, barely able to stand.

She was sweating.

She reached for the bathroom doorknob, thought she turned it, but somehow missed.

She tried again.

It opened.

She ran into Brianna in the hallway.

"I don't feel good," she said.

"What's wrong?" Brianna asked.

"I dunno."

Jordyn tried walking but stumbled.

Brianna caught her. "Woah!"

"I need Bobby. Where's Bobby?" Jordyn looked around, but they were the only ones in the hall. Then she realized that they weren't in a hall. This was a bedroom.

"Okay. Just lay down here. I'll get Bobby."

Brianna held her around the waist, leading her to the bed. "Here ya' go, honey. Just lay down here. I'll get Bobby, okay?"

"Okay," Jordyn said, starting to cry, scared and confused, feeling like she was going to die.

She laid down on the bed, praying for Bobby.

Chapter 38 - Mallory Black

MAL WAS BACK in her old home, handcuffed to the bed.

She could hear a girl crying, *No!*

Another dream of Jessi Price.

But it wasn't Jessi on the floor in danger of rape and murder from Paul Dodd. It was Ashley.

"Stay away from her!" Mal screamed, struggling against the cuffs, glaring at Paul, fingers twitching, wanting to tear the skin from his bones.

He laughed.

Ashley cried, "Don't let him hurt me, Mommy."

Mal pulled at the cuffs, the metal cutting into her skin, blood forming rings around her wrist.

Paul reached out to touch the girl's hair, licking his lips as he whispered, "Soooo, pretty."

"Stay the fuck away from her!" Mal kicked, bucking in the bed, unable to break free.

Paul looked up at her and winked.

A gunshot.

The man in black came into the room as Paul fell to the ground.

The Hunter.

"Thank you," she said. "Thank you soooo much."

But he was too busy talking to someone who wasn't there.

"Who are you talking to?"

The Hunter met Mallory's eyes. "What? You don't see her?"

"See who?"

Just as the man was about to say her name, Mal woke in a cold sweat.

She reached out in the darkness for the lamp, but it wasn't there.

What the hell?

Her hand searched the darkness, then brushed against something cold and wet.

She brought it to her face and smelled blood, tasted copper in the back of her throat.

A light came on.

She looked down to see the source of the blood. Her daughter's dead body, blood seeping from her open mouth, soaking the front of her pajamas.

Mal screamed, falling backward off the other end of the bed.

Hands grabbed her.

She spun around to see Paul Dodd, smiling.

"So pretty."

Mal screamed.

Then she woke in her hotel room, lamp on, heart racing, trying to catch her breath.

She looked over in her bed, fully expecting to see Ashley's bloody corpse.

But Mal was all alone.

She stood, frantic, searching for her purse, fumbling past everything, hands desperate for the bottle's familiar, comforting shape.

She found it, pulled it out, hands shaking, unscrewed the cap.

She dumped two pills into her trembling hand and stared at the enemy.

Don't do it.

Don't do it.

Don't do it.

Chapter 39 - Jasper Parish

JASPER RAN over his mental checklist.

He was reasonably certain that he'd done everything he needed to do.

He'd flown into Miami and rented a hotel room for two days to establish an alibi on the off chance that this was somehow traced back to him.

He'd bought a car from a used lot, paid cash, and showed a fake ID.

Then he drove eight hours north and parked outside Tony's house, watching and waiting.

He'd brought the kill bag — with the ski mask, gloves, lockpick, knife, and gun.

He had everything he needed.

Jasper stared at the light in the man's house, waiting for it to die for the night. He waited for Carissa to show up and tell him not to do it. Tell him that he was risking everything to murder a man in cold blood.

"You're not a killer," she would say.

And then he would argue, asking the point of seeing a

murderer butcher his family if he couldn't do a thing about it?

But Carissa didn't show.

And Jasper wasn't having any second thoughts.

He was more committed to his course than ever before.

In the three nights after he'd started taking the pills, he'd had another three visions of murders. All of them true.

Two were solved.

But Tony Alvarez had walked free. CCSO was still looking for a black suspect in a hoodie.

Jasper wasn't sure how Tony wasn't a suspect. Did he know someone high up in the DA's office? Did he have incriminating photos of someone important?

Or were the detectives simply lacking the evidence?

Whatever the case, Jasper couldn't allow Alvarez to walk free.

The man's light finally died. Tony was next.

Jasper waited.

He wished he could call Jordyn to check in on her, but he'd specifically left his cell phone at the room in South Florida. If someone ever checked his GPS records, they would back up his alibi, saying he was in the hotel all night. Besides, Bobby had proven not to be the irresponsible asshole he first seemed to be. He appeared to be a decent kid who cared about Jordyn.

And while a part of Jasper hated to admit he was wrong about the kid, he was also happy to be wrong if it meant Jordyn's happiness.

He drove around the neighborhood a bit, checking to see any sign of deputies watching Tony. Seeing nothing of note, Jasper drove back to an abandoned lot one block over, on a quiet street with only two other homes at the beginning, and empty wooded lots the rest of the way.

He parked at the end of the street, got out, slipped on his ski mask, grabbed his kill bag, and headed through the woods into Tony's back yard.

JASPER STARED down at the man, sleeping more soundly than he had any right to. In the very room where he had butchered his family. He looked at the scar on Tony's stomach, where he'd stabbed himself with the machete. A stupid place to stab yourself. He was lucky he hadn't died.

That luck had run out.

Jasper looked around the room. No photos of his wife or son on the dresser or walls. In fact, the walls were all empty. And the room smelled of paint.

"How can you sleep?" Jasper asked.

Tony's eyes opened, startled.

Jasper turned on his flash light, blinding the man. "Don't move or I will shoot."

Tony froze, his eyes wide and terrified. "What do you want? I got money in my office safe. Just take it."

"I didn't come for money."

"What do you want, then?"

"A confession."

"What?"

"I want to know what happened to your wife and child."

"What? Is this a joke? Ain't you watched the fucking news?" Tony tried to get a look at Jasper, but couldn't see anything beyond the bright light.

"Oh, I saw the news alright."

"Then you know what happened."

"I saw a liar lying."

"What the hell are you talking about?"

"Oh, you know. I just want to hear you say it."

"Say what? That some fucker came in here and killed my wife and son, tried to kill me too? Are you him? Did you come back to finish the job?"

Jasper laughed. "Wow, you almost seem like you believe that bullshit yourself."

"What are you talking about?" Tony said, starting to sit up.

"Lay down!" Jasper bashed his knee with the flashlight, crunching bone when it landed.

"Fuck!" Tony cried out, reaching down to cradle his knee.

"I said don't move."

"What do you want?" he repeated, curled almost fetal, clutching his knee.

"I already told you, I want the truth."

"I told you."

Jasper brought the light down again, this time on the man's shoulder.

"Fuck!"

"Stop lying. It's time to tell the truth, Tony. What happened to your wife and son?"

He growled, "I told you. That fucker murdered them."

"The black man in the hoodie?"

"Yeah, him!"

"What did he look like?"

"I dunno, he was fucking black. They all look the same in the dark."

"Wow, that's one hell of a description, Tony. A lot for a sketch artist to go on!"

"Sorry if I can't remember the exact fucking details of the man that killed my family!"

"Oh, I think you can. You're just not trying."

"Get up."

"You broke my knee. I can't!"

"I'm not asking again."

Tony gingerly set his feet on the ground.

Jasper took a few steps back to keep a safe distance in case he tried anything. He also kept the light on Tony's eyes so the murderer couldn't see what Jasper was holding in his other hand.

"Ow!" he cried out, putting weight on his foot.

"Walk to the bathroom."

"I can't."

"You will. I don't care if you have to crawl. Go to the bathroom. Now."

Tony winced, limping forward, his hand on the wall to keep himself from falling over. Eventually, and with much whining, Tony made it.

He stood just inside the bathroom where he killed his wife and child. But he wasn't looking at the ground.

"You want to see who killed them? Turn left."

The man turned to his reflection.

"Fuck you," he said.

"Why did you do it?"

"I didn't do it. Are you fucking deaf?"

"If you lie to me again, I will break your other knee."

Tony winced as he leaned against the sink, taking the weight off his bad leg.

"Sit down," Jasper said.

"What?"

"Sit where they were sitting."

Tony shook his head. "Fuck you."

Jasper stepped forward and barked, "Sit!"

Tony stumbled backward and fell on his ass.

"Good. Now tell me why you killed them. And if you tell me again that you didn't do it, or say anything other than the one hundred percent unvarnished truth, I will chop the fucking head from your body."

Jasper allowed his light to flash on the machete in his right hand. Then he flashed it back into Tony's weeping eyes. "Talk."

Tony cried. "I don't know what happened. Something dark came over me. I was pissed at Elena. Just in a dark place and she kept egging me on."

"So you killed her?"

"I don't know why. I loved her, I swear." He cried, but Jasper had no patience for crocodile tears.

"And you killed your kid too. What the fuck?"

"I don't know," Tony blabbered. "I think it was the meds. I was taking these pills for depression. I think they … they made things worse."

"Bullshit."

"I swear. Look in the medicine cabinet," Tony said, pointing up above him. "Things just got dark, man. I don't know what came over me. It wasn't me. Ask anyone who knew us, man. Please, don't hurt me."

Jasper was sick in his gut, suffering the man's pitiful begging. Even if his pills had made him go to a damned dark place, black enough that he murdered his wife and child, that didn't excuse his covering it up.

"Okay, if your meds made you do it, why not tell the detectives? Why put it on someone that doesn't even exist? You set into motion a manhunt for a 'black guy in a hood-ie.' Do you realize how irresponsible that is? How many 'suspicious looking black dudes' are gonna get pulled over and interrogated, hell, maybe wrongfully charged for your cowardice?"

"I'm sorry. I'll call the police now and confess every-thing. Just please, don't kill me."

Tony fell to the ground, crying, touching the ground

where his wife and child had cowered. "What did I do?" he cried, over and over and over.

Jasper felt pity for the man and hated him for it.

He didn't want to pity Tony.

He didn't want a possible explanation that removed some of the man's guilt. An explanation that made him any less of a monster.

Jasper had come to the house to kill a demon, not a man who may have been wrong in the head.

He moved toward Tony, gripping the machete. He'd fantasized about the kill many times in the past couple of weeks while watching the case unfold with the sheriff's office no closer to the truth.

He'd fantasized how he would make Tony beg in the same position as his wife.

How he would chop through the man's arm, then straight into his head.

He would deliver perfect justice.

But, as he stood over the bawling man, Jasper no longer felt like someone dispensing punishment, but rather like a criminal cleaning his own mess, not all that different from Tony.

He wondered how the hell he'd gotten here. He thought he was doing the right thing. Delivering justice that nobody else could or would.

But it sure the hell didn't feel like that now.

Fuck.

Jasper drew a deep breath and raised the machete, staring down at Tony, angels and demons in his shoulder battling over the man's punishment.

The walls were closing in.

Jasper had crossed the line between good and evil.

But maybe it still wasn't too late to cross back the other way.

He hadn't murdered anyone yet.

He'd broken into the man's home and assaulted him. Yes, he'd had the intention of killing him, but no one could prove it. And he was wearing a mask.

How could he murder this sobbing mess of a man now that he saw all the shades of gray that might have factored into his actions?

This was why you had courts of law.

He wasn't capable of deciding. He didn't have enough evidence, and that made him fallible.

He thought he'd been right in coming here.

True in his mission.

But now he was clouded by doubt.

He stepped back, hesitating.

Tony lunged at him, knocking Jasper to the ground, hitting his head, hard. He felt lightheaded, darkness blurring his vision as Tony crawled on top of him.

Tony started to choke him.

Jasper tried pushing him off, but he was disoriented, weak. His head throbbing.

Tony pulled of his mask with one hand and choked Jasper with the other. "Let's see who you are."

His mask off, Jasper panicked, adrenaline kicking in and taking over.

Though his vision had blurred and doubled, he brought his fist up hard into the man's throat, sending Tony backward.

With the man off his body, Jasper desperately felt around for the machete. His hand found the handle just as he heard Tony crawling toward him, grunting.

Jasper raised the blade, straight into the man's chest.

Tony gasped, then hot blood poured from his wound onto Jasper.

"Damn it!" he shouted, extracting himself from under the dying man, drawing the machete from Tony's chest.

Jasper stared down at his blood-coated shirt, his arms, his gloved hands. Then he stared down at the double images of the dying man.

"Damn it! I was going to let you live!"

But it was too late.

Jasper had crossed a line that rose like a fortress wall behind him.

Chapter 40 - Jordyn Parish

"JORDYN? JORDYN?"

Bobby kept calling to her from somewhere in the darkness.

"Jordyn!"

She opened her eyes, and there he was.

"Bobby, where were you?"

"I'm right here."

"I don't feel so good."

"What the hell did you give her?" Bobby yelled at someone she couldn't see.

JORDYN WOKE up to colored lights and the pitter patter of rain.

The place felt familiar, but nothing made sense.

Bobby lay beside her, his eyes open and staring.

She looked around and remembered.

The treehouse.

She sat up, her head swimming, hurting. Her throat

was dry and screaming.

"How are you?" he asked.

"What happened?"

"You drank too much and passed out at Calum's party. I brought you here because I'd rather not be murdered by your father."

Something felt off, but she wasn't sure what. Maybe because she couldn't remember a thing. She barely remembered going to the party. She did remember asking Bobby not to leave her side, though.

"And that's all?"

"What are you talking about?"

"I can't remember anything, like at all."

"At all?"

"Nothing. I barely remember pulling up to the house, but it's all a blur. What happened?"

"I told you, you drank too much and passed out."

"How long was I out?"

"I don't know."

"How long were we there? At the party?"

"I dunno. A couple of hours? You told me to stay by your side, but I got pulled away by the guys. When I found you with Brianna and the girls, you looked like you were having a *lot* of fun."

"Me? Having fun, with *them?*"

"I know. So I tried to give you an out, see if you wanted to go, but you chased me away, told me to go back to my boys, that you were fine. Brianna told me that you all were bonding."

"*Bonding?*"

"Yeah. You were drinking some fruity shit that the other girls were tossing back. And giggling a lot."

"I was giggling, and you just left me there?"

"What was I supposed to do?"

"I dunno, maybe not leave my side?"

Bobby sighed. "How are you?"

"Head is pounding. I'm dizzy. And I think I might puke."

"Not sure you got any puke left in you."

"What do you mean?"

"You threw up in my car."

"Oh, God. I'm sorry."

"It's okay. So, what do we do about your dad?"

"Shit. Did he call me?"

"No idea. I don't know your password. And your phone was dead, but I'm charging it now."

He scooted over to the fridge, got out a bottle of water and handed it to Jordyn. "Here, drink this."

She unscrewed the top, took a sip, then chugged a quarter of the bottle, surprised by her thirst.

Bobby pulled Jordyn's phone from the charger and handed it over.

She punched in her code and saw, to her surprise, that Dad hadn't called.

"He didn't call."

"So, maybe he's asleep?"

"I dunno. He went to South Florida on business."

"So, you didn't even need to be home tonight?"

"Um, yeah, just because my dad's not home doesn't mean I'm going to stay out all night and party."

"That's not what I meant. But, hey, maybe this is good news? When's he due back?"

"Not until Sunday."

"Sweet!" Bobby smiled, dramatically wiping at his brow.

She wanted to smile, but something felt off, something she couldn't identify. An anxiety under her general nausea, as though something terrible was about to happen.

Or already had.

Jordyn remembered something from when she woke up at Calum's, something Bobby had yelled. "What did you mean when you asked them 'what the hell' did they give me?"

One of the strings casting a glow over the tree house went out, throwing Bobby in darkness. She couldn't see him but could tell that he was troubled by something too. "Did they drug me, Bobby?"

"I ... I don't know."

"What do you mean you *don't know?*" Panic swelled inside her. "You mean they might have?"

"I don't know. I mean, I doubt it. I think they just gave you too much alcohol."

"So why did you ask what they gave me?"

"I think it's best that you don't think too much about it."

"Why?"

Bobby said nothing.

"What happened, Bobby?"

"When I found you in the bed, your shirt was off, and Sammi was passed out next to you, naked."

"What?"

Jordyn couldn't remember any of it.

She shook her head. "What the hell? What happened?"

"I dunno. Someone said that the two of you were kissing."

"Who said that?"

"Brianna."

"Shit. She saw us? Who else?"

"Um ... I dunno. Brianna, Calum, Bethanee, a few others."

"Oh my God!" Jordyn couldn't breathe. "No, no, no."

She began to hyperventilate.

Bobby crawled next to her, putting a hand on hers.

"Breathe slow. It's going to be okay."

She swiped his hand away. "No, it's not!"

She got up, stumbling toward the treehouse door, wanting to leave, desperate to go home, crawl under her covers, and forget the entire night.

Bobby grabbed Jordyn before she could start climbing and pulled her back into the tree house.

"Let go of me!" she yelled, trying to pull away.

"You need to relax. You're in no shape to be climbing down the tree. Just breathe."

Tears streamed down her cheeks as Jordyn tried to remember what the hell happened, how she ended up topless in bed with Sammi. "Did … did anything happen between us?"

"I don't know. I haven't talked to anyone since we left."

She collapsed against Bobby, crying, "I can't remember anything. God only knows what the hell else I did."

"I'm sure we'll find out."

"Yeah, that's what I'm afraid of. Everyone from school was there. *Everyone.*"

"Yeah, but most of 'em were downstairs. They all knew better than to go upstairs at Calum's. It may be a wild house party, but they know not to fuck with his rules. Only our crew is allowed upstairs."

Jordyn shook her head, "Yeah, but they know. You think that Brianna or Bethanee can keep a secret?"

"First off, it doesn't matter. Whatever happened, you were drunk. It wasn't you. Kids do dumb shit at parties all the time. You're supposed to get crazy and have a little fun. I'm sure that was some of the tamest shit all night. Did you see what was happening in the pool? And as far as the Two B's, I'll make sure they keep their mouths shut."

He held her face, sweetly, meeting her eyes. "It's going to be okay."

"I'm not even into girls. I like you," she said this partly in disbelief of what happened, but also as an apology. She wondered what horrible things Bobby must be thinking. That she was some loose party girl that got the slightest bit drunk and started fucking around with whoever, boy or girl.

"You don't need to explain to me. I know how you feel. It's okay. You're not used to drinking, or whatever else they gave you."

"So, you think they *did* give me something else? Who would've done it? Sammi? Do you think she *raped* me? I trusted her."

The thought of someone else, even someone like Sammi, getting her wasted just to take advantage of her made Jordyn furious enough to punch something.

"I don't know if anyone gave you anything. Maybe you were just drunk. Do you remember who—"

"I barely remember anything."

"I don't think Sammi would get you wasted on purpose. I've never heard her talk shit about you, and I can't say that about everyone. You were both a bit messed up. One thing led to another. But I don't think it got much past kissing."

"How did you even know I was in there?"

"Brianna came and got me. Said that you weren't looking good."

"How long was I alone with Sammi?"

"I don't think it was more than a couple of minutes, honestly. I doubt anything happened."

"Topless?"

"Well, hell, half the girls there had their shirts off and were in the pool. Maybe you were about to go swimming?"

"Oh my God, I want to die."

"It's going to be okay, Jordyn. I promise. I'll find out what happened. And if Sammi *did* do anything to you, we'll take care of it."

"What are we going to do? Call the police?"

"It's up to you. I think we ought to know what happened before we jump to conclusions, though, don't you? I mean, you like Sammi, right? You don't want to accuse her of something serious if you were both messed up and just playing around. Right?"

Jordyn couldn't help but feel violated, but at the same time, Bobby was right. Sammi had always been nice to her. And if they were both wasted and were only kissing, did that rise to the level of a crime?

"I need to shower."

"Okay, you can use mine."

"No, Bobby. I want to go home."

Chapter 41 - Mallory Black

MAL DRAGGED ass into the Situation Room and found a spot next to Mike in the rear as Sheriff Bell and McDaniels briefed everybody on the latest details. They couldn't convince Sandra Brown to postpone tomorrow's wedding, so the FBI and CCSO were putting uniformed and undercover officers at the scene. Some of these were working a security detail, with the undercover officers and FBI agents stationed within and outside the temple, including two snipers across the street, both north and south, to cover the temple's primary entrances.

Mal sat through the questions, asking none of her own, and her pounding head thankful that nobody asked anything of her.

McDaniels read assignments.

It took a while before he got to Mallory and Mike — they'd both be working undercover inside the temple, the last line of defense if nobody stopped Jeff before he got inside.

Mal hoped they could stop him before another bloodbath.

THE TEMPLE WAS PACKED with the couples' friends and family. Despite the presence of so many deputies, everyone was lively and chatting while waiting for the service to start. Mal was most surprised by the bounty of kids.

Mal would never let her child go anywhere near such a high profile target. Why didn't these people leave their kids with someone for the day?

She was sitting next to Mike in a pew near the rear, struggling with the sheer number of happy people in the room. She whispered, "I expected more fear. They know about Jeff, right?"

"Maybe they think God will protect them."

Mal laughed, but Mike wasn't smiling. "You believe that?"

"I'm not saying I believe it, but I know from my church, that when you're with your friends and family in a house of worship, you don't let things like fear worry you. This is a place of love and life, celebrating the union of a man and his wife."

"Yeah, well an AR-15 and her ex-husband could change the mood pretty quickly."

"Did anyone ever tell you that you're too cynical?"

"Did anyone ever tell you to fuck off?" Mal smiled, getting up.

She walked through the temple, looking for anything out of the ordinary. Working her way through the crowd, and offering crappy smiles to strangers as she pushed past them, Mal felt out of place.

She spoke through a hidden mic and ear piece, telling the team that she didn't see anything.

She got confirmations of "clear" all around.

Mal felt anxious as the ceremony started. A fish in a

pond waiting for the spear, not knowing when or from where it would strike. She wished Jeff would just show up already.

But he never did.

The ceremony went off without so much as a back-firing car.

Afterwards, Mal met with Gloria, Mike, and McDaniels.

"Well, what now?" Sandra asked, approaching with Eugene in tow.

McDaniels said, "Maybe he knew the heat would be on him."

"Are you saying that he's going to wait and strike some other time? How long am I supposed to live in fear of my ex?"

"We'll continue to do everything we can, and we're not going to stop until we find him."

"And what do we do in the meantime? Who is going to protect us?"

The woman who wanted her wedding to go on despite the danger was worried. Maybe her initial bravery was fueled by anger, but now that reality had washed that away, she realized the true danger of her situation. Looking over your shoulder was no way to live. Mal could sympathize.

Gloria said, "We can talk about that later. For now, we'll still have deputies watching your house."

Sandra sighed. There was obviously little comfort in that answer.

But it was all she would be getting for now.

Chapter 42 - Jordyn Parish

JORDYN DIDN'T WAKE up until after one on Sunday afternoon. Both brain and body were still dragging her through hell.

How long was I out?

She remembered finally falling asleep around six in the evening, which would mean she'd slept nearly nineteen hours.

Her head pounded with the worst headache of her life.

So, this is a hangover?

No wonder Dad is always so grumpy.

She wanted to crawl back into bed and sleep until the sun came up.

But at the same time, she wanted to talk to Bobby. Wanted to find out if he'd gotten any news on what had happened.

She went to call him, but her battery was dead.

Crap!

She plugged in her phone, then got her laptop and went onto LiveLyfe to see if he was online.

She was surprised to see that she had messages.

A lot of messages.

As in 276 of them.

Her heart began to gallop.

This can't be good.

She clicked on the upper right message icon to load the messages page.

And she stared at the computer in disbelief.

Message after message calling her names.

Slut.

Whore.

Dyke.

Cunt.

Bitch.

Most were from people she went to school with but didn't know.

It must've gotten out.

Jordyn's heart pounded harder, her fingers trembling.

She looked to see if Bobby was on.

His icon showed him as active.

She messaged him.

What happened? Did it get out?

She waited, staring at the page with her message to Bobby, waiting for his response.

She saw that he was typing something. And then, suddenly, his status read: *offline.*

"What the hell?"

Jordyn looked to see if anyone else in her friends list was online.

A message popped up from a girl named Becky — one of Brianna's friends.

Kill yerself, slut.

Tears streamed down Jordyn's cheeks as she clicked on profiles for Brianna, Bethanee, and others in Calum's crew, looking to see if any of them had mentioned the party or what happened.

But as she clicked through the names, one after another, were marked as no longer her friends. She couldn't read their walls.

"What the fuck?"

She clicked on the few friends she still had: Bobby, Calum, and Sammi.

There were a lot of new friend requests, mostly from guys she didn't know. Most had messages attached saying stuff like "nice tits" and "wanna hook up?"

"What the hell happened?" Jordyn asked herself, staring at the screen.

She reached for her phone. It was charged enough to turn on.

There was a ton of voice mail, from numbers she didn't know. She was afraid to play the messages.

Nothing from Bobby.

She called him. It went through to voice mail.

What the hell?

She hung up, called again.

Voice mail again.

"Bobby, it's me. Please call. I need to talk to you."

Jordyn waited.

All night.

AT NOON THE NEXT DAY, Jordyn was still in bed, all cried out, and still nothing from Bobby.

Messages on LiveLyfe were only getting worse. The girls were mostly pissed, calling her terrible names and asking how she could do that to Bobby. *He's so sweet.* The guys were mostly coming on to her, asking if she'd like to chat, preferably on video.

Jordyn wanted to respond, but a part of her told her not to, not until she knew what was happening. She was missing some piece of information. Why would everyone be mad at her, and how did it get out so quickly—

A horrifying thought: *video.*

Someone had taken and posted a video.

She searched for links, but most of the people Jordyn suspected of posting it were behind private walls since she wasn't friends with them.

She called Bobby again, for the fourth time in the past hour, and left another message. She thought about walking to his house, but it was raining, and she didn't feel like getting soaked or hit by lightning.

She messaged Sammi: *What's going on? Why does everyone hate me?*

Though the message was seen, Sammi didn't respond.

Something horrible gnawed at Jordyn's stomach. She couldn't eat or focus on anything. She stayed in bed, watching the screen, waiting for a phone call that wasn't going to come.

Where is he? He always calls me on Sunday morning.

Jordyn had to talk to Bobby, preferably before her father came home. There was no way on Earth she could tell him about this. No way she could hide her emotions. He would find out. And then he would freak out. Then he'd punish her forever, and say "I told you so" about Bobby before banishing him from her life.

Finally, a ping on her computer.

Sammi: *You didn't see the video?*

Jordyn felt punched in the gut. She wrote back: *No. WHAT video?*

Sammi responded with a link.

Jordyn was afraid to click it. Terrified of what might be on there. But she had to see it. Had to know why she was getting so much hate. What had she done with Sammi? And why the hell were people freaking out about it when Bobby had said that tons of other half-naked girls were making out in the pool?

She clicked on the video.

There was no sound, but she and Sammi both seemed to be giggling as they climbed on the bed. Calum was there, directing them to kiss.

They did.

Jordyn felt nauseous.

Sammi took off her top. Then Jordyn lost hers.

Sammi licked her breasts, kissed her more, pushed Jordyn down to the bed. They laid there for a few moments. Then the video jumped ahead.

Sammi was face down, either asleep or passed out.

Jordyn was sitting next to her, blindfolded.

And then a guy, naked except for a camo mask, climbed onto the bed.

It wasn't Bobby.

She couldn't tell for certain, but Jordyn thought it was Calum.

He touched her, then went down on her.

Jordyn wasn't stopping him.

No, no, no.

What the fuck?

She stared at the screen as the guy with the mask had sex with her.

No, no.

She shook her head, tears streaming down her burning cheeks.

And then, within a couple of minutes, the guy was done.

But the video wasn't.

Jordyn stared at the screen, at her lying there, wishing she could somehow talk to herself in the past and tell her to get up. To run.

She couldn't tell if she was even conscious.

Then things got worse.

A second guy with a mask appeared.

No.

And then a third.

Jordyn screamed.

Chapter 43 - Mallory Black

MAL WAS in the break room resting her eyes. She heard her name and looked up to see Carrie Thompson holding a coffee. "Long night?"

"Long month." It had been two days since the matrimonial no-show. Brown hadn't posted anything since his failed attack. The task force was intact, everyone still following tips and leads, but all evidence pointed to Jeff going into hiding. If he didn't strike soon, the task force would be suspended, and things might return to normal.

Mal didn't want that. She wanted the bastard caught. She needed closure.

"Can we talk for a minute?"

"Sure," Mal said, pushing out the chair across from her. "What's up?"

Carrie sat, then updated her on Katie's status. She was leaving the hospital in the morning, and Carrie lined up a temporary foster family.

"How is she?" Mal asked.

"Physically, she's good. Her wounds are healing fine. No lingering effects from the coma or head injury. But mentally, I'm not sure. She's going to need a lot of love to get through this."

"How's the family you're putting her with?"

"One of the better ones. The Andersons. They're near capacity with three foster kids already, in addition to their own two children. But they're good. They're patient. And their family is good with the fosters."

"Does she still hate me?"

Carrie nodded. "Katie needs someone to blame for now. It's the only way she can make sense of this. And I'm sure deep down she's condemning herself."

"That's fine. I'd rather she hates me than blames herself. That fucker Kincaid probably did a number on her too."

"No doubt. We're going to get her therapy for both what happened with her parents and the molestation from the coach."

"Good. Let me know if she needs anything, anything at all."

"Thank you. I will."

As Carrie left, Mal thought about the way Katie had yelled at her. How much hate she was holding. Mal had beat herself up about it for a while, but in the end, she had to consider the cold hard facts: Katie wouldn't have been better off had her father lived. Yes, her mother would still be alive, and the family would be together, but was it really better to live under an oppressor's thumb? Maybe her mother was better off dead. And maybe Katie was better off with a fresh start?

For one moment, Mal considered asking if she could take Katie in as a foster child. Maybe adopt her. But she dismissed the idea quickly. As much as she would love a chance to help the girl, and an opportunity to have a family again, Mal also knew that she wasn't in a good place to be a parent.

Her job required long hours and a dedication bordering on obsession.

She would hardly ever be home. And when she was, she wasn't going to be good company.

Plus, Mal was an addict. How the hell could she take care of a kid when she couldn't even trust herself?

Mal's phone rang.

Another private call.

"Hello," said the Hunter.

She sat up, her heart racing, wondering what he was calling about. Did he have info on Brown?

"You didn't catch him."

"He wasn't at the strip club," she said.

Silence on the other end. She let it go, waiting for him to speak.

"She's not safe," he said.

"Who?"

"His wife. He's going to strike tomorrow."

"Where?"

"Her house. I don't know when other than it's at night. And one other thing. When he tells you to put your gun down, *don't*. You have to shoot him instead."

"What do you mean?"

"If you don't shoot him, he'll kill her."

"Sandra?"

"Not Sandra. I don't know who she is. A girl. Don't ask me how I know, just remember what I told you. If you put your gun down, he'll kill her, then you."

"Why are you telling me this? What's your deal?"

"I'm just someone tired of seeing the monsters win."

"Is that why you killed Wes Richardson?"

"Wes was a monster. He created Paul Dodd who killed God knows how many kids, including your daughter."

"So why not turn him in and let us handle it?"

"Sometimes monsters walk free because of mistakes, because of an unfair system, or maybe because a butterfly flapped its wings somewhere and set into motion a chain of events which led to a killer walking free. Someone has to catch the monsters you can't."

"And that's what you are, a *monster hunter?*"

"I never thought of it like that, but sure."

"How many monsters have you caught?" Mal asked, feeling like she was getting closer to some truth that might tell her who he was.

Silence on the other side.

"Come on," she prodded, "if you believe in what you're doing, why not tell me?"

"Because you *don't* believe. You think I'm the bad guy. That *I'm* the monster."

"No, I think you're a frustrated man. Maybe someone who has had a serious injustice done to him or someone he loves. You're fed up with excuses. Hell, I can understand more than most people can. I lost my daughter."

"Then why didn't you make him pay? You had a chance to end it, but you didn't."

"You think I didn't want to kill Paul Dodd? Do you know how damned hard it was not to pull the trigger? Doing that would turn me into a monster like him. And I refuse to let him define me."

"He was in your house. He was a threat. You could have killed him without punishment."

"You still don't understand. Yes, I could have killed him. That's something for the lawyers to argue. But, at that moment, I didn't want to kill him. I wanted him to pay for what he did. To my daughter, to the other kids, to Jessi Price. I wanted him in prison, on death row, whatever the system decides. The law decides who lives and dies. And I have to have faith in that law. Without it, what do we have?"

"I can respect that, Ms. Black. I truly can. But a wicked world needs some lawless monsters. If that's what I need to be, then so be it. I'm willing to sacrifice so that others won't be asked to."

The Hunter hung up the phone.

Mal called Aanya immediately.

"I need a trace on the person that just called my department issue cell."

Aanya called back minutes later and gave Mal her home address.

MAL AND MIKE pulled up to her house, with a backup patrol unit, went inside, guns raised, and searched. But no sign of the Hunter. Nor any sign of anything being disturbed. The locks were secure and the system still armed.

She could check the video surveillance, but doubted she'd find anything. Mal didn't think that the Hunter had been here.

Mal had not been in her house since Paul Dodd had nearly killed her. She looked around the living room, anxiety warring with pleasant memories from before her daughter's death.

The Christmas tree in the corner, decorating it as a family. Lingering meals at the table. Sitting in the living room, helping Ashley with school projects. Coloring, side-by-side.

Her chest constricted. She had to get out.

Mal walked outside without a word, and stopped in the front yard, leaning on her knees, trying to catch her breath. A moment later, Mike was behind her.

"You okay?"

Mal nodded, shooing him away.

She was embarrassed and didn't want to put on a show for either Mike or the deputies coming out of the house.

As Mal took a moment to gather herself, she noticed something peculiar — the flag on her mailbox was raised.

She straightened her posture and headed toward the mailbox, her heart racing. She opened the mailbox and saw a phone, with a Post-it taped to the side.

It read, *I'M NOT A MONSTER.*

Chapter 44 - Jordyn Parish

"I'M HOME," Jordyn's father called from downstairs.

She wasn't ready to see him. She didn't know what to say or do. And there was no way she could hide the pain in her face. One look at her, and he'd know something was horribly, terribly, awfully wrong.

Jordyn was about to crawl into bed and pretend to be sick. But her phone buzzed with a text from Bobby: *We need to talk. Meet me at the park by your house in 20 minutes?*

She texted back. *Okay.*

Moments later, a knock. Jordyn ran to her bathroom and closed the door. "I'm in the bathroom."

"Okay, just checking in. How's it going?"

"Okay. About to go meet Bobby at the park."

A momentary pause. "Okay. What do you want to do for dinner?"

"I dunno. You choose. I should be back around six."

"Okay. Let me know if you want Bobby to come."

"Okay," Jordyn said.

⁓

DRESSED AND READY, Jordyn shoved her emotions down as low as they would go. If her father detected anything, if he asked what was wrong, she would likely crumble into a heap and tell him everything.

Not a good move before seeing Bobby.

She went downstairs wearing her widest possible smile. "Hi, Daddy."

He was at the kitchen bar, working on his laptop. He turned to her, distracted. "Hey, honey. Going out?"

She *just* told him she was going to the park. Had he forgotten already?

"Um, yeah, to the park."

"Oh, yeah. Have fun. Text me if you think of something for dinner. Otherwise, I'll probably just order pizza."

"Okay. Love you," she said, giving him a peck on the cheek.

Jordyn reached the front door.

"Wait," he called out.

Shit.

She turned, the faux smile still fixed to her face. "Yes?"

He stood, went to his suitcase in the dining room, then returned with a pink Miami Marlins hat. He put it on her head.

"Got you that while I was down there. One of the pink ones for breast cancer awareness. You still like the Marlins, right?"

Jordyn hadn't seen a game since they'd stopped watching them together more than a year ago, but she wasn't about to make him feel bad.

"Yes, thank you," she said, hugging him.

Then Jordyn left, walking as fast as she could to the park while the knot in her stomach tightened enough to throttle her breath.

Jordyn was glad to see Bobby parked near the jogging path rather than the always-busy playground area. He was leaning against his car, hands in his pocket.

As she approached him, the knot in her stomach only worsened. He wasn't coming to hug her. He was just standing there, watching her walking, like a stranger. Or an enemy.

"Hello," she said, stopping a full foot away.

Bobby approached with his arms open.

She hugged him, trying not to cry, then failing miserably.

"Did you see the video?"

"Yeah," he said, still hugging her.

"I didn't do that. I mean, I don't remember any of that. You believe me, right?"

"I believe that you don't remember, yes. But, damn, Jordyn, *three guys?* Do you know how that looks?"

She pulled away from him, shocked. "Wait. You think I wanted to do that?"

"I dunno, I didn't see you exactly pushing them off of you."

"I was wasted. You know that!"

"Yeah, but you know what they say about drunk people? They don't do anything they wouldn't do while sober. Alcohol just removes inhibitions."

She stared at Bobby, unable to believe that he could be so cold. "What happened to 'It's no big deal? Parties are supposed to be fun?' Was it only okay when you thought I was just kissing Sammi? But if it's two guys, then I'm a slut?"

"I didn't say that," Bobby said, raising his hands. "But, you have to admit, this looks bad. Makes *me* look bad, you cheating on me like that. Everyone's laughing at me. They're calling me a cuck all over LiveLyfe!"

"Are you fucking serious? *You* look bad? I'm the one in that video. I'm the one being called a slut! And I'm the one being raped!"

"Woah, woah, careful throwing that word around."

"Why? Afraid I'll get your *bros* in trouble? Tell me, Bobby, who was it that raped me? Do you know?"

"Nobody *raped* you. It's just a party that got out of hand."

"Who was it?"

"I have no idea. They were wearing masks."

"Someone drugged me."

Bobby rolled his eyes. "Who?"

"I dunno. Maybe Calum? Maybe Brianna or one of her bitch friends? I don't know, but I do know one thing. There is no way on Earth I'd *ever* let two guys do that to me! I was a virgin when you and I did it. A virgin, Bobby! I was planning to stay a virgin a lot longer than that. But I love you."

Jordyn couldn't say anything more.

She turned away from him, burying her crying face in her palms.

Silence from behind. She couldn't believe how cold he was being. How he was questioning her.

"If you think you were drugged, why didn't they do anything to Sammi? Why did they only rape you, as you call it? If they were looking to take advantage of a passed-out girl, why not do both of you?"

Jordyn spun on Bobby. "Are you serious?"

"I don't know what to think. That's why I wanted to talk to you, to see if maybe you remember more now."

She shook her head. "And what if I did? What if I

remember someone drugging me, raping me? Would you stick up for me then? Would you out your bros?"

"Yes, yes I would."

"Yeah, right," Jordyn said, throwing her arms over her chest.

A long and agonizing silence sat like roadkill between them.

Jordyn wished he would just go away so that she could go home.

But she *couldn't* go home now, not like this. Her father would interrogate her immediately. And, as mad as she was right now, Jordyn might say just about anything.

She wondered if Bobby was right. Was it her fault? Did she drink too much and bring these guys to bed? She was awake while making out with Sammi. And she might have been awake with the first guy. But what about the second? She didn't seem to be moving in the video then, but at one point, the other guy was in the way, blocking most of the picture, so it was hard to tell.

If she *was* unconscious, that was definitely rape. Hell, the whole thing was rape if she was too drunk to consent. But what if they were all wasted? Where did the blame lie then?

Jordyn wished she could remember anything, anything at all. "Who put the video out there?"

"I dunno. It was posted by someone calling themselves Slut Exposer."

"Are you serious?"

"You said the only other people in the room were your friends, right? It had to be one of them who recorded it and released it. Maybe they also know who raped me."

"Please, stop with the R-word."

"Why, is it making you uncomfortable? Rape, rape, rape!" Jordyn screamed into his face.

Bobby grabbed Jordyn by the shoulders and shook her. "Stop it. Acting like a child won't make things any better."

"Let go of me," she practically spit at him.

He did.

She glared at him. "You're right. Maybe acting like a child won't make things better. But going to the police will. Fuck you and your bros."

"Don't."

"Why?"

"Because that's not the only video."

A sledgehammer to her gut. "What?"

"There's another one. One that shows you wide awake and quite the slut."

"No. You're lying."

"No, I'm not. I saw it. You downstairs, *very drunk*, flirting with a bunch of different guys. You grabbing one of their dicks. It doesn't look good."

"Are you threatening me?"

"No. I'm just telling you not to push this, or it'll only get worse for you."

"Or your friends?"

"Fuck them, Jordyn. I am looking out for you. Cross Calum, and he'll make your life a living hell."

"I don't think he could make it much worse."

"Oh, you don't know."

"What does that mean?"

"He has shit on everyone. Fuck with him; he'll fuck you harder."

"What's he got on you?"

Bobby looked at the ground.

"What's he got on you?"

"He knows I deal."

"Deal? Deal what?"

"Drugs to the rich kids. Weed, Oxy, H, coke, E, Molly, you name it."

"You're a drug dealer?"

Bobby nodded. "How do you think I can afford to keep my mom in our house?"

"I thought your dad left you money."

"My dad was in debt to his eyeballs. The only thing he owned was that fucking car. Calum started giving me money after my dad died. Then he turned me onto the wonderful career of drug dealing."

"So, what are you saying?"

"That if you go to the police, Calum will fuck you. Then he'll fuck me. His dad knows people who will make sure my name is dragged through the mud. No school will give me a scholarship after the shit hits the fan."

"So, what am I supposed to do? Drop this? Pretend it never happened, so that you can play ball in college?"

"It's not just about me. He will find something else. Maybe that other video, or something worse. Maybe he'll go after your dad; I don't know. Skeletons are his specialty."

Jordyn considered her father's skeletons. How hard would it be to find out about his disorder? And what could Calum do with that info?

Bobby approached, parting his arms for a hug.

Reluctantly, Jordyn accepted.

He hugged her tight. "Let this pass. People will forget soon enough. Hell, I'm sure the next party will have someone blowing a donkey or something that'll make this seem like nothing!"

"What's going to happen in school tomorrow?"

"I don't know, but we can get through it."

"So, you don't think I'm a slut?" Half of her wanted to shove him.

Bobby kept hugging her. "No, Jordyn. I think you drank too much, but I don't think you're a slut. I love you."

Those three words somehow dulled the pain. Somehow made her think that perhaps she'd get through this. That *they* could get through this.

Still, Jordyn couldn't help but wonder why he'd been so cold to her when they first started talking. Why was he only now saying that he loved her? Did he mean it, or was he playing every possible card to save his friends from a rape charge?

Jordyn pulled away. "I'm sorry, but I have to tell him."

"Tell who?"

"My father."

Bobby went pale. "Please, Jordyn. Don't. He already said he'd kill me."

"I'll tell him that you had nothing to do with it."

"He'll go to the police. We'll all be fucked."

"I can't just forget that this happened."

She turned and started to walk away.

He called after her, "Jordyn!"

She kept walking.

Bobby chased her, begging at her side, "Please, Jordyn. Don't do it. My life will be over."

"If I don't, then my life is."

"Come on, don't be so dramatic!"

"Dramatic? Really?" Jordyn yelled, unable to believe the words coming out of his mouth. "Goodbye, Bobby."

She kept walking.

Bobby didn't follow, but he kept right on yelling.

Jordyn kept walking, crying as the pleading perished behind her.

❦

Jordyn approached her front door, steeling herself for confession.

How does one tell their father that they got raped at a party? Or that maybe she was so wasted that it was consensual sex she didn't even remember?

Jordyn imagined his anger. Demanding to know why she'd put herself in that situation. Why she drank anything at all. Had she *already* forgotten the last time? Hadn't he warned her, repeatedly, of how awful boys could be? How the only way to steer clear of situations like this was to avoid them in the first place?

He would be disappointed. Maybe ashamed.

What if he went looking for the video?

How would he react?

How could he ever look at her the same again?

She wondered if there was another video. And if so, how much more was on there? How many other kids had recorded her doing God only knew what?

Her stomach was sick. It was all Jordyn could do not to duck into some bushes off the sidewalk and vomit. But she kept walking, now just a block from her house. She kept thinking about Bobby's plea. How Calum would destroy not only him, but her, and maybe even her father.

Jordyn couldn't imagine what Calum might do to her dad, but she could see the avalanche of hate tumbling down the LiveLyfe mountain. It would only get worse if another video, or more, came out.

Calum could turn the entire school against her.

He was the star quarterback. And his daddy was the most powerful man in town.

What would going to the police even do?

Could Jordyn prove she was drugged? Maybe. But how could she prove she was raped, when even she wasn't sure?

An ugly gray line, the kind of thing she'd seen on the

news a hundred times or more, but never imagined could happen to her.

Jordyn was too smart. Too cautious.

She didn't hang out with people like that.

And yet here she was.

She was almost to her house when her phone rang.

She looked at the screen.

Calum Kozack.

Chapter 45 - Jasper Parish

JASPER HAD HOPED that Jordyn would want to hang out. He needed to spend some time with his daughter to feel human again.

He hated what had happened at Tony's.

It was supposed to have felt like deliverance, but Jasper had killed a man. Yes, the man was a murderer, but there was unknown data he'd not expected to find, information that shaded Jasper's ability to determine guilt. And while Tony was attacking Jasper, and one could argue self-defense at that point, Jasper should never have been in the man's house.

He'd never hurt anyone unnecessarily or compromised his principles. He never took short cuts like some of the other officers around him. He trusted the process and did his job, regardless of the results. He could look himself in the mirror because he'd done the right thing. All Jasper's life, he'd done the right thing.

But, in an instant, everything was different.

He felt dirty, with the breed of filth you can never wash out. The kind that stains your soul and stays forever.

The kind that robs your humanity.

A giant void had opened above him at Tony's. Now it was slowly descending to swallow him whole. The void had recognized him as a good man on the brink and wasn't about to let him sneak away.

It prompted Tony to attack him, to remove Jasper's mask.

It forced Jasper's hand.

It forced him to enter the darkness.

And then it claimed him.

But being with Jordyn could help Jasper rediscover the light. Father daughter time would remind him of better days. Convince him that he wasn't a monster.

But Jordyn was going to meet her boyfriend at the park.

He'd have to find something else.

Jasper found that something else in the garage refrigerator, a 12-pack of beer he'd almost forgotten about.

He carried the 12-pack into the living room, sat on the couch, and let the darkness swallow him. He cracked one can after another, searching for something, anything, other than the emptiness inside him.

Chapter 46 - Jeff Brown

JEFF WASN'T WEARING a camera to livestream tonight's murder.

Nor was he logged into NonAMus or a hijacked Live-Lyfe account to share in the delight of his kill.

Tonight was about Jeff, his wife, and Eugene. A long overdue reckoning.

He had hoped to stop the wedding, but Jeff was smart enough to know that he couldn't get within fifty feet of the temple. With his name out there, he'd be cut down in seconds.

Jeff waited a few days until the attention died down. His name and photo were still all over the news, but his profile was sinking beneath the weight of fresh scandals.

He was dressed head to toe in body armor. Moving through the woods was more difficult, but the extra protection was necessary.

He had performed recon the night before using a drone from a few blocks away and determined that there was only one pair of deputies watching the house, across the street from their parked car.

Jeff flew the drone around the back of their yard, and over another block, but he found no one else. But a flyby of his old home revealed that Sandra, Eugene, and Liam were inside. He didn't see anyone else in the house. It seemed like he'd have only two hogs to slaughter.

He held the same AR-15 he'd used in his prior attacks, this time fitted with an ACOG scope so he could fire from a distance, subsonic ammunition, and a suppressor to eliminate the CRACK that came from firing.

He also carried two pistols in a side and back holster outside his armor.

Jeff stepped out of the woods, about twenty feet behind the unmarked car where the deputies were watching.

He lifted the AR-15, balanced it on his shoulder, looked down the sight, and fired two shots into the backs of their heads.

Direct hits, both deputies slumping down and hitting the dashboard.

A whisper from the shots. Soft enough to keep Sandra and Eugene feeling safe inside the house.

A dog barked a few doors down.

Jeff walked as fast as he could toward the—

Something wasn't right.

He pulled a small flashlight from its pouch on the front of his armor, then shined it into the car.

Two mannequins.

The window shattered beside him.

Fuck! A sniper!

A spotlight shined on Jeff, from a car parked just ten feet away.

He raised his rifle and indiscriminately emptied his magazine at the car.

Someone returned fire, holes punching the unmarked car behind him.

Jeff raced into the woods to escape, dropping his rifle as he fled.

Chapter 47 - Jordyn Parish

IT FINALLY STOPPED RINGING.

Jordyn kept walking, planning how to tell her father everything, about the party, about the drinking, and about the videos. He'd be mad, but he would know what to do. He'd know how to handle this.

She had to trust him.

The phone rang again.

"Hey, Jordyn," Calum said, his voice sickly sweet.

"What?" she asked, expecting his begging.

"My boy, Bobby tells me you're throwing around some heavy accusations."

"They're not accusations if they're true."

He laughed. Her stomach rolled.

She couldn't believe she'd endured his presence for so long.

"I don't know what you think happened, but I do know what I saw. What half the school has seen by now. If you think that proves anything, you're a crazier bitch than I thought."

"Tell it to the cops."

"Oh, I will. My father is friends with half the sheriff's department, so good luck with your little fairy tale. I have another one. Wanna hear it?"

Jordyn said nothing.

"My story is about a jealous little bitch who was trying to ruin her boyfriend's friendships. She wanted him all to herself, enough that she decided to seduce his friends and call it rape."

Jordyn imagined him smirking and wanted to kill him.

She said nothing.

"She even had her friend Sammi set up a camera to record it, but then Sammi felt bad about betraying her real friends, and told Calum what she and the little bitch had planned."

"That's a lie, and you know it!"

"No, it's not. *You're* the liar, Jordyn. And now everyone knows it. Game over. Why don't you and your crazy daddy run back to South Florida."

Crazy daddy?

Bobby must've told him.

Damn it! He promised.

"By the way, there is one more thing you ought to know."

"What?"

"I'm sending the pic to SnapChat. And let me just say, there's more where this came from."

Calum hung up.

Moments later, her SnapChat indicated a new picture.

Jordyn clicked.

Her, Calum, and Sammi. In bed. All of them topless, a sheet covering them from the waist down. They were all smiling, eyes wide open.

She stared at the photo, shaking.

Then she threw up.

JORDYN COULDN'T GO HOME. Not like this.

She kept walking, trying to figure out what to do, to make sense of everything.

Date rape drugs knocked you out, at least from the little she knew. Was it possible that she'd been drugged and was not only conscious but getting naked and having sex with Calum and whoever else? Or was it possible that she was just drunk, intoxicated beyond the point of control? And if that were the case, who was to blame?

Her father would say that whoever held the party and provided the alcohol was to blame. But it was a party filled with teenagers. It wasn't like some pervert adult had tricked them into drinking so he could take advantage.

Everyone was drinking of their own free will.

Still, there was no way she would knowingly sleep with Calum or anyone other than Bobby. Nor would she make out with Sammi. And the fact that she couldn't remember any of it only added to Jordyn's conviction that she'd been drugged.

She circled her block, then went onto the next one, searching alcohol and drugs and their effects on Google without a single concrete answer. People could do crazy things on drugs or alcohol and have no memory of it afterward. She read horror stories of other girls and boys, who'd been raped after blacking out. A recurring, terrifying theme.

Accusers were rarely believed. And, more often than not, perpetrators were never punished. The grayer the area, the less likely anyone would ever be held accountable.

And that was in normal cases, not taking into account when these things happened with people like Calum Kozack.

The more Jordyn read, the more hopeless she felt.

After walking for nearly half an hour, it started to rain. She headed home, unable to hide her pain. And now Jordyn wasn't sure that she should tell her father.

She opened the front door. Fate could decide. If he asked her how she was, she'd lie and say that everything was fine. If he were paying attention, he'd ask her what was wrong.

If he did, then she'd tell him.

But her father wasn't in the living room or the kitchen. He was upstairs, talking to someone. Maybe he was on the phone with his client from South Florida. She started up the stairs. His voice got louder.

Her father was yelling.

Then he heard the last name she expected. "I don't care, Carissa. It isn't for you to say!"

Jordyn froze on the stairway, her face feeling like it was going to crack.

No, no, no. I don't need this. Not now.

"No, it doesn't matter. And nobody is going to find out."

Jordyn finished climbing the stairs, saw her father in his bedroom. He stared at his bed as if her mother were sitting on it.

"Find out what?" Jordyn asked. Her father turned, eyes wide as if he'd been busted. Before he could answer, she snapped, "Did you stop?"

"Stop what?"

"Taking your pills?"

"Jordyn, honey, it's complicated."

"You promised! You promised, and you lied!"

"I didn't lie. I just—"

"What? You what?" He was speechless. And now she

was close enough to smell his breath. "And you're drinking?"

His face went from sheepish to angry in a flinch. He turned to where he imagined her mother to be and yelled, "Butt out!" Then he spun on Jordyn. "I'm the parent here. You are the child. I don't need to explain myself to you."

"You said you'd stop! If you're not gonna stop, I'm calling the doctor."

"No, you won't."

"Try and stop me." Jordyn reached into her pocket. He smacked the phone out of her hand and sent it sailing into the hallway.

She stared at him, a hard knot in her throat.

"Go to your room."

"What?"

"I said go to your room!" He pointed.

Jordyn burst into tears. Everything inside her was about to come out, all at once — her anger, her confession, and her accusations against Calum.

But as she was about to speak, her father pushed Jordyn out of his room and slammed the door in her face.

She bent down and scooped up her phone, then ran down the stairs and out into the rain.

Chapter 48 - Mallory Black

"OFFICER DOWN!" Mal shouted into her radio, leaning in to put pressure on Mike's leg.

Captain Wilson was on the radio calling for air support and more officers, stationed just outside a three block perimeter, and road blocks around the neighborhood.

She repeated her call into the radio. The dispatcher finally responded with a promise that help was on the way.

Mike sat up and leaned against the car. "Go get him."

"You sure?" Mal asked.

"I got this."

The shot looked clean, in and out. It had missed any major arteries. Still, she hated to leave him bleeding.

"Go!" he said, again.

Three deputies had a thirty-second head start, but the woods connected several vacant lots on both blocks, then led to a wide swath of woodlands surrounding the neighborhood.

It wouldn't take long to lose someone in the woods or on one of the streets.

She raced into the woods after Jeff, her eyes scanning for movement.

Lights bounced ahead, the other three officers to her left and right as they spread into the woodlands. Behind her, darkness.

Rain fell harder.

CAPTAIN WILSON UPDATED them on the radio. "Weather has grounded the chopper, so we've got no eye in the sky. That means it's on you all to find this bastard."

Mal ran through the woods, and out onto a long street lined with homes, most with sleeping residents. A handful were lit, but no one was out. No yells of intrusion, no signs that Jeff had taken cover in one of the yards.

The darkness could bury him anywhere.

She had to follow her gut. He was still running, not hiding out this close to where he'd fired the shots. If he knew the area, he also knew that there was a train track a half mile west of them, and beside that a river fronting several hundreds of acres of forest.

Mal would run west, as far as she could get from the city.

A Honda Civic sat on the roadside, in front of one of the empty lots. It had a sticker on the window from the sheriff's department, telling the owner they had 24 hours to move before the vehicle was towed, meaning it had likely been there at least a day.

She was about to approach the car when branches crunched to her left, across the street. She followed the sound to where the brush was thicker, scratching at her face and hands as she pushed her way through it.

Her radio was filled with the chatter of deputy updates.

The crunching stopped.

She turned her radio to silent and killed her light. She fell to her knees behind some brush. She listened.

Lightning cracked and strobed the woods in white. Thunder exploded.

She could hear officers in the distance. Dogs had arrived, giving them a desperately needed edge.

The circle was closing around the area, but even if they called in every agency in the northeast, they still wouldn't have enough officers to stop Jeff from slipping through. Not without a chopper.

She waited for the sound of branches again but heard nothing.

Another flash of lightning, then Mal headed through the woods to the next street, continuing west. Instinct told her to stop.

She thought about the car sitting on the street.

Just sitting there.

The sticker meant it had probably been there all day. But what if Jeff had taken a sticker off another car to make the car look abandoned?

She raced back the way she'd come, exploded out of the woods and into the street, just as Jeff was approaching the car.

She didn't tell him to stop.

She fired.

Missed. Cracked his windshield.

Startled, he turned and fired back.

Mal ducked behind a fence, no protection, but at least he couldn't see her. She peeked out, ready to take another shot, and saw him running toward the house he'd parked in front of.

Shit!

This was about to turn into a hostage situation. And

given his propensity for stacking the body counts, Mal didn't hold out much hope for a positive outcome.

She turned on her radio, updated his location, and called for backup.

Screams and gunshots as Jeff forced his way inside. Mal couldn't see him from two doors down, but as the bellows multiplied, and a child's was among them, she couldn't wait for backup.

Lightning flashed. Rain poured harder. Mal raced toward the chaos.

She cornered a row of cars, nearly wiping out as she pounded sidewalk on her way to the house.

The front door was wide open. Jeff stood in the living room, aiming his gun at the people inside — a Hispanic family of five, screaming at them all to back away.

He would try to make his way toward the rear of the house.

Mal was going to duck behind a car and sneak around to the back, but she was too late.

Jeff looked up, locked eyes with Mal.

She raised her gun.

He grabbed a teenage girl and pulled her in front of him, putting a pistol to her head. "Gun down!"

The girl screamed.

The men yelled at him to let her go. The women cried.

The scene was a cluster fuck. The kind of shit that went sideways fast, before three days writing reports explaining how the hell it went so wrong.

"Gun down!" he yelled again.

Mal wasn't sure how long it would take for backup. She had no choice, but to put her gun down. But then she remembered the mystery vigilante's advice *not* to put the gun down or else he'd kill the girl. Not Sandra, specifically a girl.

How could he have known it would go down like this?

Every ounce of training told her to lower her weapon, wait for hostage negotiators to talk him out of the house.

Her heart raced as she stared down the sight of her pistol.

She was twenty-five feet away. But it was raining, and her target was mostly concealed by a crying teenage girl with a gun to her head.

Her radio crackled with Wilson calling for an update.

She didn't have time to answer. Or think. Mal only had time to act.

Put the gun down or fire?

She locked with the crying girl and felt her aching. She'd let Katie down. She was already responsible for more pain than she wanted, so it made sense to heed the gunman. Put the gun down, and let the hostage negotiators handle this.

Jeff screamed, "Put the fucking gun down or—"

Mal fired.

Lightning crashed, so close and blinding that everything was white for a moment.

Then, when her vision returned, Jeff was on the ground and the girl was in her family's arms.

Mal ran inside the house. "Police, step away from the body."

She went in, gun aimed down at Jeff. But as she drew closer, Mal saw that he was down for good. Thanks to the perfect hole in his forehead.

Chapter 49 - Jordyn Parish

JORDYN DIDN'T KNOW where she was going. She just wanted to be far away from everything.

She tried to call Sammi, the only person who might be able to help her. At first, the calls went straight through to voice mail. Jordyn texted:

Please, Sammi. I don't know what to do. Please call me.

She was about a mile away from the beach. There were a few diners on the other side of the intracoastal overpass where she could go to escape the rain. She had a few dollars in her pocket, enough for something to eat. After puking up the next-to-nothing she'd had all day, Jordyn was famished.

She wasn't sure if a diner would let her in soaking as she was, but it was worth a shot.

A car full of teenagers in an SUV passed in the westbound lane, honking.

She thought it might be someone offering her a ride. Then the window rolled down and a bunch of girls and guys yelled, "Slut!" in unison, with middle fingers to follow the slur.

Jordyn flipped them off in return.

She kept walking, anger boiling. This was her life now.

Her phone pinged again. More LiveLyfe alerts, people messaging, calling her skank, whore, slut, and other not-so-creative names.

The insults weren't just coming from strangers; some were coming from kids she'd thought she was friends with. Kids in what used to be her circle, but didn't seem to be in Brianna's. Kids that had been down-to-earth. Nice, until now.

More people had posted to her wall, including links to the now infamous video, as well as Photoshopped pictures of Jordyn's body on porn stars. There was Jordyn in a gang bang, Jordyn and lesbians, Jordyn getting pissed on, Jordyn getting raped by all sorts of celebrities and cartoon characters.

The flood of hate showed no signs of slowing or stopping. There was nothing she could do. The only thing Jordyn could think of was to tell her father and go to the police. But that wasn't an attractive option, not with her father's current state of mind.

She *could* call 9-1-1, but didn't want to without telling her father first. She thought of him slamming the door in her face. Remembered the anger in his eyes.

He'd never looked at her like that.

That wasn't just anger; it was something closer to *hate.*

Jordyn had often wondered if he resented her mother dying and leaving him to care for her on his own. He'd never said it, of course. But there were times she could feel it over the years, in an exhausted sigh or a rising voice of annoyance, times when his actions told the truth that she was a burden. That he would've been happier on his own.

Maybe he would've returned to the force after the injury. Maybe he wouldn't have turned drunk and crazy.

The job had kept him grounded. But he left South Florida because of her when she was having trouble at school with other kids.

Jordyn hadn't fit in for years.

And after she went to the police, she'd be ostracized like never before.

She'd never have another friend.

School would be an endless hell.

And where could she go now?

Homeschool?

If her father wasn't sick of her before, that would certainly do it.

And it wasn't like they could go running back to South Florida, even if they managed to sell this house.

Her phone rang at the top of the bridge. *Sammi.*

Jordyn sighed with relief. The girl that had always been nice. The girl that Bobby claimed had never hurled a single ill word her way. The one girl that she felt might really be her friend.

"Hello?" Jordyn answered.

"Hey, you called?"

"I need help. I don't know what to do."

"About what?" Sammi sounded weird, not what Jordyn expected. It wasn't the comforting voice of someone returning a call to someone in obvious distress. It was almost matter-of-fact. Clipped.

"The videos. What happened to us. I don't know what to do."

"Just tell the truth."

"What do you mean?" Jordyn asked, confused.

"Tell Bobby the truth. That you were trying to get him away from his friends with a fake rape charge."

"What?"

"Come on, Jordyn. Just tell them the plan you told me and then apologize. They'll forgive you."

"I never said anything like that."

A sound of the phone brushing up against something, then another voice — Brianna's. "Listen, you little bitch. The game is over. And you are fucked. You come at my man and me, you come at our friends, we will fuck your shit up. I suggest you don't ever show your face again or we'll release everything. And I do mean every little thing. You got that, cunt?"

Brianna hung up the phone.

Jordyn's face felt like it was going to crack. Tears streamed down her cheeks as she stood paralyzed.

How had it come to this?

How could everything in her life all crumble at once?

The cold rain pelted her. She looked out at the churning dark waters, barely visible in the intense rain, barely able to make out the lights on passing boats beneath the overpass.

It would be so much easier to end things.

It wasn't the first time she'd thought about suicide. She'd considered it a few times in South Florida. Her father thought the problem was with their home, and the memories that were haunting them both. Other kids. A shitty community.

The problem is me.

Jordyn looked down at her phone.

She called Bobby and raised the phone to her ear. If she could get him on the line, maybe she could find a way to work through this. Find a way that didn't involve the police or throwing her life in the garbage.

But even if she could somehow return things to the way they were, things could never be normal again.

Even if she could go back to people pretending to be nice, she knew the truth. Everybody hated her.

Jordyn was an outcast.

Same as she'd ever been.

The world would be better off without her.

She climbed to the top rail of the bridge and looked down.

She called her father.

She wasn't sure if she was calling so he could talk her down or calling to say goodbye.

It didn't matter.

He didn't answer.

"Sorry, Dad," she said to his voicemail. "I know you tried. Tried real hard. But I can't do it anymore. It's too hard. I'm going to see Mommy."

Jordyn hung up.

She put the phone in her pocket and looked down at the churning darkness below. A long drop. If it didn't kill her, it would paralyze her for sure. Either way, she didn't care.

Jordyn just wanted something other than the pain. Because now she knew the brutal truth. There was no escape.

She jumped.

As she fell, the phone trilled in her pocket.

But it was too late to answer.

She—

Chapter 50 - Jasper Parish

JASPER CARRIED the plate with the peanut butter sandwich and bottle of water down the darkened stairwell to the cellar.

He set it down, grabbed his pistol, then unlocked the padlock. He opened the door, gun aimed, just in case his prisoner had slipped free from his chains.

Calum Kozack was still leashed to the iron bed post, the collar still around his neck, hands still cuffed. He had just enough room to reach the toilet. There wasn't a sink.

Calum's eyes widened when he saw his meal. His only one of the day. He was salivating as Jasper pushed it toward the bed.

Jasper stood in the corner, watching Calum turn animal, shoving the sandwich into his open maw fast enough to choke himself.

"Slow it down, Cal, there ain't gonna be another one for a while."

"How long?"

Jasper turned to the plastic clock mounted on the wall behind him, also out of Calum's reach. 6:15. "About this time tomorrow. Or maybe the next day."

"You fucker."

"Tsk tsk, Calum. That's no way to talk to the only person keeping you alive. The only person who *knows* you're alive."

"My father will find me. And when he does, you're dead. Do you hear me? Dead!"

"Like my daughter?"

"I already told you, I had nothing to do with that."

"Except that you did. I talked to Bobby after it happened. He told me everything. Told me how your girlfriend drugged Jordyn. I went to the sheriff's office. But you and your scumbag friends are still walking the street."

"Bullshit! He's lying. Your daughter got drunk. Plain and simple."

"Really? So, if I were to ask Brianna, that's her name, right? If I were to ask Brianna, she would back up your story?"

"Go ask her! Then when she tells you the truth, you can come back here and let me go!"

"Hold on a second," Jasper said, smiling, already on his way to the door. He turned back at the threshold. "I'm leaving this door open for a moment. If you scream or try anything, I *will* use this." He held up the pistol. "Are we clear?"

Calum nodded.

Jasper ascended the stairs.

"Don't do this," Jordyn said, following him. "Please, Daddy, they're going to catch you."

"No, they're not."

He reached the top floor and shook his head at the

large sack that had moved a few inches closer to the door. He bent down and threw the heavy sack over his shoulder.

It kicked and cried out, cries muffled by a gag and tape.

He carried the bag down the stairs, dropped it gently to the ground in front of Calum, and untied it.

"Brianna!" Calum yelled.

She cried out, her words muffled.

Jasper pulled the bag off of Brianna, made sure the many layers of duct tape around her hands and feet were still intact, then sat her up.

Brianna's eyes were bugging out as he touched her. Tears smeared her makeup. He reached down to rip the tape from her mouth, and she flinched as he touched her.

"Relax. I'm just taking out the gag. You can scream, but I assure you, as I just told Calum, no one will hear it."

He ripped off the tape, then yanked the cloth from her mouth.

Brianna cried out in pain.

"Calum!" She moved toward him.

"Stay put." Jasper reached into his back holster and put the gun on her face.

"Don't you hurt her!" Calum said, face red, neck muscles straining as he rushed toward Jasper.

His restraints yanked him back a full foot short.

Jasper turned to Calum and smiled. "Such a tough guy, aren't you? What position did you play?"

"Fuck you," Calum spit.

Jasper cocked his arm back and slapped Brianna across the face.

She cried out.

"Stop!" Calum screamed.

Jordyn stood in the corner, staring at Brianna, silent. Jasper could tell from her glare that she was somewhat delighted to see Brianna, the architect of her misery, here in the room.

Jasper grabbed Brianna by the back of her hair and turned to Calum. "Here's the deal, Romeo. I'm going to ask you both some questions. If either of you lies or says anything I don't like, I will hurt the other one. Do you follow?"

Calum glared at Jasper. "You're fucking crazy!"

"You don't *even* know," Jasper laughed, yanking Brianna's hair. She cried out. "Now, do you follow? Or do I need to start hurting her now?"

"I follow!" Calum said.

"How about you, Blondie?" Jasper asked, still holding a fistful of hair. She glared up at him, nodding. "Good."

Jasper let go then stepped toward the door. He looked down at Brianna on the ground to Calum's left, just out of reach.

"Now, we're going to play a little game called What The Fuck Did You Do to My Daughter. Are you ready?" Neither of them nodded or said a word. "Well, I'll take that as a yes. The first question, is for you, Brianna. Which one of you drugged my daughter?"

They exchanged nervous glances.

Calum shook his head. "I already told you she wasn't drugged."

"Not your turn to talk!" Jasper returned the gun to its holster then ducked outside the door to retrieve an aluminum bat. "Last chance to tell the truth."

Brianna stared at him, her back to the wall, knees to her chin, trying to make herself as small a target as possible.

Jordyn still stood in the far corner of the room, observing.

"Hmm, I guess she doesn't love you," Jasper said, swinging the bat hard just below Calum's right knee.

"You fucker!" he screamed.

Brianna cried out, "I did it!"

Jasper turned and smiled at her. "See, it wasn't that hard, was it?" He turned to Calum. "Hmm, I guess I was wrong. She does love you. She just needed to see how serious I was."

"Now, next question is for you, Calum. Whose idea was it?"

Calum bent over his leg, straining not to bawl.

"I asked you a question. Five, four, three, two—"

Jasper raised the bat over Brianna, trying to decide the best first place to hit. He didn't want to deliver a killing blow and end the game early.

Perhaps he'd hit her in the back.

"One."

Jasper was about to swing when Calum spit it out.

"It was her idea!"

"Liar!" she yelled. "It was his idea!"

Calum glared at her, "No, you came to me all pissed off, saying that Jordyn was trying to fuck with you and Bobby, working to turn him against us."

Jasper slung the bat over his shoulder. "Hmm, you all better get on the same page. I'm going to ask you one more time. Whose idea was it?"

They stared at each other, both of them crying.

"Five," he started the countdown.

"Okay," Brianna said. "It was my idea. But we had no idea that she'd kill herself! We just wanted to break her and Bobby up."

Jasper walked over to her. "You lied to me. I'm afraid I'm going to have to hurt Calum again."

He swung at Calum's foot. Bones crunched, and

Calum screamed again. "Fuck!" He whimpered, clutching his ankle.

Brianna asked, "You think Jordyn would want this?"

"Oh, so now you care what Jordyn wants?" Jasper spun toward her, feinting a swing, but holding up after she flinched. "You're right; she wouldn't like this. But she's not here to weigh in, is she?" He turned to Calum. "Okay, next question is for you. Why didn't the District Attorney's office press charges against any of you?"

"There wasn't evidence," Calum whimpered.

Jasper swung the bat, hitting Brianna beneath her left knee. She screamed. Unable to touch her leg, given that her hands were cuffed behind her back, she put her head down, sobbing.

Calum screamed, "Stop!"

"Tell the fucking truth!" Jasper roared at him.

"Fine. My dad knows people. He pulled some strings with someone at the DA's office."

"Who?"

"Lyle Dobson."

Dobson was the District Attorney, confirming Jasper's suspicion that the fix was in.

"Good, good, we're getting somewhere. Next question is for …. um, let's see. Let's go with Brianna."

She didn't look up.

She was still crying.

"Who raped my daughter?"

Brianna's head shook back and forth as she cried even louder.

"That doesn't sound like a name to me. Come on. There were three people in the video, right? Names. Now."

He slammed the bat against the wall beside her.

She jumped, crying out, "Calum and his cousin, Perry."

"You bitch!" Calum screamed.

Jasper took a step forward, gripping the bat tightly. "That bitch just saved you some more pain. You might want to be a bit more grateful."

Calum glared at Jasper. "I didn't rape her. She was into it. I got more video that'll prove it."

"Bullshit!" Jordyn yelled from the corner.

Jasper turned, saw his daughter crying.

He turned back to Calum. "My girl says you're lying. You know what that means, right?"

Instead of the bat, he kicked Brianna in the ribs. Just hard enough to get her screaming.

Calum yelled again, "You're fucking crazy!"

Jasper laughed, swung the bat at Calum, hit him in his right arm.

He screamed.

Jasper turned to Jordyn. "Should I continue?"

Tears were streaming from her eyes as she nodded.

"Alright, Jordyn says we keep playing! Next question, Calum! Who recorded the video? Who spread it around?"

Calum glared at Jasper, his eyes full of hate and impotent rage. "She did."

"It's all coming together now. I feel like we're getting somewhere. Now, I've got just one more question. This one is for Brianna. Who else was in on it?"

Brianna looked up. "Please, we'll tell you whatever you want to know. Just please let us go."

"You answer my questions, then maybe I'll answer yours."

"He's not letting us go," Calum said, spitting toward Jasper.

"You're wrong. I am going to let one of you go." Brianna's eyes widened with a glimmer of hope. Jasper smiled.

"It all depends on how you play the game. Now, tell me, who else was involved?"

"Nobody," she said. "I mean, we sorta twisted Sammi's arm to back up our story when Jordyn threatened to go to the police."

"Of course you did," Jasper said. "What about Bobby? Was he involved?"

He stared at Calum, who said nothing.

Then at Brianna who shook her head.

"No. Bobby didn't know anything. We told him she was drunk."

Jasper sighed. This explained why Bobby said he wouldn't testify against his former friends.

Jordyn asked, "Why didn't Bobby stick up for me?"

Neither of them answered.

Jasper said, "Hey, she asked you a question."

"Who?" Brianna said, looking around.

Calum said, "He's fucking crazy. I told you!"

Jasper yelled, "Shut up!" then turned to Brianna, "Jordyn wants to know why Bobby didn't stick up for her."

Brianna stared at Jasper, a look of confusion, fear, and something else, maybe sadness washing over her face.

"Because Calum told Bobby that he'd destroy him if he didn't stick to the story."

Jasper turned to Calum. "Is that so?"

Calum glared back at him.

"I asked you a question."

"Yeah, I threatened him. What does it even matter anymore? None of this is going to bring her back."

Jasper nodded. "You're right. This isn't about that. This is about justice for my daughter."

Brianna cried, "Can you please let us go, Mr. Parish? We answered all of your questions."

"I've got one more question. Why?"

"We already told you," Calum said, "she was trying to fuck shit up. We were all doing well before she came along, trying to put thoughts in Bobby's head, turn him against us."

"So, this was jealousy?" Jasper laughed. "Wow, I've heard a lot of stupid reasons for people killing one another, but this is pathetic."

"It wasn't meant to come to this," Brianna said. "If we could take it back, we would."

Jasper looked at her. "I think I believe you. But all the sorrow in the world doesn't change things. You're both ugly. *Animals*."

Brianna cried.

Calum just glared.

Jasper started to leave.

"Wait!" Brianna said. "You said you'd let us go."

"No, I said I'd let *one* of you go. Which one should it be? Which one of you deserves it?"

"I'm not begging you for shit," Calum said. "Let her go."

She looked at Calum, tears streaming down her face, "Please, sir. We won't tell anyone what happened. Just, please. Let both of us go."

"No, I said *one* of you. And the best way to decide who that should be is by treating you like the animals you are. You're going to fight for your freedom."

He reached into his back pocket, retrieved the pocket knife, and tossed it between Calum and Brianna. "Whichever one of you is left, I'll let go. You have the advantage, Brianna, seeing as he can't reach the blade. I'd get it fast if I were you."

He closed the door and locked it, ignoring Brianna's cries, "Please don't make me do it!"

~

JASPER SAT across from Jordyn in the sparsely furnished home in the middle of nowhere.

"She's not going to kill him."

"Then I guess he'll kill her."

"Why did you do this?" Jordyn asked, wiping tears from her eyes.

"For you. Justice."

"This wasn't for me. This is a sickness in you. Don't use me to justify killing them."

"I'm not using you. I'm just ensuring that they never hurt anyone again."

"You're going to get caught."

"No, I'm not."

"How can you be so sure?"

"Because I'm careful."

"Not that careful."

"What do you mean?"

"When you saved that detective? You said my name."

"No, I didn't."

"Yes, you did. And how long do you think it'll be before she ties you to this?"

He shook his head. "She won't."

Jordyn shook her head. "You don't know that."

"I see things? Remember?"

She smiled. "Well, I see things too, now. And I don't see this ending well. I see that detective catching you. I see you rotting in jail."

"Then so be it."

A scream downstairs.

Jasper stood, grabbed his gun, and started toward the stairway.

"Don't do it, Dad," Jordyn cried out. "I swear. If you do it, I'm gone."

"What am I supposed to do? Huh? Let him or her go? You're so worried about me being caught that I would think you'd see the wisdom in ending this here."

"The jury would go lighter on you for kidnapping than murder."

"Fuck juries," Jasper said, heading down the stairs.

He reached the door and unlocked it. He raised the gun, just in case they were trying to trick him — which would've been the wise thing to do.

But they weren't wise. They were fucking idiots.

Jasper opened the door.

Brianna was lying in a pool of blood.

Jordyn stared at the girl, crying.

"Why are you crying?" Jasper asked, thoroughly confused. He thought she'd be happy to see the bitch who had set this all into motion lying dead on the floor.

But she wasn't.

Calum glared at Jasper, smiling, still holding the knife.

"Come to let me go, Mr. Parish?"

"No," Jasper said, raising the pistol.

"Don't do it, Dad. I swear, I'll leave you."

"I'm sorry," he said to his girl. "I'll miss you."

He fired the gun, six times.

He watched as the light flickered from Calum's eyes.

Jordyn stared at Calum, then at her father, shaking her head.

And then she was gone too.

Chapter 51 - Mallory Black

MALLORY ENTERED the hospital room holding a teddy bear with a shirt that read, *Sorry You're Sick. Get Well Soon!*

Mike looked up. "Mal! I thought you were never going to visit me."

"Well, no thanks to you, I had a mountain of paperwork to get through alone. You need to get better fast. I refuse to do all your work. Here, I got you a teddy bear. They didn't have any that said 'Sorry you got shot.'"

Gina hugged Mal and said, "Thanks for coming" before taking the bear and putting it next to his bed which was filled with cards, flowers, another bear just like the one she'd gotten in the gift shop downstairs, and enough balloons to start a parade.

"Jesus, what the hell is all this? You'd think you were seriously injured or something."

He laughed. "I can't help it if people like me."

"Are you saying people *don't* like me? People fucking love me. I'm a nice girl. And those that don't love me can fuck right off."

Mike laughed.

"So, when are you coming back?"

"I dunno. It was a bit worse than they first thought. Might be on crutches for a month."

"A month? Fuck. They better not put me with Skippy. I swear to God, I will shoot myself in the leg to get out of that."

Mike laughed again.

Gina said, "You did good, Mal. You saved that girl."

"Yeah, well, I'm not sure the brass is thrilled. The media is bashing us, saying how we fucked up and let the killer slip out of our grasp. How I risked getting that girl killed and never should've taken the shot."

Mike shook his head. "They writing you up?"

"Not yet. I guess it depends on which way the political wind is blowing."

"Well, we caught the fucker. And the girl is alive. That's all that matters."

Mal nodded.

Mike asked, "What made you take such a shot? Was it clear?"

"You wouldn't believe me if I told you."

Mike looked up at the muted TV as an insipid used car commercial ended, and the news anchor showed a picture of Calum Kozack alongside a Sheriff's Department toll free number.

"They still haven't found him? Fucker is probably on a coke bender, banging super models in Aruba," Mike said.

"No," Mal said. "It's with Missing Persons. Say, do you remember a few years ago when that guy came in wanting us to charge Calum with rape, saying his daughter killed herself because of him? Do you remember who worked that case?"

"I think it was Peppers in Sex Crimes. She turned it

over to the DA's office, but they said there was nothing there."

"Do you remember the daughter's name?"

"Shit, I don't. I think it was something with a J. Joanna? Jennifer? Hell, I don't remember. I think her body was found in Jacksonville, so they worked the case. Why? You think her dad had something to do with this?"

"I dunno."

"I doubt it. He killed himself."

"What? When?"

"Last year, while you were off duty. He burned his house down, with him still inside it. Arson ruled it a suicide."

"Shit, I don't remember that."

"Well, it's not like you didn't have your head somewhere else, what with Ashley dying and all."

She nodded, staring at the television, feeling like she was looking at a puzzle with half of its pieces still missing.

She made a mental note to call Peppers tomorrow.

Epilogue

MAL WOKE up in the nightmare again.

But this time the Hunter was there. He'd already broken in and saved her.

She was untied and sitting on the bed.

He wore a ski mask and held a gun. He stared at Paul Dodd, who was quickly bleeding out.

Sirens were screaming.

She had to keep him there so they could arrest him.

She tried to compliment him. "You did it. You killed him. You've had your revenge."

He stared at her confused, then down at his gun.

Something was happening behind his eyes. Some realization was confusing him.

He looked back at Mallory, then aimed the gun at her.

"Do you really see someone behind me?"

"Who do *you* see?" she asked.

"My daughter."

"What's your daughter's name?"

He paused and looked behind him, as if the imaginary person were talking to him.

"Her name is Jordyn."

I think it was something with a J.

Joanna? Jennifer?

Mal woke up from the dream like a shot.

"Jordyn."

THE END

The story continues...

A young girl is found dead in the woods, and the horrors are just beginning …

Mallory Black isn't the only one with something to hide as she seeks justice for the child. And Jasper Parish finds himself drawn back into a world where it's kill or be killed. A world with no hope.

No Hope is book 3 in the *No Justice* series.

GET NO HOPE TODAY

A quick favor...

If you liked *No Escape*, then *would you kindly** consider taking a few minutes to leave a review on your favorite bookselling site. If you're a book blogger, we'd love any mentions on your blog or YouTube channel, also. Every bit of word-of-mouth helps to introduce us to new readers.

As always, thank you for reading,
    David Wright (and Nolon King)

(* *Bonus points if you got the* Bioshock *reference.*)

About the Authors

Nolon King writes fast-paced psychological thrillers set in the glitzy world of entertainment's power players with a bold, insightful voice. He's not afraid to explore the darker side of human nature through stories featuring families torn apart by secrets and lies.

Nolon loves to write about big questions and moral quandaries. How far would you go to cover up an honest mistake? Would you destroy your career to protect your family? How much of your soul would you sell to get the life of your dreams? Would you cheat on your husband to keep your children safe? Would you give in to a stalker's demands to save your marriage?

~

David W. Wright is the co-author of edge-of-your seat thrillers including the best-selling post-apocalyptic series *Yesterday's Gone*, the paranoid sci-fi *WhiteSpace* series, and the vigilante series, *No Justice*, as well as standalone thrillers *12*, and *Crash* which was recently optioned for a movie.

David is an accomplished, though intermittent, cartoonist who lives in [LOCATION REDACTED] with his wife and son [NAMES REDACTED.]

He is not at all paranoid.

He is "the grumpy one" on the *The Story Studio Podcast* with fellow Sterling and Stone founders, Sean Platt and Johnny B. Truant.

You can email him at david@sterlingandstone.net

We swear, he almost never bites. Unless you feed him after midnight.

Also By Nolon King

Hidden Justice

Hidden Justice

Hidden Honor

Hidden Shame

Hidden Virtue

No Justice

No Justice

No Escape

No Hope

No Return

No Stopping

No Fear

Once Upon A Crime

Once Upon A Crime

Twice Upon A Lie

Three Times a Murder

Dead For Good

Dead For Good

Left For Dead

Dead Of Night

Wake The Dead

Dead For Life

Stand Alone Novels

Pretty Killer

12

Blown

Miserable Lies

The Target

Secrets We Keep

Close To Home

Heat To Obsession

A Simple Kill

Tell Me No Lies

Red Carpet Black

Fade To Black

Victim

Also By David W. Wright

Hidden Justice

Hidden Justice

Hidden Honor

Hidden Shame

Hidden Virtue

No Justice

No Justice

No Escape

No Hope

No Return

No Stopping

No Fear

Karma Police

Jumper

Karma Police

The Collectors

Deviant

The Fall

Homecoming

Yesterday's Gone

October's Gone

Yesterday's Gone Season One

Yesterday's Gone Season Two

Yesterday's Gone Season Three

Yesterday's Gone Season Four

Yesterday's Gone Season Five

Yesterday's Gone Season Six

Tomorrow's Gone

Tomorrow's Gone Season One

Tomorrow's Gone Season Two

Tomorrow's Gone Season Three

Available Darkness

Darkness Itself

Available Darkness Book One

Available Darkness Book Two

Available Darkness Book Three

WhiteSpace

WhiteSpace Season One

WhiteSpace Season Two

WhiteSpace Season Three

Stand Alone Novels

12

Crash

Emily's List

Threshold